The Palm of Judah

How one woman's courage transformed the story of Israel

Viktoriya Lorimer

A STORY OF HOPE
BOOKS

For anyone who has been abused

Face the past, let God heal, and be free; then soar into your future, brighter than the summer sun.

Forward

The first time I had the honor of meeting Tori Lorimer, I was not only struck by her beautiful heart and ease on the outside but also by her bravery and courage on the inside. Her hunger and passion for living to the full is truly infectious and a gift to so many people, whether they've been friends for years, or whether she encounters a stranger for the first time.

This book is a product of the way Tori lives her life in a passionate, enthusiastic and brave way. As I read the way that Tori has interpreted the powerful story of Judah and Tamar, she drew me into a new and compelling perspective- the Biblical account came alive to me in such an interesting and imaginative way. Tears of sadness, of joy, coupled with moments of beautiful reflection and healing were enjoyed as I read along, almost hearing Tori speak out the words, and at other times, clearly hearing and seeing the hand of Jesus all over her writing.

I know that this book is incredibly powerful, and will bring healing and hope to many, as well as fun times in an enjoyable read. I also know that this will not be the only book Tori will write- she evidently has a beautiful gift, and I for sure am thankful for the time and commitment she has poured into this and for the many people who I know have poured into Tori's life personally. She is a woman of an incredible heritage of courage and perseverance, and a present full of possibility, and the future- well wow, that's very exciting!

Together with her husband Ricky, the Father has created an exceptionally creative household whom we (Andy, Noah, Anna and I) are immensely proud to call family, in the wider, Jesus sense of the word.

Love, Rhoda, Andy, Noah and Anna Fearon

Pastors and Dreamers at Carlise Vineyard

Book of Beginnings

Many of us have heard the stories that were passed down for generations and then recorded in the Bible. One particular story, the short tale describing the lives of Judah and Tamar, placed right in the middle of the well-known story of Joseph, fascinated and confused me when I first read it. I felt that God was asking me if I wanted Him to show me more about Himself through this story, and I said yes. Out of that 'yes', this book was created. So I've spent this past year researching everything I possibly could about what really happened there, and asking myself, 'What was that like?' to the situations they encountered.

The lives of Judah and Tamar are extremely messy; at first I couldn't believe this story was actually in the Bible. But the more I studied and researched, the more I saw not only their flaws, but the restorative love of Jesus permeating every word in this chapter. Even in their darkest moments, He held in mind the possibility of their great future: to be the mother and father of the great tribe of Judah, and the great ancestors of Jesus, the one who every single story in the Bible points straight to. I've grown to love this particular tale so much, mostly because God surpassed all the mess and wove it into an incredible story of hope.

Whatever situations and circumstances you find yourself in life right now, good or bad, easy or hard, or somewhere in between, the good news is that Jesus, the Lion of the tribe of Judah, is offering the same restorative hope to you. Because of His love, there is always a space for us at His table. Genesis means, 'the book of beginnings', so let this book be a new beginning for you.

Healed

When Jesus speaks, healing comes. As I was writing this book, something I felt Jesus whisper into my ear was that He wanted to bring healing to some of those reading these words. His request was very consistent with the Jesus I have grown to know and love, the same Jesus who walked in the Bible. Wherever He went, He brought hope, life, restoration and healing, just as did those who loved and followed Him. I battled including this section for months. I felt, rather feel, scared. It seems to me like too much of an act of faith to pray for healing through the mere means of a book.

I've seen many healed before as part of my church, and I've also seen people prayed for where no apparent change happened. I've seen Jesus heal people and them dedicating their lives to him, and people still turning away from Him even after receiving a miracle. I myself have been healed from an affliction that caused me pain and discomfort for years, and at the same time I am still deaf in one ear. But what I've learned is that it's not my job to perform the miracle. All that Jesus asks is for me to be obedient, and to have faith that He really is the same God that I read about in my Bible: the One who is always faithful, who can do the impossible.

Here are some specifics that I felt God was showing to me as I write this book. Isn't it just like the Jesus in the Bible to stop for the one person in the midst of the crowd? I believe that some of you will be healed right in this very moment. I see the incredible Jesus, who is loving, powerful, and righteous, standing right in front of you, stretching out His hand. He is inviting you to experience the thing we were made for: seeing Him for who He is. Open your eyes. He is looking straight at you. His gaze is one of unconditional love. And then He speaks. Tune into His voice. At His word, healing comes. I declare backs aligned into place, eyes seeing for the first time, the immobile getting up and running, even dancing, deaf ears hearing, headaches fleeing, sleep coming to the insomniacs, shoulders and knees return to their full range of movement. Open your heart and sit still for a moment, and allow His mercy to grace any area of sickness, weakness, or affiliation. He knows *exactly* what it is.

I see fingers that are in a cast being able to wiggle again. I see breakthrough for cancer and scars of self-harm fading. I see anaemia restored, growth stunts becoming growth spurts, limbs that were lost or severed regrowing before your very eyes. I see skin conditions disappearing, and you being able to touch your newly smooth skin.

If you feel a heat or tingling coming down your body, that is just the power of the Holy Spirit. Do not be afraid, God is just showing you His love. All sickness must bow at the name of Jesus. You are deeply loved by a good God, a great Father, and a faithful Friend. He loves each one of us so deeply that He makes His awe inspiring power available to us.

If there is something you couldn't do in your body before, try it out. If you were healed of anything or have any improved mobility, or have less pain, I praise God! Now go get your healing confirmed by a doctor, and then exclaim His goodness to those around you! Sometimes healing can come gradually, but regardless of the outcome, He is the good God of miracles, the same today as He was when Judah and Tamar lived.

Note:

Although 'The Palm of Judah' is based on the Biblical narrative, this book is mostly fiction. I have done my research to keep as much accurate as I can, but many of the different conversations and emotions are my best interpretation. Please keep this in mind as you read. This fictional story is designed to whet your appetite, so you can discover what really happened in the lives of Judah and Tamar. At the end I have included every Bible passage used, so you can see the real story that God Himself authored.

Part 1

Chapter 1

Judah

It was one choice which would change the rest of our lives.

"Look, there comes the dreamer!" yelled my older brother, Levi.

"We couldn't miss him even if we tried, with that colorful coat of his," chuckled Gad, elbowing Reuben in the side. The coat should have been given to Reuben, the oldest of my eleven brothers by our father, Jacob. But after Reuben slept with my father's fourth wife, that little tattletale, Joseph, got it instead.

While my brothers and I despised Joseph, Reuben had always tried to defend him. We spent the majority of our time trying to make his life miserable, as he did ours. Many nights around the campfire were spent talking about how we could make Joseph suffer. This hatred was more than just a feeling. It shaped the way we saw everything: a hatred so deep, it haunted us from waking to sleeping.

"I say we kill him," said Dan.

"The only question is...how? I am so tired of him telling on us and getting us in trouble," replied Asher.

"Yeah, 'cause you get in the most trouble," said Naphtali, smiling.

"We could cut off his head, then he definitely wouldn't have any more dreams!" exclaimed Zebulun excitedly, like a little child.

I looked around at my brothers, their eager faces looking more and more like those of ravenous wolves. It was disgusting and grotesque, yet somehow so fitting. The plans got more creative and more absurd.

"We can tie him down and then set him on fire!" yelled Simeon. He was the cruelest of all my brothers. Sometimes, when we weren't watching, he liked to torture oxen just to see them suffer. I shivered.

"Come on now, brothers, settle down. Let's just kill the little dreamer and throw him into one of these cisterns," I said, pointing to one of the deep holes in the ground which were full of water. A black abyss, it looked like a gateway into another world. Just yesterday one of our sheep had fallen into one of the cisterns; the poor creature had bleated and cried as death came slowly. None of us could rescue it without jumping in ourselves.

"Yes! Nice and simple," said Issachar. "Then we can tell our father that a wild animal has eaten him, and we'll see what happens to his dreams."

The sun was high in the sky and Joseph had almost descended into the valley in which we were pasturing our father's flocks. He was very easy to spot with his curly red hair and colorful coat. Even from a distance, I could see the size of his smile. He waved at us. Clearly, the boy had no idea what he was walking into. Like an innocent sheep about to be slaughtered, he came closer and closer. But he wasn't innocent. I clenched my teeth as a new wave of hatred washed over me.

Reuben, with his small, sturdy frame and unruly black hair, walked out of his tent. I knew what he was going to say before he even opened his mouth.

"Look, boys, I know we all hate Joseph, but let's not kill him. Why should his blood be on our hands?"

The force of Levi's reply took us all by surprise: "No way you are talking us out of it this time, like you've done before! This time we are far away from our father. It's happening, Reuben, whether you like it or not." The rest of us nodded in agreement.

"Alright, alright," replied Reuben, raising his bushy eyebrows and smiling anxiously. "Then let's just throw him into a cistern here in the wilderness. He'll die without us having to kill him."

I felt a stab of guilt. Were we really going to go through with this? I pushed the thought aside as quickly as it came. We had planned Joseph's death many times before, but it had never happened. There had always been an obstacle, whether a lack of courage, being too close to home, or being intercepted by Reuben.

"Fine, Reuben, but we're still going to hit him a few times," whispered Simeon as Joseph came within earshot.

"Hello, brothers! Father sent me to see how you are doing. I brought you some roasted lamb and freshly baked bread. I hope the sheep are all okay. How are you surviving with these cold desert nights? I stepped on a tumbleweed and almost tripped, and..."

Before he could say anything else, Levi and Simeon grabbed Joseph by the arms and legs and slammed him onto the ground, causing a cloud of sand to rise into the air. As it settled, and the sun lowered, we crowded around our victim. Joseph's face was made dark by our shadows, and he strained his neck to look up at us, his eyes widened.

"What kind of a game is this?" he whimpered, panicking, as Dan threw the first punch. Someone stepped onto Joseph's arm and he whined in pain as the bones cracked. He resisted fiercely as Asher began to tie him up. "Please, I won't tell on you again! I won't tell you about my dreams! Is that what this is about? Please, don't hurt me!" Joseph looked to Reuben, whose eyes remained downcast, then to me. "Tell me what I did! I'm so sorry! Just let me live! I won't tell on you again! You can even have my robe!"

Did he really not know? Our father's affection towards him had given Joseph a skewed view of life. He didn't know hard work, hatred, or pain, the very things permeating our existence.

"Is this about my dream where you all bow down to me? You don't ever have to do that! Please, just let me live! Tell me what I need to do and I'll do it!" He looked even more like a child as he began to cry. When tears didn't work he fought, kicked, and screamed.

Finally, Joseph was tasting justice. He had spent his entire life rubbing our father's affection in our faces, only to claim that he didn't know what all this was about. I was surprised by the rage - pure bone-chilling rage - washing over me.

Revenge felt very sweet. We threw Joseph into the cistern, not only for every moment of pain he had caused us, but also for the misery he had inflicted on our mothers. Leah, Bilhah, and Zilpah had always been in the background. Father Jacob only had eyes for Rachel, Joseph's mother. When we were still living with our uncle Laban, I couldn't help but notice the way my mother looked at Jacob. I was only a little boy, yet I could still see her pain. She looked like a withered flower, and there was nothing I could do to help her.

As the last streaks of daylight disappeared behind the mountains, I squinted my eyes to appreciate the grotesque scene before me. Joseph was soaked in blood and urine, with two very black eyes and marks all over his body, which was still restrained by the ropes. We tossed him into the empty cistern and, for that one moment, we weren't invisible any more.

Just minutes later, it was finished. I could hear Joseph's staggered breathing from deep down beneath us. My brothers and I were left standing in a circle, peeping into the darkness. The glee, exhilaration, and hatred which had filled us was draining away. There were no sounds, not even from the cattle or birds. The silence was eerie. My knuckles were raw and our camp was filled with the foul stench of blood. Suddenly, Reuben, who had said nothing the entire time, quickly turned and ran towards the hills. With our leader gone, none of us knew what we were to do except keep peering into the darkness which now held our brother.

Whether minutes or hours passed, I couldn't say. Then, one by one, my brothers went back to their duties, starting the fire or bringing in the sheep. Dan was the first to take out the lamb-meat and bread Joseph had brought. The smell of it cooking helped mask the stench of revenge. Naphtali brought out some wine. Soon the nine of us were sitting around the fire, eating our supper in silence. By now the only light was coming from the fire, for there were no stars in the sky tonight. No one dared to speak a word. Who would break the silence first?

Suddenly, Levi sat up, startled. "Do you hear those voices?" he asked as we squinted into the darkness. The sound of bells and camels' hooves: must be Egyptian traders. We had seen them on this path before, speaking with the accent of Ishmael, trading their exotic foods and expensive clothes. As they approached I could see six men walking alongside their carts, and a few naked slaves chained to the caravan.

Earlier, I had suspected that Reuben would try to rescue Joseph after our departure. Maybe there was a way I could outsmart him? I got up, an idea forming quickly in my mind.

"Brothers, what do we gain by killing Joseph? Someone could find the body, and we have been seen making camp here. We cannot carry him anywhere else. Why don't we sell him to these Ishmaelite traders? After all, he is our brother. The price of a slave is thirty shekels; maybe we could sell him for that?"

My brothers agreed, but there was still one problem.

"Who will get him out of the cistern?" asked Issachar in a quiet voice. Everyone looked to me. "It was your idea, Judah, so you should do it." I saw I wasn't going to get out of this.

"Okay, I'll carry him up, but then you all need to stop the traders and convince them to take the dreamer."

Zebulun and Dan went with me to get Joseph out of the cistern, while the rest of the brothers went to negotiate with the foreigners. Zebulun looked at me with eyes full of unspeakable guilt. My two brothers didn't have to say anything for me to know how they felt. They took a rope, tied it as a harness around my waist, and lowered me into the cistern. I could hardly see anything in the darkness.

"Father, is that you?" said Joseph, his voice cracking.

There was that pang again. *What am I doing?*

I picked up Joseph and put him on my shoulder, the way I used to when he was little. I tugged on the rope and Zebulun and Dan pulled us up. It was no easy task to hoist us out of the cistern, and eventually two more brothers had to help pull us up. Joseph cried out in pain as his blood spilled all over my robe.

When we finally got out I shuddered as I looked back down into the depths of the cistern. The darkness was all consuming and overwhelming. At the top, I quickly cut the ropes that bound Joseph.

Joseph's puffy eyes opened to see the traders standing there. We hadn't told them this was our brother, so when they saw his condition there were no questions. It wasn't the first bruised and broken slave they had seen. The traders' skin looked leathery from years of walking in the desert winds and sand. They wore very expensive cloaks, bought from the profits they made trading.

"Take off his tunic so we can inspect him," said one of the traders in his harsh Midian dialect.

Again, my brothers looked to me. Joseph didn't say a word as I undressed him. My hands shook as I took off his colorful robe, and I remembered Father Jacob giving this to Joseph, as well as his excitement as my brothers and I stood bitterly in the background. I threw what was left of the garment to the ground. The Ishmaelite approached Joseph, took out his whip, and lashed Joseph as hard as he could. Joseph cried out and fell to the ground, but did not protest.

The trader smiled approvingly. "We'll give you twenty shekels." He cast the money onto the ground and whipped Joseph again. "Get up, slave!" he yelled. Shaking violently, Joseph slowly struggled to his feet.

I noticed the naked slaves at the back of their caravan. Their wrists were chained to the saddles on the camels and they didn't even look up as Joseph was shackled amongst them. I saw their tattered backs and the scars on their chained wrists. They reminded me of animals.

I knew I was making a decision I might regret, but there was no turning back now. The traders didn't look back as they headed towards the direction of Egypt. Moments after they set off, I heard a familiar cry echo through the desert night. It was the same cry I heard from Joseph's tent when his mother had died giving birth to his younger brother, Benjamin. Most nights the stars shone brightly, but tonight there was complete darkness. Joseph's dreams were dead.

~~~

We had planned to stay near the town of Dothan for the next few days, but none of us could last that long. I heard one of my brothers screaming during the night. When we woke up in the morning, no one dared to speak. The valley that just yesterday had been filled with grass for our livestock and a sanctuary for us now seemed dull and bleak. There was a heaviness in the air I had never felt before.

We packed up our tents, got all our animals ready to leave, and headed back towards the Valley of Hebron, where our father's tents were.

We hadn't got very far before Reuben came running up to us. his face red with anger. "Where is Joseph?" he demanded. Silence. "Tell me, where is Joseph?" he shouted at the top of his lungs, grabbing Levi by the tunic, pulling him off his feet and close to his face, his breath heavy.

"Judah wanted to sell him. Look, we got twenty shekels!" replied Levi. "Think of what we can do with this money! Father doesn't pay…"

"Enough! Where is he?"

"Probably halfway to Egypt by now! It was Judah's idea," replied Simeon.

Traitor.

Reuben threw Levi aside onto the desert sand and squared up to me. "Have you sold your own brother?" My mouth opened but no words came out. "This is on you, Judah."

Defeated, Reuben's shoulders slumped as he walked away.
~~~

~~~

I held the goat's fat legs as Naphtali began cutting its throat. The goat was kicking, the panic in its eyes not unlike Joseph's when we had thrown him into the cistern. The creature from our flock bleated loudly, squirming in our grasp. As its blood poured out and drenched the ground, we were left with a lifeless carcass on the desert sand. I knew exactly what my brothers were thinking.

Dan took Joseph's special robe and rubbed it into the pool of blood, cutting into it with his knife. When he was finished, the garment really looked like it had been destroyed by a wild animal. Simeon had found a servant in the local village and paid him to give our father a message: "Look at what we found. Doesn't this robe belong to your son Joseph?"

As the messenger started off towards the Valley of Hebron, we tried to find the longest possible route home.
~~~

Chapter 2

Judah

Before Joseph was born, our father took me and my brothers to pasture the sheep with him. He asked our mothers to bake us bread and pack us some olive oil to dip it in. They were glad for a few days peace from their ten boys, and packed us an entire camel's load of food. Along with our servants (no one man would be able to handle us alone), we set off to the pastures with our father.

A few hours later, we arrived at Dothan. The first thing we did was jump into the river to cool off. The sun had been beating down on us the whole journey, and it felt so good to dive into the cool, clear water. Dan and Asher began splashing each other and trying to catch fish. Simeon and Levi took turns sitting on each other's shoulders and trying to tackle the rest of us. Reuben, who could hold his breath the longest, would dive right down to the riverbed and pull an unsuspecting victim under the water. I looked over at the shore and saw father taking off his robe. Was he really going to join us? Slowly, he walked into the river as my brothers and I stood in the water, up to our bellies, anticipating his next move. His expression was as serious as stone.

"Sons, all of you against me."

I looked at Reuben and he returned my gaze. Father was clearly not messing around. He began to run, his battle cry echoing throughout the surrounding valley. Jacob was chasing us with the biggest smile on his face as we scattered, unsure of how to react. He swam after Reuben first, but the boy was too quick and wriggled free. Then he managed to grab Gad and Issachar, pushing them under the water as the rest of us yelled in protest. By the time father swam up to me, I was laughing so hard there were tears rolling down my face and mixing with the river water. I could feel his arms on my back, pushing me down towards the sandy riverbed. Those three seconds underneath the water were blissfully perfect. He was there. Finally, I could feel his slender arms lifting me out of the water, my hair stuck to my head and my smile widening from ear to ear. Father looked at me and winked.

Before I knew it, Naphtali was on father's back, dragging him under. All ten of us were cheering and hollering. When we finally allowed him to come up for air, Jacob coughed and shook the water from his dark hair. "Okay, you have defeated me," he said, still smiling. "Now let's go eat."

We did not need any more convincing. As we sat warming ourselves around the campfire, father began to tell us stories of his childhood; stories which had us howling with laughter and shaking with excitement. He told us of his hatred for his brother, Esau, our grandfather's favorite, and how his mother, Rebecca, had talked him into obtaining his father's blessing through trickery, impersonating his older brother by covering his arms with goat hair and wearing his clothes! We all laughed at how Esau had traded his inheritance for a pot of stew. "It *was* a delicious stew, my sons," father added, grinning.

His face hardened as he told us how he had been forced to leave his mother and run away, fearing for his life. Then he told the story that would become my favorite: his dream of a staircase winding up to heaven, with heavenly beings ascending and descending. At the top, father said he had seen God, who had declared to him that we were now His chosen people. God promised that our family would be as numerous as the sand on the seashore and the stars in the sky.

Jacob's face shone as he related the vision. "That promise goes for you too, my sons." Mesmerized, my brothers and I hung on every word, our eager faces reflected in the light of the fire.

Father was everything I believed a man should be. Even though his skin was light and he was small in size, I knew he was strong. He was the head of the household and respected by everyone. He was our protector, and I knew that when I was older, I wanted to be just like him. I loved, perhaps even worshipped, him.

When I was slightly older, father had planned for us to leave for one of our camping trips. I was so excited to hear what stories he would tell us this time, and couldn't wait to sleep under the stars instead of an old tent crowded with my smelly brothers, Levi and Simeon. The food was prepared and my brothers and I were packed and ready to go, sitting down outside our tent, waiting for father to come. But he never came. Deep disappointment showed in all of our faces, from the oldest, Reuben, to the youngest, Zebulun.

By evening we had given up and returned to our mothers' tents. Leah, my mother, enfolded me in her arms. "Why didn't Jacob take us camping?" I asked her, tears stinging my eyes.

"Judah," she began, searching for the right words, "your aunt Rachel is going to have a baby."

That was the moment everything changed. We never went on another camping trip. After Joseph was born, it seemed that my brothers and I were diminished in our father's eyes. He would walk around, carrying the red-haired infant, declaring over and over again: "Behold, the son of my old age!" He would brag to every visitor about how beautiful his new son was.

Father spent hours playing with Joseph, making him little animals out of wood and taking the boy everywhere with him. From Joseph's first breath, we were ignored. Whenever father did speak to us, it was to tell us what we needed to do: take care of the animals; fix the well; cut firewood; carve more plates and cups; make more toys for little Joseph. Demand after demand, without a single word of thanks.

For the next seven years, my brothers and I were little more than a pedestal for Joseph. It was all about him. Our aunt, Rachel, would strut around as proud as a peacock, her head held high, telling everyone to be careful around her firstborn son. If Joseph knocked over a bag of grain, he would point to me and start crying, earning me a lashing. Once, he let all the animals out of their pens, forcing Issachar and Asher to skip their supper and wander through the night to retrieve them. Joseph never failed to tell on us: when Simeon and Levi snuck out in search of entertainment, when Gad cheated people at the market place; or when Manasseh stole an animal from Jacob's flock to cook for his friends. Even when it was clear that Joseph had stolen the gifts we brought for our little sister, Dinah, there were no consequences. "Let him have it," Father would say. While we got in trouble for everything, Joseph was never rebuked.

Then came the day we took away our father's dignity, after which he stopped ignoring us, but instead began treating us as enemies.

~~~

It happened when Joseph was ten years old. We came home one day from pasturing our father's sheep to see large camels draped with brightly colored saddles standing near our tents. We could hear male voices from inside.

"My son longs to marry Dinah. Please name any price, and we will pay it," said one of the men in a deep, full voice.

A suitor was asking for Dinah's hand in marriage! Our little sister was the darling of the family. The only daughter among eleven boys, she was beloved and spoilt by her older brothers in every single way. Even at thirteen she was a beauty, even more lovely than Aunt Rachel, with long dark hair, hazel-green eyes, and bright soft skin. I loved seeing my brothers' affection for her. None of us would admit it, but she had us wrapped around her little finger. We would buy her bracelets, nose rings, and oils whenever one of us went away for a few days to
~~~

Shechem or Dothan. She was the opposite of Joseph in every way. While our younger brother was made proud by all the attention, Dinah seemed to blossom and become more lovely with every compliment and gift.

Who was this man who thought he was worthy to marry our only sister?

"I will wait until my sons come back from the fields to give you and your son any answer, Hamor," replied Jacob, his voice sounding tired.

With Reuben leading the way, my brothers and I entered the tent, one by one.

"Who is this suitor, father?" asked Reuben.

"This is Shechem, prince of our land, and his father, Hamor. It was Hamor who sold me the land we are living in. Shechem is in love with Dinah and wants to marry her." There was definitely more to this story. I raised my eyebrows as I waited for father to continue. "Well, when Dinah went to visit some of her friends from Shechem's kingdom, he saw her and...lay with her. But now he claims he loves her and wants her to be one of his wives."

I could not believe what I was hearing.

"He defiled our sister? He raped and humiliated our little flower?" I yelled. I wanted to hurt this man until he was covered in blood, to take away his breath. This animal did not deserve to see another second of sunlight. As I imagined all the things I wanted to do to him, Levi ran up to the prince and placed both hands around his throat.

"You have disgraced our family! You have dishonored our sister!" spat Levi, knocking Shechem to the ground. With little enthusiasm, the rest of my brothers restrained Levi, throwing wary glances at Shechem and Hamor.

"Please," begged Shechem, "I know I was wrong to take her by force. But I fell in love with her afterwards. I am willing to pay any price for what I have done; just name it and I will give you anything you ask for. Your sister will be the most cared for and revered woman in the entire land of Canaan. She will lack nothing. Please, I'm asking for a second chance. I'm asking for forgiveness."

"And let's not stop there!" Hamor added, a little too brightly. "Let's join more of our sons and daughters in marriage. There are plenty of beautiful women in Canaan you men can take as your wives or concubines."

Suddenly, an idea began to form in my mind. "This is impossible, Hamor. We could never give our sister to a man who is not circumcised. Why, we would be disgraced; it is against the customs of our ancestors. The only solution, if you want to talk business, is that all your men will become circumcised like us. Then we will freely exchange daughters in marriage and make ourselves at home among you. But if this is not an acceptable condition, we will take our sister and leave, and you will never see her again."

As my brothers opened their mouths to protest, one sharp look from me told them I was up to something.

"What is 'circumcision'?" asked Shechem, hesitantly. As we explained to the two men, the color drained from their faces. Then, looking at each other, they nodded. "We will do it!" Shechem exclaimed, trying to hide his fear and disgust. "So will all the men in our village, so we can intermarry with you."

Jacob looked surprised, but said nothing. Outside the tent, Levi and Simeon confronted me. "Judah, what are you doing? We can't let our Dinah marry that filthy rapist."

"Brothers," I replied, calmly, "what happens to a man after he is circumcised?"

Levi and Simeon looked at each other with wide smiles. We had all been cut as infants, but when a new male servant joined our household, he too had to be circumcised. Levi and Simeon always found it extremely amusing to listen to the servant screaming like a woman giving birth. And everyone knew that circumcision would make a man immobile for at least a few days afterwards.

Simeon giggled like a little child receiving a present. "Say no more, Judah. We know exactly what to do."

A few days later, as all the men from Shechem's land lay recovering from their ordeal, Simeon and Levi wreaked their revenge on the village. First Shechem and Hamor, then the rest of the men, were all slaughtered by their sword, their heads and limbs cut from their bodies. Then I and the rest of my brothers joined the raiding party, taking everything we could lay our hands on. We took their women and children for slaves, and their animals and gold to add to our riches. Then Dan and Naphtali set fire to what remained. Revenge was sweet and exhilarating. We did it for Dinah.

When father found out what we had done, he was furious. "You have ruined me! You have made me an outcast before all the people of this land," he cried. "They will think I have stolen all my wealth in this despicable way. You have not only disgraced my name, but that of our entire family. What you have done to me is even worse than what Shechem did to Dinah. You have tainted the name of the God of Abraham and Isaac!"

After that, our father's attitude towards every son of Leah, Bilhah, and Zilpah - and to Simeon and Levi, especially - was marked by bitterness. But we didn't care; we had defended our sister, no matter the cost. Yet, if that was the day our father stopped loving me and my brothers, it was also the day I lost what was left of my respect for him. How could he have allowed his only daughter to be disgraced like a prostitute? Instead of my hero, he had become some pathetic, cowardly old man.

Soon after that, Jacob moved our entire family to Bethel. He claimed God had spoken to him, but I thought he was just running away from the shame we had caused him. He made us get rid of all our idols and purify ourselves. No one was happy about giving up our household gods, earrings, and other jewelry; now we would stick out like a camel at a cattle market. Jacob even took our wealth and buried it under a tree near Shechem. Because of the slaughter, I thought the surrounding nations would be out to get revenge. Much to my surprise, however, none of the tribes we encountered as we travelled attacked us. Jacob said God was protecting us and had given him a new name, Israel. I thought he had lost his mind.

Some time later, we left our home in Bethel and the entire family moved towards Ephrath, near Bethlehem, which was little more than a collection of tents set in a desolate wilderness. Aunt Rachel went into labor with her second child while we were still some distance away. It was an awful place to give birth, with no midwife to help, only my mother and the two servant-wives.

With the women occupied, chaos ruled; no-one knew what to do. I heard the screams from the tent, sounding at first like the sounds of a woman in great pain, later as if an animal was being killed in some barbaric and inhumane way. Jacob paced around outside the tent, neither eating nor sleeping. Three days and nights passed like an eternity, and on the third night we discovered that, not only was Rachel dead, but we had another brother. I heard my mother and the servant-wives whispering that, with her dying breath, Rachel had named him Benoni, meaning 'son of my sorrow'. The grieving Jacob soon renamed him Benjamin, meaning 'son of my right hand'.

There was no joy at Benjamin's birth, as there might be over that of any other infant, only deep sorrow. Rejoicing over a new brother felt wrong when we had lost one of our mothers. After Jacob held his son for the first time, tenderly kissing his cheek, he tore his clothes in mourning and laid on the floor to weep. I looked from Jacob to my mother, who was holding Benjamin. She would become the mother he never knew. I was amazed at my mother's strength. She, who was so unloved by her husband and treated with contempt by her sister, would raise their son, Benjamin, with as much love as she showed to the sons of her own womb. We buried Rachel and set a stone monument over her grave in Bethlehem, the place where she had died. Jacob was never the same.

We all wondered if Benjamin would be treated the same way as Joseph, or if he would become one of us, knowing the rejection of our father. I hoped he would be treated well, but as life went on and we settled at Ephrath, Joseph became even more adored, as if Jacob was channeling the love he had for Rachel - the love he was supposed to give Benjamin - into Joseph. He never said it out loud, but it was clear that Jacob blamed Benjamin for having killed his favorite wife.

~~~

Amidst my memories of our childhood, one thought kept returning to me over and over again: if not for me, Joseph would now be back at our father's house, bruised, but alive. Reuben would have rescued him. Now, as we approached our tents, I saw Jacob's figure waiting for us in the distance, as was his custom if Joseph had gone away with us.

Normally, as soon as he spotted us, Jacob would start walking toward us, searching for Joseph. He was always so concerned something would happen to him. Once, Gad had made a joke about how Jacob wouldn't notice if one of the other brothers was missing, to which Jacob had retorted: "You men can take care of yourselves. I don't worry about something happening to you, but I do worry about you hurting someone else." Now, his words had become the truth.

We first saw him waiting outside the tents. As soon as he saw us, he picked up his robe and started running towards us. It was such a strange sight to see the elderly Jacob running. He stumbled on the rocky ground a few times, but didn't fall. We slowed down, unsure of what to do. He had torn his usual robes, and instead was covered in the burlap he would wear at times of great mourning.

"Is it true? Is Joseph gone?" Jacob's white hair and beard were smeared with black ashes. It was terrifying to see the head of the household - father to twelve sons, husband to four wives, with enough wealth to last a lifetime - as an
~~~

unrecognizable mess. We all looked at each other. Would anyone dare tell the truth? The tension hung in the air.

I spoke with my last bit of failing courage. "Yes father, we found the robe along the side of the path from Dothan to Shechem."

Everything in me wanted to tell father Jacob the truth, but I just couldn't. Jacob's whole body collapsed as if a great gust of wind had pushed him to the ground. We quickly gathered around the old man.

"I will go to my grave mourning for my son," said Jacob, his voice sounding like the very definition of true sorrow. And then he wept. I had never seen a grown man weep so, not even when Rachel had died. It was like watching hopelessness take human form, as waves of sorrow washed over his whole body. He wept as we picked him up and carried him back to the tents, and for the next three days the sounds of his sorrow hung over the entire camp, from dawn to dusk. He was broken. I hated myself, but I wondered how much more the God of my father hated me for what I had done.

~~~

That first night back at my father's tent, I dreamt of Joseph lying in the empty cistern. Suddenly, the walls broke and water came gushing in, drowning him. "Help me, Judah!" called Joseph. He stretched out his hand to me, his green eyes looking straight into my soul. "I beg you, Judah, help me!" I looked back but turned away, the sounds of his screams still piercing my ears. I woke up, my body drenched in sweat. That scream filled the void in my heart with overwhelming grief and guilt.

Maybe all Joseph had wanted was to be included by his older brothers. Maybe he sought our affection the same way we sought our father's; or, perhaps he had taken everything as a joke, thinking we were messing around with him because we liked him. Maybe he hadn't known he was provoking, humiliating us. Maybe he
~~~

hadn't deserved this, and we were the ones who had been wrong for seventeen years.

I wept.

Chapter 3

Judah

I could barely see my sandals as I ran through the dark night. With a small tent and a few days' worth of bread on my back, I ran as fast and as far as I could from what I knew as home. I never wanted to see my father or any of my brothers again. I wanted nothing more to do with my family, or to hear Jacob's cries of anguish and see my guilt mirrored in my brother's eyes. My departure would break my mother's heart, yet I just ran.

Where I was or how far I had run, I did not know. I stumbled a few times and my sandal strap tore, leaving the worn sole to be buried by the sand. With one bare foot I had to slow down, trying to avoid the rocks and thorns littering the dry terrain. Suddenly, I stepped on something sharp and cried out. I looked down to see a wooden splinter sticking out of my foot. It was painful but I didn't care, I just kept walking.

There were caves along the way in which I could have taken refuge, but the damp darkness of the cavern reminded me of Joseph's cistern, so I took my chances with the wild animals and slept right out in the open. I could hear wolves howling in the distant hills, and a few crows tried to steal the remains of my bread. I woke up every few hours in the night to put more wood on the fire; I could not bear the cold if it were to go out. At least my foot had stopped bleeding, but it was beginning to turn red.

There was a strange silence in the wilderness. I was so used to hearing my brothers running around; the women going about their daily chores; or the livestock making their noises. The sounds of family. What if it wasn't all bad? Even though our father didn't care about us, our mothers certainly did. The three women adored their children. My mind recalled the delicious meals of roasted meat, bread, cheese, and olives, prepared for us by Zilpah and Blidah, or the beer brewed by my mother, Leah. My stomach gurgled at the thought of their cooking. I loved the taste of the sweet dates we often picked from the two big trees near our camp.

Life at home was good. Reuben and I were especially close, and while Simeon and Levi enjoyed their notorious nights filled with women and drinking, Reuben and I much preferred a quiet night swapping stories around the fire. My heart burned when I thought of my mother. While some women were like butterflies, gentle and lovely, Leah was more like a camel: large, sturdy, and very useful. There was nothing she couldn't do. What did she think now I was gone? How had I never noticed the good parts of my life before? My frustration and bitterness towards Joseph had colored the way I viewed everything. Now that Joseph was gone, presumably dead, I spent the rest of the cold night wishing I could take it all back; that I could go back to that awful moment and choose a different path this time. It had happened only days ago, but already it seemed like a lifetime away.

~~~

The sun was already high in the sky when I opened my eyes. How long had I slept? The desert sands had completely covered what was left of my fire. As I stood up, I tried to take in my surroundings, wiping sand from my bleary eyes. My stomach churned; I had eaten all my bread on the first day, and nothing since. As my eyes shifted into focus, I saw a village in front of me, tents and a well surrounded by trees, as green as can be. Water. I ran as fast as I could towards the village, my mouth bone-dry with thirst.

"I hope you aren't stealing our water."

The voice made me jump. I was so consumed by thirst, I hadn't even noticed this strange man approaching me, speaking in some dialect I had not heard before. He looked ten years older than me, and while most people's skin was
~~~

darkened by the sun, this man's skin was whiter than milk. His skin was so white it was blinding. I put my hand above my eyes, shielding myself from the light. Unlike my brothers, this man's facial hair was short and light, and I couldn't help noticing his sturdy jaw and broad shoulders. Something about him made him seem important and respected.

"Actually, I was," I replied, my voice cracking. "I haven't had anything to drink for over a day." He pointed to the pail of water at his feet. In a moment, I was on my hands and knees, lapping the water like a dog.

"Who are you and why are you here?" asked the stranger as I arose.

No point in telling the truth. This is a new start, after all. The story I told him was told with such conviction that I almost believed it myself. I told him how my brothers had spent their whole lives mistreating me, of their attempt at my life, and how I had run away for my protection.

"I'm just going to live out here until I can figure out what to do next," I said, pointing back to the wilderness.

We stood in silence for a few moments. Strangely, it was not at all uncomfortable.

"Follow me," said the stranger, at last. "What did you say your name was?"

"Judah. My name is Judah."

"Judah," he said, his smile widening, "I think you'll find what you are searching for right here."

He led me through tents filled with women and children going about their daily tasks, as livestock grazed outside. These women were so different from any I had seen before. All the women in my father's house covered their bodies, but these women wore only a sash around their breasts and fabric tied around their hips. They didn't cover their heads, and left most of their bodies exposed. I wasn't sure quite where to look. I had seen jewelry - nose rings and bracelets - before, but these bodies were entirely adorned with gold and their skin was covered in strange dark writing and patterns; some had many rings in their ears or noses. The men of the town had none of the long beards worn by the men of my father's house, and the children wore black kohl around their eyes. It felt like a different world. I could see the influence of Egypt on this land, and all the things Jacob had protested about.

As we walked into the stranger's tent, I saw three children sitting inside - two boys and a girl - carving animals from wood. They looked like siblings. "Father Hirah, you are back!" exclaimed the younger boy, jumping up into his arms.

"Welcome to your new home," said Hirah, turning and looking at me.

Over the next few days, I learned that Hirah acted as a gatekeeper in this village, which was called Adullam. All who entered, left, or passed around the village had to go through him. Sometimes, people would stop for a cup of water; at other times, Hirah would prepare an entire feast for his guests. He had no wife, and his home was definitely lacking a woman's touch. There were no tapestries or little artifacts; no rugs or little trinkets. Everything was simple but clean. Later, I learned that these children weren't the first Hirah had taken into his tent. Their parents had died, and he had taken them under his protection until they reached maturity. Hirah's was a home where strangers were welcome. Here, wealth and hospitality were united.

Although we never spoke about it, as the months drifted by it was clear I had become another member of Hirah's household, and his close friend. The only friends I had before were my brothers, and everyone knows how brothers argue and fight. My friendship with Hirah had all the good parts of having a brother, without the rivalry. He was a good man, doing good to all regardless of social standing or family heritage. He also never missed an occasion for a celebration, showing me the things of this world I had been denied under my father's roof. He often laid on feasts for the whole village, where wine and beer flowed as freely as water.

During those months, my whole perception of right and wrong was shaken. There was no sanctity to marriage here, and sex was often used as a prize to be had with the many prostitutes and dancers (male and female) provided at Hirah's feasts. The entertainment would begin with women dancing in nothing more than their hip-cloth. That stirred something in me I hadn't felt before. Oddly, I kept feeling out of place, knowing my mother would not approve of my presence here. I pushed away the thought every time. I was a grown man of twenty-five, after all, and I could make my own decisions.

Since I had become Hirah's right-hand man, I had my choice of pleasures. I didn't care much for the men, but the female prostitutes were beautiful and their bodies were captivating. They would lead me into their tents and show me what had been hidden from me by my protective family. As I left, Hirah would wink at me, holding up his goblet of wine.

Somehow, these revelries accomplished their purpose; I wasn't thinking about anything, much less my family. Every time my feelings of guilt about Joseph rampaged into my mind like a raging animal, I would push them aside and tell myself that my old life was behind me. And then I would drink myself into a stupor.

The nightmares continued, although they became less frequent. I would sometimes wake up in the middle of the night, my sleeping mat drenched with sweat and my head spinning from last night's drink. Even as I ran from everything I had believed in, I was being pulled back to that moment in the darkness of the cistern. I could see Joseph tied to the back of the Ishmaelites' caravan: naked, beaten, bruised. As time passed, these feelings became a constant companion, always lurking in the background of my thoughts. I knew that one day, the God of Jacob would catch up with me. I would have to pay for what I had done.

Chapter 4

Judah

One night, after we had eaten dinner and were sitting around the fire, I told Hirah the truth about my family. I just couldn't hold it in anymore. It felt like a huge weight was lifted from my chest once someone know the entire truth about me. After I had told the story of my brothers and what we had done to Joseph, Hirah was silent for a while.

"Judah," he said, finally, "you really need to put this behind you. I can see the guilt that is eating you up. Right and wrong is just an opinion, no matter what your family may have taught you. People make up gods to make others do what they want, and the desperate cry out to their god because they have no-one else to turn to. I may have done many bad things in my life, but also I try to do good where I can. That's all that counts in the end, right? Let go of this guilt. I know you didn't really want to hurt your brother, but there is nothing you can do to fix it now. Just move on with your life, and stop thinking about it."

Hirah said this and much more. When he had finished talking, he gave me a friendly pat on the back, and left me alone with my thoughts, the bright fire, and the even brighter starry night.

His words made me question everything I believed. I doubted what I knew about right and wrong, about my guilt and shame. Was there really a God or had my father just invented Him? Even if there was a God of Abraham, Isaac, and Jacob, did he only care about our family? Why were we the chosen ones? The more I thought about it, the less credible it all seemed. I began to wonder if I had been lied to my entire life to force me into behaving in a certain way. The thoughts were painful.

But, as much as I wanted to cast my beliefs aside, something deep inside of me remembered how I had felt when Jacob had told us about his vision of the ladder to Heaven and all of God's promises. God had promised my father that his descendants would be equal in number to the stars in the firmament. And now here I was, many years and miles apart from that moment, looking up at the starry sky. Part of me wanted to believe that the God of my youth existed, but I was also afraid that He would have to punish me for how I had treated my brother. I tried to shake these thoughts out of my head as the first light began to streak through the dark clouds. Had I been wrestling with my thoughts for an entire night?

In the following months, Hirah and I became like brothers. Now that he knew the truth, I could tell him what it was like to grow up with a full household of four women, eleven brothers, and one sister. I told him of all the tricks we had played on Joseph and of the tension which had followed Benjamin's birth. Recalling my ancestors, I told Hirah about how my great-grandfather, Abraham, had to pretend that his beautiful wife, Sarah, was his sister in order to save his own life. Twice. Hirah laughed as I related the marriage of my grandparents, Isaac and Rebecca, which had only been made possible by Rebecca drawing water for a whole caravan of camels, something most men would never be able to do. Then, Hirah looked on in amazement as I told him the stories of Jacob: how he had won his brother's birthright through trickery; how he himself had been tricked into marrying my mother; finally, how it took Jacob fourteen years of work to pay for Rachel, the woman he had desired all along. Hirah would shake his head disapprovingly and keep asking questions long into the night.

~~~

"A sheep-shearing festival?" I asked in astonishment.

"If you think you've seen a good time at my feasts, Judah," replied Hirah, "just wait until you see this!"
~~~

We were walking along the road from Adullam to Timnah. Noticing the many prostitutes touting for business, I raised my eyebrows at Hirah, but he just smiled. "Hold onto your sheep, Judah, and have a bit of patience."

The festival was full of people from all the surrounding towns. Some had even travelled from Egypt. They brought their sheep for the shearing and celebrated the plentiful harvest of that year, worshipping their many different gods and goddesses: of fertility, of the sun and moon, and of abundance. As the offerings were made, everyone filled their cups as hundreds of women danced with their tambourines. It was a joyous occasion, a time for everyone to rest after the sheep had been sheared.

I was still a little afraid of these kinds of festivals; my father had made it very clear that his God demanded that He alone should be worshipped. Although I wasn't sure what I believed any more, something in me kept me from offering sacrifices to the other gods along with the rest of the people.

In the midst of the festivities, I thought about Joseph. Once, I saw a man in the crowd with curly red hair and my chest tightened. The man looked like an older version of Joseph. Was my brother still alive? He never got to go to a festival like this; his lips had never sipped wine in such abundance; his body had never known the pleasure of a woman. Somehow, even though I was surrounded by people, I felt very alone. I looked over at Hirah. He was surrounded by two women and a man, and they were all heading into one of the tents together. He gave me a look as if to say: "What are you doing? Go have yourself some fun!" I shrugged, and Hirah rolled his eyes and walked into the tent. The rest of the festival passed in a blur of color and noise.

After we returned to Adullam, I could see that Hirah was thinking seriously about something. A few days later, I was just about finished roasting the meat for that night's dinner when I saw Hirah approaching, cast in the shadows of sunset. It was dusk, but I could make out two other figures with him. Hirah introduced them to me as Shua and his daughter, Reya.

Reya was the most beautiful woman I had ever laid eyes on. She had smooth dark skin and long black hair flowing all the way to her waist. Her deep hazel eyes caught mine. It was like holding the gaze of a wild and beautiful deer. I was struck dumb in amazement. She was so full of life, and for this one moment when our eyes met, I saw home.

"Smells delicious! I am very excited to eat whatever you are making!" said Shua, bending over the roasting duck. "Reya and I live on the outskirts of Kezib. Hirah invited us over for a meal, I hope you don't mind."

Reya's eyes were locked on mine. All I could do was shake my head. Yes, no, I didn't even remember the question.

I ran back into the tent to get the rest of the wood, and as I stood there, with my heart pounding out of my chest, it felt like I needed Reya's presence in order to keep breathing. She stirred something so much deeper than any of the other woman at the festival had. Her appearance was breathtaking, but she was so much more than that. The way she smiled, the way she laughed, the way she rubbed her hands together when her father was introducing her; all of this mesmerized me and I had only known her for a matter of minutes. I took a deep breath and brought out the platters of food. The others were sitting under the shade of the palm tree in the late evening sun, the conversation flowing as if among a group of friends who had known each other for years.

As we talked through the rest of the evening, I discovered that Reya was surprisingly funny. She told me about her job, making clothes for the women in the town, and of the gods she worshipped. She told me about her half-sister, Niya, born to her father's concubine, who also made clothes, but for the servants. When she told me her dream of becoming a mother, with a dozen sons to adore her, all I could do was look down at my feet. After the meal, we sat around for another hour as the night drew on, sipping wine and eating dates. When it was time for Shua and Reya to go, I knew I had to see this woman again.

"Can I see you tomorrow, Reya?" I asked, hesitantly. Surely such a beautiful girl wouldn't want to spend time with a fugitive who lived with his friend, with no possessions of his own.

"If you make me a dinner like that again, I won't let you out of my sight," she replied, running her fingers down my arm and setting my whole body on fire.

After three months of seeing Reya every couple of days, I decided I wanted this woman to be my wife. Thoughts of Joseph only appeared to me at night, and somehow she made me do what I ran away to do: forget. I would never tell her that, though. She would never know of the guilt I carried around. When I asked Shua for his daughter's hand in marriage, he only chuckled and said, "Hirah was right about you."

~~~

The wedding was a quick but luxurious affair. Reya wore a colorful robe she had made just for the occasion. The violet garment went around her chest and shoulder, showing off her bare midriff and pierced navel, and her legs were covered with a long flowing skirt. Her hair was all pulled back with flowers and she had black kohl around her eyes. I knew, without any doubt, that I loved Reya, and would do so until my dying breath.

Hirah took charge of the entire day, making sure the servants were keeping everyone plied with wine, speaking to every guest in the room, and making everyone feel relaxed. I had only known the people seated around the tables for a few months. As I scanned the faces, I wished my mother could be here. I had never really thought about my wedding day, but at the very least I had assumed my mother and brothers would be there. I pushed away the thought as I drained another cup of wine. I looked around at Shua and his family; at Hirah's orphans and
~~~

house guests; and the rest of the faces I recognized from the feasts and festivals. Everyone's bellies were full and their eyes sparkled from the wine.

As night fell, Hirah led Reya and me outside. "For your marriage, many children, and your everlasting happiness, here is your wedding present." He pointed towards the south of his property and in the distance I saw a luxurious living-tent: our new home. Hirah looked very pleased with himself as Reya gave him a kiss on the cheek. Then he winked at us and left.

Hand in hand, we walked slowly towards the tent. A gentle breeze was blowing, and Reya took the flowers and ties out of her hair, which now fluttered behind her in the wind. As I opened the door to our new home, Reya saw in the middle of the tent the bucket of water and cloth I had asked Hirah's servants to prepare. She looked at me with curiosity and anticipation. I took her hand and gently sat her down, took off her sandals, and held her feet in my hands. They were dark and lovely, covered in dusty sand, tired from dancing. Keeping my eyes fixed on hers, I began to wash her feet. She was surprised at first, tickled by the water and by my rough hands, but then she smiled and began to relax.

Making love to Reya through the night, I felt passion and ecstasy unlike anything I had known before. We took our time enjoying each other's bodies, lying as close to each other as possible and dreaming of the rest of our lives together.

I resolved in my mind that I would be a better husband to Reya than my father had been to my own mother, never disregarding her or making her feel unloved. I would see to it that Reya would never shed a tear, working hard to build my fortune so I could afford to give her everything she could ever want. I would let her worship her own gods; she didn't have to know about Joseph, my family, or the God they served. I would never let this mighty woman know my dirty secret. Unlike my own father, I would be close to my children, never playing favorites and giving my love equally. They would have everything I had lost.

Chapter 5

Judah

Reya was crying out in pain, and I could do nothing but pace around the birthing tent. Between her screams, I could hear the women beginning to panic. This was not going to be an easy delivery; the baby was turned the wrong way, and my wife's life was at stake.

Earlier that day, I had walked into the tent and saw the look of horror on Reya's face. "What's wrong, my love?" I asked as I rushed to her.

"I think I wet myself," she replied, bowing her head with shame, putting her hands over her enormous belly. I exhaled and smiled. It was time for her to give birth.

I quickly sent my servants to call the midwife, as well as Reya's mother and Niya, to help with the delivery. Niya brought her husband, Sergad, the shepherd of my flocks, and their two-year-old daughter, Tamar. Since Niya was inside the tent with her sister, Sergad was left to pace around the tent with me, holding Tamar in his arms.

Even between her contractions, Reya's screams echoed in my ears. I felt so helpless, and the minutes dragged on like decades. Surely having a child was not worth this pain, or a new life worth putting an existing one at risk?

I was taken right back to Benjamin's birth. I could almost see Jacob pacing around the tent, the women hustling about, and my brothers and I unsure of what to do with ourselves. I remembered sitting by a nearby river and dipping my feet into the cold water, clasping my hands over my ears to shut out Rachel's cries. I had waited for someone to notice I was missing, but nobody came. When I returned, I saw Jacob laying face down on the floor in the darkness. Frightened, I tapped his shoulder and asked, "Father, are you okay?" He said nothing as he looked up at me, his face covered in black ash; then his face turned to the floor and he began to weep.

"Father, why auntie yell?" asked little Tamar, her eyes full of fear. Her voice shook me from my memories and I was back in the present, realizing that now I was the father and it was my wife who could die. Sergad stroked his beard nervously, obviously unsure of what to say to reassure her. He had delivered hundreds of my animals, yet had no idea how to explain a human birth.

"Tamar, could you help your father feed my camels?" Just as the words left my mouth, Reya cried out again. Tamar nodded silently and, as she walked away with her father, Sergad turned to me and mouthed: "Thank you."

The women ran in and out of the tent, fetching more water or another knife, their hands and cloaks covered with clots of blood. Niya presented herbs which were supposed to speed up the delivery, and Reya's mother brought in the bucket of water heating over the fire, then another bucket straight from the well. I ordered one of my servants to bring food for the women. At dusk they took turns coming out of the birthing tent to eat and rest.

As the hours crawled by, Hirah arrived to offer me support. The man's eyes were as wide as a cow going to slaughter. He flinched at every scream, his head twitching to one side. The two of us sat outside, helpless, not speaking. I just stared at the floor, making lines in the sand with my feet. Was my wife's death a punishment for my sins against Joseph? Restless, I paced back and forth, my path marked into the dirt. I couldn't leave, and I couldn't stay. There was nothing I could do but wait.

After two tortuous days and nights, the loud shrieking of an infant finally filled the night air. I heard the women whispering over the cries of the baby, but I could not hear Reya's voice. Had the infant taken her life? At this point, I didn't even care if had a child; I just wanted my wife to be alive. Hirah placed his hand on my shoulder and squeezed it.

Finally, the midwife emerged from the delivery tent. The old woman's work was done.

"Is she alive?" I asked timidly, afraid to hear the answer. She nodded. Relief washed over me like a river.

Then, in the moonlight, I saw Niya walking out of the tent, holding a large baby wrapped in swaddling cloth. "It's a boy," she announced quietly.

He had patches of black hair on his head and his puffy eyes looked around angrily at the world that disturbed him. The wrinkles on his face made him seem like he was already troubled, and his already bushy eyebrows didn't quite separate in the middle. Gently, Niya placed the unusually large infant in my arms, and as I bent down to kiss my son, he began to shriek. I swallowed hard and drew him closer. He was faultless.

"His name will be Er," I declared. "As my first born son, he will be the guardian of all my possessions. My son. I have a son!" The word was as sweet as honey on my lips. I wanted to jump, dance, and scream with joy. But all I could do was stare at my son's beautifully grumpy little face.

I was a father.

Suddenly remembering about Reya, I rushed into the birthing tent. It was dark, with only a few flickering candles casting shadows on the walls of fabric. My wife's face seemed even darker; her mouth hung open and her breathing was heavy and strained. She was still wet with sweat, and I could see patches of dried blood all over the floor. I sat down near her mat, and took her hand in mine. She stirred. I pushed away the thought that she could have died, instead leaning down and whispering into her ear, "You made it." It was incredible to me that, somehow, this woman and I had created a child; a child that would grow up to love us, to hate us, and maybe be just like us.

As I was sitting there, Niya came in and placed Er into Reya's arms. Hastily, he began to suck at her breast. I was completely in awe at the scene before me. When Reya finally opened her eyes, long after Er had stopped feeding, I whispered, "This is just the beginning, darling Reya."

~~~

One year later, on what must have been the hottest day of the year, my second son was born. We named him Onan, meaning 'vigor', for we knew he would need strength to deal with his older brother. Whereas Er's birth had been long and painful, Onan was born in just a few hours. He was much smaller than Er, and his eyes were filled with mischief. The first time I held him, I could hardly believe that Reya and I had created such a handsome little face.

Er, the firstborn little prince of our household, did not like having to compete for our affection. When he saw Reya holding Onan for the first time, just a few days after the birth, he furrowed his thick brow and wailed for the next hour, throwing anything he could get his hands on.

As Er and Onan grew up, they took over our entire lives, from waking to sleeping. Sometimes I would be awake the whole night trying to stop Er from beating Onan, who had a habit of wandering into his older brother's tent. There was barely a day when the boys weren't fighting, hurting one of the animals, or breaking something. Er demanded that things went his way; if Onan ever tried to share his brother's wooden soldiers, Er would begin yelling and hitting him. Despite being younger, however, Onan was the stronger and smarter of the two, and he usually found a way to escape and get his revenge on Er.

Reya loved our sons selflessly and sacrificially; she surrendered her life to them. I lost my patience with them almost every day, but Reya kept her calm. I loved Er and Onan, but sometimes I had to admit that I strongly disliked them. Once, Er took my staff and began beating Onan, who found a sharp rock and
~~~

began hitting back. The result was a broken staff, and I was furious; that object was one of the few things I had brought with me when I left home. My sons had no respect for anyone or anything! I knew they needed to be punished, but if ever I threatened to give them the beating they deserved, Reya would appear and take one boy in each arm. Always, it would be me who would end up being yelled at.

If I ever tried to take away the children's toys or privileges, Reya would get defensive. She thought her sons were little angels, and no-one in the village, myself included, were allowed to discipline them. For what my brothers and I would have earned a good lashing, Er and Onan got away with by charming their mother. They were like the sun to her, the light of her life, but to everyone else they were like the unbearable midday heat. The only time she lost her temper was when Er broke Reya's expensive bottle of wine which she kept near her sewing supplies. But even then, their only punishment was an earlier bedtime. Every time I was about to punish the boys behind Reya's back, however, I remembered that what I had done to my own brother, Joseph, was worse than anything Er and Onan could imagine doing to each other. After that, I kept my own counsel.

Years crept by, and I could see that the lack of discipline was making Er and Onan self-centered and cruel. My promises to be a good father seemed long forgotten. Seeing my sons growing up made me wonder about my own father and brothers. How had we behaved as children? How did our four mothers deal with all of our silly arguments? Were my brothers' children as hard to manage as mine?

And then there was Joseph. I still dreamt of him often, and one nightmare in particular haunted me. I saw Joseph from behind, his wrists chained and his back whipped so many times that much blood was gushing out. He was sitting in a dark prison cell made of stone, crawling with filthy rats. The cell became smaller and smaller, and Joseph was crying out into the blackness. Then the prison transformed into the cistern we had cast him into.

Joseph turned around to me, his eyes as dark as the cave: "Judah, you did this to me."

~~~

Every couple of weeks, I would walk over to see Hirah on his side of the camp. His life had not changed much; he would have his favorite prostitutes spending the night, but clearly saw no need for any greater commitment to a woman. His three orphan children had grown up and moved to Egypt, and he lived alone with his servants, with the occasional traveler spending the night.

On one visit, after he had greeted me warmly, Hirah asked me about the boys. Clenching my jaw, I gave him a look of resignation and sighed: "How about a drink?"

Hirah laughed and ordered his servant to bring out his finest beer, brewed in the plain of Kezib. As the alcohol took hold, I told Hirah all about the recent dramas with the boys, and how it was interfering with my relationship with Reya. For the past few months, every time I would try to be intimate with my wife, Er and Onan would find some way to divert her attention to them.

"Judah," suggested Hirah, "why not take Reya away to Kezib for a night? I have a friend who lives there by the river with a spare tent for people traveling by. Take her there, spend an evening together. I'll watch your little lizards for you."

Maybe this was exactly what we needed. When I came home, I told Reya we were going away for a night. As I knew she would, her first thought was to ask about the boys. Rather than get annoyed, I decided to tell her how I really felt.

"Reya, I miss you. Since the boys were born I feel like we haven't been able to spend time together, just me and you," I began, taking her hand. "I miss your jokes, the way you cuddle up to me as we watch the stars; I just miss spending time with you, dear wife." I pulled her in close. "Come away with me for one night. Hirah will take care of the boys."
~~~

To my great surprise, Reya burst out laughing. It was a sound I hadn't heard in years. "Did he really say that? He obviously hasn't seen much of them together!"

"I know," I replied, chuckling. "That's why this is our one and only chance to escape."

~~~

Kezib, a few towns east of Adullam, was a quiet settlement set among rolling green hills. It was the perfect place to forget about the usual distractions and responsibilities of life. As we were sitting near the river at dusk, I could see that Reya's cheeks were flushed from wine. She looked older, her long black hair now marked with silver streaks. Her body had grown larger from bearing children, but she still looked so beautiful, like spring in full bloom. I realized that, somehow, I hadn't really *seen* her for a long time. We gazed into each others eyes, and I surprised myself again by reaching out and releasing the piece of twine that bound up her hair. It flowed down like a waterfall.

She leaned over and kissed me, igniting a fire like the first time she had touched my arm. Then, she got up, took off her robe, and jumped into the river. The last warmth of the day radiated from the sand and the dying fire. Soon, I too was playing around in the water, feeling like a man twenty years younger. This love was even deeper than the first.

Nine months later, our third son was born. We named him Shelah, meaning 'to prosper'. Reya and I decided even before he was born that we would be different this time around. We would take time to be together, and not let our lives be solely focused on the boys. His name also meant 'ease', and we hoped his birth would mark the end of our hardest times.

After his birth, we decided to move to Kezib. It was time for another new start. We packed up our tents, fed our animals, and moved all our possessions. I
~~~

joked with Hirah about leaving the boys behind, but he didn't find it even remotely funny. The time he had volunteered to watch them, the boys had found his knives, cut an ear off one of his sheep, and stabbed holes in his tent. Then they had sat down, awaiting their dinner with little smug faces. His look to me was one of pity, but which also seemed to say: "Never again."

As we settled at Kezib, Er and Onan seemed too busy with their constant rivalry to pick on their little brother. As he grew up, we saw that Shelah was very quiet and reserved, never speaking unless he really had to, and obeying his brothers without complaint. This way, they would leave him alone. Shelah's only friend, Belhan, was the son of one of my servants. The boys played together, but Belhan did most of the talking, while Shelah seemed content to listen. Reya and I were slightly concerned, but we had to admit that a quieter child made our lives easier.

The move to Kezib did everyone well. Reya and I spent the nights cuddling and talking, about everything and nothing. Years went by in the blink of an eye. The fights, the arguing, and dreariness of everyday life seemed bearable when she was in my arms.

Chapter 6

Tamar

My father's clenched fist was held up high, next to his face.

"Tamar, I have something for you," he said to me.

I felt nervous and excited, and began biting my lower lip, a little too hard. Father's hand lowered, his fingers loosened, and I saw a gold nose ring in the palm of his hand. Where did he get that? I had seen other girls wearing these precious rings, but never had anyone in my family of servants owned something of such value. I swallowed to try and clear the lump in my throat.

"Happy tenth birthday, my little date palm," said father. "You have brought your mother and me so much joy. We love you with our entire hearts, Tamar! Happy birthday, dearest daughter!"

My father worked so hard to make sure my mother and I had food to eat, spending each day herding sheep for one of the richest men in Kezib: Judah. Even though Judah's wife, Reya, was my mother's sister, father never came home with more than a few shekels to show for his hard work. Sometimes he would not eat so that mother and I would have enough. This gold ring must have cost him at least a year's salary from Judah! I looked up at my papa, and slowly reached out to touch the smooth metallic surface. Tears came to my eyes as I noticed the eager look on father's face. His shoulders were held back with pride, and as I ran towards him, he swept me into his arms and spun me around.

"Okay, Tamar, go into your mother's tent and she will pierce your nose for you." Only at this point did I realize I was actually going to have a hole in my nose. My stomach churned at the thought of the sharp piece of hot metal piercing the skin. But, I thought, it would all be worth it once my friends saw my new piece of jewelry.

I walked into mother's tent and saw her spinning on her loom. She sewed clothes for the servants and peasants in our village. My auntie, Reya, the *real* daughter - the word my mother taught me is 'legitimate' - also made clothes, but for rich people. My mother was born to a concubine, so she had very few rights: about as many as an average camel, she once told me. I never heard her complain, however, and she would often tell me it was an honor for her to help make the less wealthy feel beautiful. Somehow, she always found material at a good price, and would sell the clothes for just slightly more than they had cost to make. My auntie and my mother were not at all alike, but the one thing that united them was their love for fabric and needles; they delighted in seeing people trying on a garment for the first time, knowing they would be wearing it for years to come.

Mother looked up from her loom, her eyes shining as she saw me holding out the nose ring. "Tamar, darling, you will soon be a woman. Let's celebrate your last year of childhood," she said.

Oh no! Was she referring to this bleeding again? I was sick of hearing about it. How disgusting! Mother had told me that, when a girl becomes a woman, she has to bleed for a week every month for the rest of her life! In this heat, the thought seemed so dreadful. I absolutely, positively, refused to accept this fate, and would just walk away anytime she tried to tell me about it!

Seeing me squirm, mother laughed and said, "No, Tamar, I'm not talking about your menstrual cycle again; I'm talking about your piercing!"

She sat me down as her skillful, calloused fingers quickly pierced a small hole in my nose. I felt the hot needle, but before I even had a chance to cry out, the ring was inserted. My nose throbbed, but I felt extremely grown-up. A piercing! But as I looked down at the needle and saw my blood, my stomach tightened and I threw up all over the ground, just like every other time I had seen blood. I wiped my mouth and, looking up at mother, I could see her trying to suppress a giggle.

~~~

That evening, as the sun was setting and the desert breeze cooled the village, father made a fire under the date palms and mother brought out our food. Normally we would just have dry bread for dinner, but since it was my birthday, mother had also prepared cheese, olives, and dates. My mouth watered. I liked the dates best of all. My name means 'date palm tree', and I lived up to it by eating as much of the sweet fruit I could get my hands on.

After we had finished our food, I begged mother and father to tell me the story of their wedding day.

"Tamar, you've heard this story so many times! You could tell it better than us by now!" father replied.

"I know, but it's my birthday and you love me!" I pleaded, beaming.

Father shook his head and returned my smile. "Okay, but we are only telling it once."

"The first time I saw your mother', father began, between sips of wine, "her face was hidden under her wedding veil. Even though I couldn't see these big brown eyes, I could tell she was petrified. As I approached her, slowly, I didn't have a clue about what one should say to their future wife; the first thing that came out of my mouth was: 'Want to see my baby camel?'"

I giggled. My papa was so silly.

"You definitely caught me off guard," mother added. When she smiled the lines around her eyes became even deeper. She was a plain woman, but I thought she was the most beautiful person in the world. "I expected an introduction, not a baby camel! He turned around and slipped through the tent door. I guessed I was supposed to follow him."
~~~

"I took her outside," father continued, "and proudly showed her my newly acquired baby camel, sitting underneath the shade of a tree with his legs tucked into his furry body. I took care of Judah's sheep for an entire year to buy that creature! And I was so glad I did. Your mother bent down to pet the camel's head, then looked up, took off her veil, and smiled at me. When I saw her face something new was born in my heart, a love like I've never felt before. It was a love that is fierce, that wants to protect and fully accept. That fire was sparked, and just like this fire," he said, gesturing at the blaze in front of us, "my love burns for you and your mother." I smiled and glanced over at the old camel, now all grown up and happily chewing some leaves, tied to the nearby palm tree.

It was mother's turn. "Whenever we realized we were starting our wedding day with a baby camel instead of wedding guests," she said, taking father's hand, "we gave each other a smile and headed back into the tent. No words were needed." The way she looked at him, I knew there was a lot more to this story I didn't know, but it didn't bother me. I was so happy.

It was the sight of them telling their story, going back and forth like this, that made me never tire of hearing it. Every time they would finish it, something deep in my heart told me I was loved. My father's love for me burned like the fire, he had said, and it would never go out. And one day, when I was ready, my father would find a man to cherish me the way he did.

When it was time for me to go to bed, father picked me up in both hands and carried me to my corner of the tent. "Aren't I getting too old for you to carry me to bed like this, papa?" I asked.

"Maybe one day, and one day soon. But not yet," he whispered back.

As he set me down, I could feel a familiar feeling of panic creeping up my throat. I swallowed hard, knowing what was to come very soon. I wished he wouldn't leave, but I couldn't say that. I was ten years old now, and it was time to be a big girl.

I pushed away the scary thoughts and imagined what it would be like when I grew up. Who would daddy choose for me to marry, and what kind of a man would he be? What would our lives be like? Mother said that girls needed to marry when they were twelve or thirteen, but that seemed like such a long way away! I was ready to be married now! I tried to hold on to these beautiful thoughts to distract me from what I knew was coming.

I had never told anyone about it, not even father and mother. I didn't want them to know what happened to me at night. I would fight to stay awake as long as possible, trying not to notice how sweaty my palms were getting and how difficult it was to breathe. My shoulders would get tense and pressed up to my ears; nothing I did would relax them. *I need to stop biting my lip so hard*, I would think. Ugh, blood. Even the thought of it made me queasy. I was always scared to fall asleep because every night, as soon as my eyes closed, there were footsteps. I smelled the smoky fire. In the dreams, whatever the fire touched turned into blood. I was petrified.

And then, sometimes, I would hear the voice. *My daughter,* it would say.

The voice was my only comfort after these night terrors. Slowly, the heat returned to my body, and I could feel myself breathing again. The darkness gave way to the light. Who did that voice, the one who chased away the darkness, belong to?

Names

Viktoriya

In the society described in the book of Genesis, the choice of a child's name was itself a prophetic act, by which parents believed a chosen name declared their child's destiny.

My name means victory. As far back as I can remember, my mom and dad have always reminded me that I am made for victory. I was born in Kyrgyzstan, and my entire family moved to the USA on refugee visas when I was six years old. I remember my first day of first grade; I was dressed up in my puffiest dress, my shiniest black shoes, with big bows in my hair. Little did my mom know that kids in America didn't dress up for the first day of school like they did in Kyrgyzstan. I remember walking into that room full of thirty kids that didn't speak the same language as me, looking around and thinking, "I don't fit in here," From the fact that I needed a translator, to the fact that I brought exotic smelly Russian foods for lunch when all my friends were eating their PB&J sandwiches, it already seemed to my six-year-old self that I would have a lot to face.

I could not read or write very well. My brain was completely full of Russian letters and sounds (a thirty-three letter alphabet, really?), and there was simply no space for any more! Well, at least that's what I told myself. I was the slowest reader in my class. Not only because English was new to me, but also because the way words worked together didn't make sense in my head. Did you know that a Russian "r" and an English "p" are written exactly the same way? I was quickly falling behind in my classes as time went on. I spent many afternoons after school crying because I could not imagine anything worse than being forced to read and write. I understand now that my hurdle was small. Nonetheless, for me it was significant.

There were two teachers who noticed me struggling and decided to help me. One of them took me aside every week and helped me to journal. I wrote to her every day, and no matter how many mistakes I made, she encouraged me with notes like, "Brilliant! Fabulous! Keep writing!" My second grade teacher kept me behind after class every day for an hour for extra reading lessons. Progress was slow but she didn't give up on me. I had nothing to give her in return but she did it anyway, because she believed in me. Slowly, I started to gain confidence; I could master this whole reading and writing thing! Gradually, my grades improved and I would go on to be top of my class in high school, take honors classes, and go to university two years earlier than normal.

Today, journaling is still my primary means of communication with God, and reading is my means of relaxation, whilst reading the Bible is a place of adventure and discovery of my Creator. I found my passion, my hobby, and a way to express and recharge. All of this, God's plan for me to know and praise Him through writing, was made possible by my teachers who helped me overcome.

I love to write. I love the way my heart feels when it overflows with inspiration, feeling my fingers working furiously and filling an empty page. But the victory my parents declared for me is not confined to reading and writing. I believe that God's plan for my life is to bring victory into the lives of others. The name Viktoriya was my parents' shout of hope for my destiny. I have come to know the God of Victory, that same God who walked alongside Tamar and Judah.

Tamar's name means 'date palm tree', one of the few trees which can flourish in Palestine's arid climate. It does so by adapting to its surroundings. With a trunk that can tower as much as eighty feet above the ground, the *tamar* demands to be seen, even respected.

Jewish celebrations involved carrying and waving palm tree leaves and branches, as the people did when Jesus entered Jerusalem on 'Palm Sunday'. I loved it when we would act out this scene in Sunday school, standing in line and turning our little palm branches into swords and spears to poke each other with. Then when the music started we would become little smiling angels again, waving our branches at the adults making their procession along the red carpet of the church hall.

Palm trees also appear at the very end of the Bible, when Jesus returns and gathers his beloved ones back to Him.

After this, I looked, and there before me was a great multitude that no one could count, from every nation, tribe, people and language, standing before the throne and before the Lamb. They were wearing white robes and were holding palm branches in their hands. (Revelation 7:9)

I believe that Tamar's life was an act of celebration, just like those palm branches. She was not a descendant of Abraham, God's chosen people. She was a Canaanite, the very nationality Abraham wished for his sons not to marry. It was through unorthodox circumstances that she joined the tribe of Jacob, yet she is one of the matrons of the Christian faith. The Bible doesn't tell us much about her, but I can only imagine the incredible woman that she was.

Judah's name means 'praise'. When Judah was born, his mother Leah praised God even though her husband didn't love her. Judah's birth is a praise in the midst of messy family situations and sibling rivalry.

When the LORD saw that Leah was unloved, he enabled her to have children, but Rachel could not conceive... Once again Leah became pregnant and gave birth to another son. She named him Judah, for she said, "Now I will praise the LORD!"
(Genesis 29:31,35)

As you later read the Biblical account of Judah's life, keep the significance of his name in mind. Judah and Tamar were both people God chose to carry on the lineage of Jesus. It gets messy, it gets awkward, and there are many parts of the story I still don't understand. But God knew all of this, the mess, bitterness, anger, and the sins; he saw everything, and he still chose them. The unlikely, chosen for the incredible task of being the forerunners of Jesus.

On the very first page of the New Testament, where the lineage of Jesus is recorded, we meet our beloved Palm and Praise,

> *Jacob was the father of Judah and his brothers.*
> *Judah was the father of Perez and Zerah (whose mother was Tamar).*
> *(Matthew 1:3)*

Unlikely people, with a messy past, covered by grace and chosen to be the ancestors of Jesus. And what about the sweet, powerful name of Jesus? His name transcends definitions. His name is royalty that came down from heaven to earth, something we can never understand, and become everything that's wrong with this world, in order that we could carry us out of our brokenness and into his light. His name means that our sin has been defeated, and death has lost its sting, that everything in the world belongs to him.

Because of His name, what can your name mean?

54

Part 2

Chapter 7

Tamar

Why doesn't my father just accept a marriage proposal on my behalf already? Many men have come to him in the last five years; there have been sons of servants, sons of shepherds, even a slave boy who wanted to marry me. Some have offered a bride price; others have offered next to nothing. I am ready to be married, but father always says no. I am nineteen years old after all! Most of the girls my age in Kezib are long married, many with children on the way.

I know that father wants the best for me, but if he doesn't accept any offers for my marriage soon I will end up in his house forever, a virgin with no future! The thought makes me shudder. It's not that it bothers me to live with my parents, but I do care how the people in our town treat unmarried women. A woman who isn't ready to bear children or who is born into a poor family is not allowed to do anything for herself. It annoys me that my mother has the same value as a slave just because she is born to a concubine. "Just the way things are, Tamar," mother always says when I try to tell her what I am thinking. I was taught from a young age that it is my job to learn how to be a good wife and mother. That is the epitome of my existence.

On one hand, I want so much to fit in with my friends, sitting around in the marketplace talking about all the silly things their husbands get up to. Some have good men who love them, while others have husbands who hurt them, take concubines, or who are always traveling to the city. Either way, each accepted her fate. I want to know what it feels like to be loved by a man, to have a tiny baby wrap its chubby little hands around my fingers and say, "mamma." On the other hand, I get so bored of doing housework - cleaning, cooking, repeat - that the thought of my life being reduced to these tasks makes me want to vomit.

My thoughts press hard on my head, just like the water jug I carry to the well twice each day. It is one of my household jobs I like the most; I certainly mind it a lot less than washing clothes or clearing up the dishes after supper. What in the entire world could be worse? I love this time alone every morning and evening, fetching water for my mother and father. As I reach the well, I set down the clay water jug, lower my head into the well, and yell at the top of my lungs. The echo comes from deep within the stone chamber, making my voice sound strong. I shake my head, as if that would help get rid of this tension, and decide not to think anymore. I begin to lower my water jug into the well, as I have done day in, day out, for as long as I can remember. The sturdy rope around its handle does its job, and in a daze I watch the vessel descending lower and lower towards the unseen water below.

"Tamar," I hear a man's voice say. Startled, I let go of the rope and the clay jug slashes into the water. I turn around and see Judah standing there, his colorful robes hanging majestically over his large shoulders.

"Good morning, Master Judah," I say quietly, looking down at my sandy feet. I can feel my cheeks flushing. Why was he here? Judah smiled, his white teeth gleaming brightly.

"Tamar, could you get me a drink of water please?"

Why was he asking me, of all people, to get him a drink of water? He had plenty of servants who could make this trip for him. Only servants and women made this trip to the well. And to make matters worse, I can't even oblige because I had dropped my water jug.

"Well you see, when you said my name...." I really don't know what to say. Judah smiles again, and this time I can see he is trying not to laugh. I feel even more embarrassed, my cheeks flushing red. And then, without saying another word, he turns around and walks away.

~~~

I forcefully pulled aside the tent door, walked in, and sat down. My mother looked confused when she saw that I had no jug and no water with me. "What have you done, Tamar?" she asked, clearly frustrated. I looked down, not knowing whether or not to tell her about Judah. "Please don't tell me you dropped it in the well. Tamar, you know we don't have enough money to buy another one, and it will take a few days to make a replacement! What are we supposed to drink now? And the rope..."

On and on she went, about how I needed to be more careful, that I needed to stop acting like a little child and start being responsible like a woman. I said nothing, still staring at the dirt below me. My mother pouted for the rest of the day, clearly still bearing a grudge against my clumsiness.

That evening, when my father came home from Judah's fields, he walked straight into my mother's tent, looking extremely excited. I could hear them whispering inside. Curious, I left the bread in the fire on its own, and crept up to them.

"Are you sure, Sergad?" whispered my mother in a concerned voice. "I don't know if he's the best choice for her."

"Look, Niya, we know this family, I trust them. I've worked for Judah since before Tamar was born. We watched Er grow up. They will treat her well, and they'll be able to give her what I could never give you."

Then there was silence followed by the sound of their footsteps approaching the door. I ran quickly back to my bread. Finally, they were talking about my marriage! Shivers went down my back, even in the evening heat. Could it possibly be true? Could Judah have asked for my hand in marriage to his oldest son? Er was the man every young girl wanted to marry. He was two years younger
~~~

than me, but as large as a bear and as majestic as a lion. I was so lost in this possibility that I didn't even hear my parents approaching.

"Tamar, were you listening in?" asked my father in a mischievous tone. I smiled back. He took my hand and led me to our campfire. "Let's have dinner first, and then we can talk."

I sat down, gulped the wine, and stuffed my face with bread as quickly as I could. Hands folded on my lap, I stared at mother and father as they slowly ate their meal, savoring every bite. Why were they taking so long? Why couldn't they just tell me now? My whole body was tense with anxious excitement.

"That was delicious bread you made, Tamar," father said as he patted his belly approvingly.

"Tamar, would you stop biting your lip? It's going to bleed again," mother scolded. She was clearly still upset about the water jug. I gave an exasperated sigh, my shoulders slumping.

Finally, they finished their bread and father began to explain. "Tamar, you know how much your mother and I love each other. Our lives have definitely been improved by our union. You also know that I have received many requests for your marriage. I was holding off because I didn't trust those men." He lingered, as if trying to hold onto something very precious that was being taken from him. "But...I trust Judah."

I remembered Judah's face at the well earlier today. Did his strange appearance have something to do with this conversation? Seeing my confusion, father explained further. "Before I came home today, Judah came into the fields and proposed to me that Er should take you as his wife." He stalled. "My little palm, what do you think about that? I want the very best for you. I don't know Er, but I know Judah. He is a kind man, and Er seems like man with a bright future ahead of him. Most importantly, their family has wealth, so you will be provided for. That's just as important as having a loving marriage. I don't want you to just eat bread for the rest of your life." He rubbed his temples, and ran his calloused fingers through his grey hair. Why did he look so ashamed? "It was something I could never do for your mother." He cleared his throat and asked quietly, "Do you trust me, Tamar?"

I was being given a choice, one I knew most women in the world would not get. I had a father who had every right to pick my husband, but as I saw him focusing his gaze on me, his look radiating affection, I wanted to trust him. How could I not? This man loved me more than he loved himself.

"Okay, father, I will marry Er."

~~~

Normally the father of the bride would prepare the wedding feast, but Judah had agreed to take care of it all, since he knew my father had very little. I didn't see Judah or Er at all during the planning, but Aunt Reya was scheduled to come over to talk over the details with my mother. We expected her to come alone, but near the time she was supposed to arrive, we saw two figures approaching our home.

I had always thought that Reya looked very similar to my mother, yet now her face looked hard and determined, her head held up high. It was such a contrast to my mother's soft gaze, her understanding eyes often downcast, not looking straight at people. Reya approached; she was wearing a little cloth wrapped around her chest and a long skirt that flowed freely from her hips. She had henna over her arms and belly, and her hair was half gathered up, the rest flowing down her exposed back. I wondered who the woman with her was, whose face and body were completely covered in a shiny black garment which only exposed her hands. She was such a contrast to Reya, who showed as much skin as a temple dancer.

As the two women arrived, mother invited them to sit underneath our palm tree, on the other side of my camel. I looked at my mother, who seemed uncomfortable, holding her hand in front of her mouth as she spoke. Why was she behaving like this? She had a few teeth missing, but I had never seen her look
~~~

ashamed before. She also kept fixing her robes, tugging them from one side to another. Seeing her like this made me feel uneasy too. My mother never said anything bad about her sister, yet now I was old enough to tell something was wrong in the way they interacted with each other. For the first time in my life, I saw how different these two sisters were. My mother's clothes seemed like rags compared to the expensive robes Reya was wearing, her tent shabby, and her dishes cracked. An anger began to rise in me. My poor mother; it wasn't her fault her own mother had been a concubine, while Reya's had been the legal wife. Reya carried herself like a queen, and the woman I saw as my confident, beautiful mother shrank in her presence.

When we sat down and Reya's companion took off her long veil, my mother and I couldn't help but stare. She was the most beautiful person I had seen in my life. She looked only a few years older than me, and her eyes were huge and blue like the sky, framed with long thick lashes. I had never seen anyone with such light skin. She had high cheekbones and her lips were full and ruby red. She was very tall, but her large frame was filled out with flowing curves. Her skin glowed in the sunlight, and when she smiled I swallowed hard. Even Reya's exquisite beauty paled in comparison.

As if Reya saw what we were thinking, she let out a deep sigh and cleared her throat. "This is Dinah, Judah's sister. She is here to help with the wedding preparations."

Though this was my first time seeing her, I had heard a lot about Dinah. She was the one who was raped by the prince of Shechem, and her brothers massacred the entire village of Shechem in revenge. The story was often told by people for miles around as they sat around the campfire. Now that I had seen her beauty, the tale made much more sense.

"So nice to meet you, Tamar," said Dinah, looking into my eyes and taking my hand. Her hands felt like smooth marble and I noticed that her nails were short and clean. "I am so excited to welcome you into our family. Sadly, I was the only sibling invited along for the occasion, as I am the only one living nearby. I am so happy to be here with you, and I will make your wedding the most festive occasion it can be."

I listened and nodded silently, still unable to speak. Then Dinah took out a white fabric I had never seen before, as smooth as the surface of a river. Silk, she called it. The fabric was elegantly turned into a beautiful skirt, which came with a shoulder wrap. I saw Reya look away as Dinah handed the silk to me, nodding in the direction of the tent. My mother and Reya stayed under the tree, while Dinah helped me to undress and try on the silk garments. Strangely, I didn't feel uncomfortable around her at all. Her beauty was so inviting, making you feel at ease.

"If you would like to wear this dress on your wedding day," she said, "it will be my present to you." I didn't know what to say. This fabric cost more than what I would fetch as a slave. Still captivated by her beauty, I bobbed my head up and down.

Aside from the nose ring my papa had given me, this was the most expensive thing I had ever owned. As the dress slid over my body, all my nerves about what it would be like to be a wife and mother faded away. I could hardly wait to wear this beautiful garment and, finally, become a wife.

~~~

On my last night as an unmarried woman I lay awake in my bed, sleep escaping me. All my life I had been waiting for this moment; now that the day was so close, the anticipation was consuming me. As my body finally gave in to sleep, I felt the darkness I had lived through as a child overcoming me. I hadn't experienced the dreams about blood and fire for a long time, yet somehow my body remembered the anxiety of it, slipping into an all too familiar pattern.
~~~

Suddenly, somewhere between sleep and reality, I saw myself standing next to a man so dark that he made my blood go cold. He looked into my soul and flashed me a vicious smile. I tried to run away but, as I looked down, my feet were chained to the ground. He grabbed me; I couldn't move. Shrill laughter came out of his gaping mouth as my beautiful silk wedding gown turned into blood.

I jumped out of bed, shivering uncontrollably, and saw that it was still the middle of the night. The only sounds were the chirping of the crickets and the wind sweeping the sands harshly against my tent. I needed to see my mother. I stood outside her tent, still shaking and covered in goosebumps from the cold night air, and quietly called for her. My father slept like a stone. I hoped my mother would hear me call above his deafening snores. After a few minutes, mother's sleepy head emerged from her tent. Her hair was tied into a long braid and she was wearing her sleeping tunic.

"Can you please come to my tent?" I whispered. The request made me feel more like a child than a woman on the verge of her wedding day. Mother looked surprised, but didn't ask any questions. She disappeared into her tent then reappeared a few moments later with her woolen blanket and followed me to my bed. Still shivering, we got under the covers and she wrapped her soft arms around me.

"I'm scared, mother," I confessed.

"My daughter," was all that she said; she didn't ask any questions or scold me like I had expected. As I looked at her gentle face, I saw my own fears, worries, and doubts mirrored in her eyes. She understood, and was perhaps even more scared than I was. She opened her mouth to say something else, but instead just sighed. Then she pulled me close and whispered into my ear, "I love you, Tamar."

With those words echoing in the fearful places of my heart, and with her arms wrapped around me, I fell asleep as a single woman for the very last time.

Chapter 8

Tamar

Though the wind howled in the night, the morning that followed was bright and warm. As the first sunlight broke through the awakening sky, Dinah rode over on her camel and the two women rubbed my body with oils, lined my eyes with charcoal, and put a red berry dye over my lips and cheeks. My mother braided my long hair into a thick braid, weaving it together with ribbons and flowers. Dinah took hours to carefully paint my entire body with intricate patterns. When the paint was finally dry, the sun was already starting to peek out from behind the mountains. My mother helped me into my dress, and as the two women held the mirror in front of my face, I almost didn't recognize the girl in the reflection.

My father brought my beloved camel for me to ride towards the tents of Judah, the place of my wedding feast. Leaving the camel tied underneath a palm tree, father walked into my tent.

"Tamar," he said gently, as his eyes began to fill with tears. "My beautiful little girl is all grown up." He cleared his throat. Seeing him gazing at me, I was overcome with emotion. Oh, how he loved me. As he focused on me, I remembered the voice I used to hear after my nightmares, a voice which stilled my fears and which was accompanied by an overwhelming sense of peace. I hadn't heard that voice for years, but at this moment I felt that same peace again.

He led me out of my childhood home for the last time and helped me to mount the camel. I patted its head and it fluttered its lips in acknowledgement. I made sure my silk dress was not dragging behind us, and then father led me towards my new home, followed my mother and Dinah. I looked over my shoulder, seeing the two little tents, side by side, and the palm tree I had spent so much time under; it seemed like every childhood memory gently surfaced, treasures for me to take to my new life. Tears brimmed in my eyes, but as the morning sun gently caressed my face, I smiled underneath my wedding veil. Today was not a day for tears.

As I approached the familiar sight of Judah's encampment, I was astounded to see that Dinah and Reya had managed to create a beautiful sanctuary for me. There were tapestries hung from the trees, large wooden tables set with metal plates, burning candles, incense, and much food and wine, all of which filled the whole camp with a delicious aroma. I was amazed at the transformation; they must have had the servants decorating and preparing for days!

As I looked around, I saw people from Kezib, Adullam, and the other surrounding towns, only a few of whose faces I recognized. As I dismounted, the crowd parted and a rush of whispers danced around the party. Unsure of what to do, I walked towards the main table with my parents close by my side. I saw Judah and Er on the other side, Judah's arm proudly around Er's shoulder, talking, laughing, and drinking. They looked over at me, waved, and returned to their conversation. The people saw their response and followed the example, returning to their festivities.

"Looking good, little sister." I turned around to see Onan standing there, two women draping themselves over him. "Good luck being married to Er! The man is a donkey with the mind of a snake." The two women laughed at his words and stroked his face seductively. He tilted his head to one of them, whispered something, winked at me, and walked towards the food table.

As the feast continued, people drank too much and then danced to the music. Judah took out a flute, leading a few men in playing a wedding melody. Some women from Adullam joined them on their wooden drums. The sound they created together was hypnotic. I watched people eat and dance, but didn't know what to do with myself. My father stayed very close to the food table that the servants constantly replenished, and mother hid in the kitchen, offering to help the servants. Eventually Judah told his servants to gather all the people for his speech, which took a long time, given that most of the guests were drunk. Eventually everyone was seated at the long wooden tables.

Judah stood there under the open skies, and spoke in his deep booming voice: "I came to these lands many years ago, looking for a new start. Thanks to my best friend, Hirah, I met the woman who became the love of my life. Let's drink to Reya!" Everyone happily obliged as Judah continued: "She blessed me with the greatest honor of all: three warrior sons. And now we get to see my firstborn, Er, taking a wife. What a joyous day it is!" He turned towards Er and motioned for him to stand up. "My son, the watchman over everything I own. One day you will own half of all that is mine. But for now, may you have a happy life, be treated with honor and respect, and have many, many descendants to fill these lands. May the God of my forefathers, Abraham and Isaac, bless you, make you fruitful, and make your children multiply to fill these lands."

A loud cheer rippled through the crowd. My father looked over at me, his brow furrowed.

Reya stood up next and gave thanks to her many gods. She offered incense, then praised her firstborn, offering a toast after describing Er's many achievements. After the speeches, more food was brought out and the guests resumed their dancing.

The sun was low when Er finally drew to my side. "Tamar," was all he said. His breath stank of alcohol, and his eyes were slightly drooping. I saw that his eyebrows were joined together as one, as thick as a caterpillar. He was not as handsome as I had heard. When he stood next to me, I saw he was much taller than I expected; I only came up to his chest. My stomach was doing flips underneath my silk dress as I tilted my head to look back at him. Somehow, he was not at all what I expected. His stench actually made me queasy. I scolded myself;

what an awful thing to think about my husband. My husband! The word resounded through my entire body, causing me to smile shyly.

"Hello, Er," I replied. I remembered the story my parents told me of their wedding day. Was this going to be part of the tale I would tell our children?

Er and I walked around together during the rest of the party, speaking to people I didn't know. He held my hand, which felt very small in his, as he guided me through the crowds. He smiled at everybody and was very charming. Sometimes his tipsiness would cause him to stumble, and it took all my strength to help him stay standing. I could see that the guests loved him; many told me how lucky I was to be married to a man like Er, to which he happily nodded. Clearly they hadn't smelt his breath, I thought, before I caught myself again.

Night finally arrived, and I was exhausted. My stomach wasn't used to all this rich food, my feet were sore from dancing, and my mouth hurt from constantly smiling. I just wanted to lay down and sleep. The day wasn't anything like I had hoped for. There was something about the way Er acted around me that made me nervous: like how he had stepped on my toe without even noticing, and when I cried out, looked at me with disgust; or how he had never really looked into my eyes. Where was the moment I had imagined in my head, where our eyes locked and we began to fall deeply in love? He had looked at me a few times, but it wasn't in a way any woman would want.

With his large hand still squeezing mine, Er led me back to our wedding tent, where we would stay for a week while the rest of our guests continued to feast. My heart was pounding so loudly I was afraid Er would be able to hear it. My mother hadn't told me much about what would happen on the wedding night, but I had heard plenty of stories from girls my age in our village. Some said the first time was really painful, while others enjoyed it greatly. Some of the girls warned me to make sure the man withdrew so that I wouldn't get pregnant right away, while others said not to be shy and try everything out. But no matter how much those girls told me, I was still nervous.

"Follow me," Er stuttered, by now completely drunk. His whole body reeked of alcohol and he was stumbling along the path, leaning on me for support. He was heavy, and I found it hard to keep upright. My knees felt like they were going to buckle. When we reached the tent, Er tugged on my hand. Shocked, I flinched, surprised at how hard he was pulling me. Seeing my resistance, an anger like fire sparked in his eyes. "You had better do as I say, woman."

My mouth hung open, and I could feel the lines on my forehead pressing together. How could he speak to me this way? Never in my life had someone used such a harsh tone with me. Father was always gentle, even when rebuking or disciplining me.

Once we were inside, Er closed over the tent door and turned around slowly. My blood ran cold, and my anxiety and nausea were becoming stronger. What had I gotten myself into?

"Listen to me, Tamar," he said, slurring his words. "My father asked for me to marry you, but you come from a family of servants. You are worth nothing. You will listen to me without questioning. Do you understand?"

Was this some sort of joke? Biting my lower lip, I remembered my mother's warnings about making it bleed, and relaxed my jaw.

Suddenly, Er came towards me and slapped me across the face, knocking me over onto the dirt floor. Stunned, I started to feel heat where his hand had been. I didn't know what to do. Should I run? Scream? I was shaking with fear, but couldn't do anything else.

Er lowered himself onto the ground next to me. Then he reached into the pocket of his robe and pulled out a knife with a crude blade. I could barely breathe as he lifted the weapon high above his head. "I want you to know, without any doubt, that you are my servant. You must do everything I say." My body began to shake, but my mouth remained clenched shut. As he lowered the knife towards me, I managed to open my mouth to scream, but in a flash he slammed his free hand over my face. I recoiled, feeling the blade right next to my mouth. "If you dare..." The look in his eyes was wild. I was horrified, but Er was clearly enjoying this; the darkness in his eyes was the image I had seen in my dream last night.

Er took the knife to my silk wedding dress, slashing it from bottom to top. He ripped off the fabric, leaving me helpless and exposed. I lay there naked, trying to make myself as small as possible.

"If you tell anyone about this, I swear to the God of my father that you will not see another day on this earth." He grabbed my long braid of hair and cut it off in one swift movement. Part of the knife had pierced my back as he did this, and I could feel blood seeping out. He laughed, dipping his fingers in the blood, smearing it all over my face.

Just like it had since childhood, the sight of blood made me nauseated, and sent my head spinning. I bent over as my body retched and I threw up everything I had eaten, covering Er's sandals and the edge of his robe in my vomit.

He was outraged. "How dare you! You disgust me!" He began to pound me with his fist as hard as he could, each blow worse than the last. It was a pain like I had never experienced. In his drunken state he missed every now and again, which only made him even angrier and the next blow even harder. "You deserve this. How dare you vomit on me, your master!"

I was too weak to move by the time his fists dropped by his side. And that's when he forced himself into me. The pain was unbearable; I could feel blood gushing out. I threw up in my mouth again. Too afraid to spit it out, I swallowed as his body continued to writhe on top of me. His large body was crushing my bones, preventing me from breathing. Finally, he cried out in satisfaction and I could feel his body relax. I couldn't have moved, even if I tried. After what seemed like an age, he pulled himself out and stood up, staring at me, bloodied and bruised on the floor. Then, after urinating on me, he turned and left without another word.

Hours later, I lay on the mat weeping, blood smeared over my legs and the floor. Every sob hurt, but I couldn't stop.

I reached my hand up to touch my hair, now hanging weakly around my ears. My hair. My papa used to brush my hair and tell me how beautiful it was. I saw the braid, still in tact, lying against the side of the tent, its flowers and ribbons mocking me. It took all the strength I had left not to faint.

Looking around, I saw nothing I could clean myself up with, only the scraps of my silk wedding gown that Er had ripped down the middle. The white fabric lay pathetically on the ground, covered in sand and dirt. I lifted it and held it close to my face, trying to wipe away as much of the filth as possible. Soon, there was no white to be seen on my wedding dress; the garment was altogether filthy, forever maimed and ruined, just like its owner.

Still lying naked in the tent, I began to shiver. It started with my legs and soon my entire body was shaking uncontrollably. I tried to cover my breasts with my arms for warmth, but the pain was too much and I quickly lowered them again. I didn't know how much time had passed; minutes or days, it was now all the same to me. Then, without warning, I heard heavy footsteps outside the tent, and Er was standing before me, smiling, as he took off his clothes yet again.

~~~

The next week of torture was worse than I could ever have imagined in my nightmares. I could hear the wedding feast going on in the background, but the music and dancing were too loud for anyone to hear my cries of pain. Hadn't anyone noticed that the bride was missing? Er would come and go, doing whatever his heart desired. All I could do was lay feebly on the floor of the tent, too weak to run away.
~~~

This first week of marriage was surreal: at first, the only emotion I felt was confusion, which expressed itself in floods of tears; but, as Er's actions became a pattern, I started to feel angry. At one point, I clenched my teeth together so hard that I felt a piece break off. Holding the tiny chip of my tooth in the palm of my hand, I wondered if this was how things would be for the rest of my life? The darkness I used to feel as a child surrounded me again, only this time I realized that the one torturing me was my husband, and that I was never going to wake up.

Chapter 9

Tamar

One month after I lost my freedom, my parents came to visit me on Er's property, on the outskirts of Judah's land. His parents had given him a large amount of animals, a few servants, and a tent to live in as a wedding present. Er was at work and I had secretly sent one of his servants to my parents' house to invite them over.

Ever since the first day after our wedding, Er insisted I wear a full body veil anytime I was around people, which was infrequent, for he didn't want anyone to suspect what kind of man he really was. The veil was black, and very similar to the one Dinah had been wearing for protection when I first met her. But Dinah's veil was to hide her beauty, while mine was to hide my shame.

As my parents approached my tent, they whispered to each other as they saw my black veil. We exchanged greetings like strangers who had run into each other at the market. I led them to the table my servants had covered with rich foods. Their eyes widened as they saw the selection of the finest produce I had requested for them; father forgot everything else and began to eat as fast as he could. We sat in silence, with just the servants bustling around, seeing to our needs.

I was resentful as I remembered how we had eaten when I was a little girl. We had so little, but somehow we had been very happy. But I wasn't that child anymore, and it was all their fault. Once they had finished eating, I dismissed the servants. What I wanted to do I knew would hurt them, but I proceeded with it.

Slowly, I took off my black veil, and instantly they gasped at the sight of my face. My lower lip was swollen, my left eye a dark blue, and there were black bruises all over my arms, neck, and shoulders. My mother jumped up and rushed to my side of the table: "Oh Tamar, what in the world has happened?"

I hesitated slightly, but proceeded to tell them exactly how Er was treating me, not sparing any details. After the initial shock, my mother continued to mourn and my father sat with his head in his hands, trembling. Battling with the memories, I finished with the accusation I knew could hurt father as much as I was hurting inside: "Father, Er was *your* choice."

He looked at me as if I had died before his very eyes. Never in my life had I seen my father cry, but in this moment, he broke down. "Oh Tamar, I know," he whispered.

I knew it was wrong to blame him like this. My father wanted the very best for me, and he would take my place one hundred times over in order to spare me Er's abuse. But I couldn't help myself. It felt so good to hurt someone instead of being the one hurting. Father reached for my hand as he said, "Tamar, let's go, right now. We'll run away to Egypt, and we'll never have to hear of Er or Judah again."

"You know we can't do that," I shot back. "You don't have any money. You couldn't provide for us if we left." I knew how he blamed himself for our poverty, and I was hitting him exactly where I knew it would hurt the most.

My mother wiped her face and whispered, "Tamar, we'll figure something out. Nothing else matters to us other than your safety, your happiness. Let's just leave right now."

"Stop it, mother. There is nothing that can be done now."

Deep down, I wanted to run into their arms, to cry until it was all gone, and to run back home with them. But it was all a lie. They wanted to protect me, but they had failed me. And the One whose voice gave me peace; how dare He make me feel so safe before the biggest tragedy of my life, where all my fears came true?

So instead of trusting my fate into their hands again, I put my veil back on and walked away from the only two people in the world who loved me. I commanded Er's servants to escort my parents out. They refused to go and, eventually, the servants had to pick up the people who had once given me life and forcefully carry them away from me. When the servants returned, I paid for their silence with some of Er's shekels and then sat down on the floor of the tent, anticipating the abuse that would soon come. There was nothing else I could do.

~~~

I often wondered if Judah and Reya knew the truth about their son. It seemed like nobody, not even his parents or the servants, suspected there was a problem. He was very good at pretending to be something he was not. Sober, he was proud and overconfident, but at least he wasn't cruel. As soon as he drank, though, he would become a ravenous lion, and I was the helpless prey.

Everyday, Er would go to oversee his father's household, bossing the servants around but not doing much work himself. One day, months after our wedding, he came home and I immediately knew something was different. He wasn't drunk. He took off his sandals and forcefully laid his head, dirty from a day's work, into my lap.

His soberness and close proximity almost shocked me more than the pain of a first blow. "Listen, I know that whenever I drink I get a little angry, but today I found out why it isn't my fault." I'm glad I was wearing my veil, because otherwise he would have seen my reaction. "This morning I went to visit my mother. It wasn't even midday and I saw she was already drunk. She cheerfully offered me a drink, and when I hesitated, she said, 'Why not? You've been drinking since before you were born.' Then she laughed and said, 'Shh, don't tell your father.' So there you go, it's not my fault I like to drink so much, okay? I've never known a life without alcohol," he said, sitting up with ease and staring straight at me.

The man looking back at me was one I had never seen before; frail, maybe even hurting, as if he had been drowning and had grasped his first breath of air. That proud look and the cruel darkness in his eyes were gone. But now it was
~~~

my turn to be cold. Did he expect sympathy from me after the way he had treated me? Even now, in our very first normal conversation as husband and wife, here he was, failing to take responsibility for his actions. If anything, his confession only made me despise him more. What kind of man would blame the bruises on my body on the mother he claimed to love deeply? His explanation only showed me more of his true self: a coward, a madman, nothing more than a pathetic, boneless worm.

I was not going to accept this pathetic excuse for an apology. I would never let it go. His sorrow and my bitterness hung in the air between us, moments passing into minutes. I loathed Er and would never forgive him. I stood up and walked out of the tent.

As I hid outside, anticipating the beating I knew was soon to come, I was surprised instead to see Er storming out and heading towards Adullam. That night, instead of beating me, Er brought home a prostitute and I was forced to sleep outside on the floor. For hours, all I could hear was him yelling her name, Rahab, over and over again. I wasn't jealous or angry, only glad it wasn't me as I listened to the girl struggling to escape. This had been the only time he tried to let me in, and since I had pushed him away, he fell even deeper into his darkness, dragging me with him.

~~~

As a little girl, the thought of my monthly bleeding disgusted me. I could have never imagined that, one day, I would look forward to it so eagerly. On those too few days, I was so thankful that I could retreat into a separate tent to sit on the mat and escape the drunken beatings. It was the only time Er didn't touch me, for he feared the uncleanliness my menstruation brought.

One night, while Er was forcing himself on me even more violently than usual, I comforted myself with thoughts that my bleeding was only a few days away.
~~~

But, as the days passed, the blood which I had come to love never came. The horrible possibility loomed in my mind, more horrible than any bruise Er could have inflicted on me: was I really pregnant with this monster's child?

~~~

As weeks went by, and the bleeding still didn't come, I realized there was no way around it. I was certain I was with child. My already bruised breasts ached even more, and I felt queasy and nauseous. But, to my surprise, hatred for my husband didn't stop me loving the growing child in my womb. Slowly and steadily, a fierce love filled me, a love like the one I remembered my father describing to me as a child. I wanted to be a mother who would lay down her life for her child, protecting it from all harm. Gradually, a plan formed in my mind. The only way I could be that kind of mother was to hide my pregnancy and escape from Er once and for all.

I began to accept Er's abuse without complaining, and he was too dumb and drunk to suspect anything. When he would begin punching and kicking me, I took the blows to my head, back, and legs, being careful to protect my growing midsection. I made sure that, whenever he would force himself into me, there were no candles lit. I needed the darkness to hide the life within me. I would lie with my eyes open, numb on the inside, trying with all my strength to ignore the pain spreading like fire throughout my body.

As my escape drew nearer and I knew the pain would soon be over, the beatings became easier to endure. I dreamed of my life after Er; I would do whatever it took, even sell myself as a prostitute or slave, to keep my child alive. Even if I couldn't find work or money, I would rather die out in the wilderness than give Er the chance to hurt my baby.

~~~

A few months passed, and I began to notice my stomach getting bigger. My plan was working. Once, after I ate a few dates, the food I craved most, I felt the baby kick. That little flutter gave me the strength to endure, to one day hold those tiny feet in my hands.

The night before I planned to run away, Er walked home in his usual drunken state. He made straight for me, and I had no time to blow out the candles. He started to rip off my clothes and I clenched my teeth. I was six months pregnant and without my clothes you could clearly see the bump on my tummy. That night, in the slight glow of the candle, he saw. First, he looked hurt, then horrified, then angrier than I had ever seen him.

Blow after blow rained down on my head and stomach. The stomach, over and over. Pain. Blood. I was being punished. For the first time since the wedding night, I fought back. I scratched and clawed, but I unable to defend myself. He was much too strong. Clumps of my hair were torn out of my bleeding scalp. Er's face was above me, spitting, swearing, biting. He took some rope and tied my hands and legs to the two side of the tent. My tied body fit just perfectly between, and I knew he had measured it all out before. A new wave of strength washed over me. I could not let him steal the life of my baby. I squirmed and tried to bite him back, but felt myself being pulled towards each side of the tent. Then, Er took his walking staff and began to hit my belly repeatedly. The pain was unbearable, stopping me from moving. I felt the child within me shifting. I lay there, rigid, tied between two poles, too sore to cry. This was my final defeat; I could do nothing to save this little life. Finally, everything went black as I slipped out of consciousness.

~~~

I opened my eyes and was relieved to see Er was gone. As my memories flooded back, I saw I was still tied to the tent poles. I felt the sharp pain in my back and on one side. I looked down between my legs, and saw a tiny figure lying there, lifeless.
~~~

A strength I did not have earlier stirred within me and I was able to rip myself from the ropes restraining me. I gently picked up the fragile body. It was a little girl.

She was only the size of my palm. Her bloodied fingers and toes were all curled up, and she was still tied to me. As I looked down on the beautiful form in my hands, I couldn't even cry. She was perfect. I saw her eyelashes, almost transparent, and the little bow of her lip that was smaller than my fingernail. With every hair on my head, with every breath I exhaled, with my very being and existence, I loved this little girl.

Seeing the knife that had fallen out of Er's pocket, I severed the cord that connected me to my daughter. Then I stood up, somehow not even feeling my own pain, and ran to the nearest well with an empty bucket. I had never run that fast before, urged on by a force pulling me back to my daughter.

Soon I was back in the tent and boiling the water over a fire. When it was just warm enough, I picked up my little girl and gently washed off the blood and sand that had gathered on her body. I decided to name her Davida, the 'one who was beloved'. I didn't even have anything I could dress her in. Taking a red ribbon I had saved from my hair on my wedding day, I wrapped Davida in it. It fit perfectly around her little figure. Then, I just sat in silence, looking at her serene face. I would have given my life one hundred times over, or an eternity of living with Er, just to see one breath coming out of those little lips.

~~~

The sun was starting to set. How had the day passed so quickly? The thought of Er's return shook me back into the present moment and I found a shovel and began to dig a hole underneath the palm tree. The hole was not wide but it was deep. I gently placed Davida into the ground, covered her in a layer of wild flowers and, with great hesitation, replaced the soil above her. With each lump of soil, I was throwing away my last hopes, my broken maternal instincts, and my will to live. I
~~~

found a rock and placed it over the grave, so that no-one could see the soil had been disturbed.

It didn't matter if Er killed me. There was nothing he could do that would be worse than burying my child. *Please help*, I cried out. My plea was addressed to the One who had calmed my fears as a child. Where was He now? I didn't care about my own protection anymore. I just wanted to know that my baby had gone somewhere safe.

Almost instantly, a warm peace penetrated my heart. A peace I didn't understand; one that didn't make sense. It was as if a warm blanket was surrounding me and my dead child. As I heard the night's breeze against the tent, I heard Him reply. Somehow it felt as if He was sitting right beside me.

My daughter, she is with me.

I lay down on the soft soil above my buried daughter and let the words sink in. Then, suddenly, I heard heavy footsteps. I turned around to see Er's shadow towering just a few feet away from me.

Chapter 10

Judah

I could sense something was wrong between Er and Tamar, and I had the worst feeling that it was my firstborn's fault. Before Tamar was married to my son, I would see her in the market as she was buying food or skipping to the well. She had the look of a lamb that had just learned to walk, exploring its world, unknowing of any dangers. That was why I chose her to be Er's bride. I thought my son needed someone who would show him the lighter side of life. I knew what a hard man Er was, and I believed that this marriage would help him turn his life around for the better.

Since the day they got married, Tamar began to cover her entire face and body with a dark veil. I knew Dinah wore a similar veil when she was out in public, but that was a precaution after the trauma of her rape. It was not our custom, and it was terrifying, especially at night, to see a black figure walking at the edges of Er's property. Now, Tamar the lamb had the resigned look of an animal right before its sacrifice; an animal that fought at first, yet eventually accepted its fate.

In the few times I had seen Tamar over the past nine months, I noticed that she walked slowly and spoke as little as possible. She didn't have many visitors and kept to herself most of the day. What was happening within my son's tent?

I sent a servant to invite Er and Tamar to come over for an evening meal. Most families that lived on the same property ate together, but Er and Tamar hadn't visited us once. The only time I saw Er was when he came to visit Reya every couple of days. I waited all day for a response, but as evening came one of Er's servants came back with the message that Er had declined our invitation. When I asked the servant what reason had been given, he reported that Er had simply refused and walked away. I could tell this wasn't the whole truth, and my curiosity got the better of me. I needed to find out if something was wrong, so I decided to go to the one person who would know.

The next day, I went to find Sergad in my fields. If anyone could tell me what was going on it would be him, the father I aspired to be. He may have had very little, but I saw how he put his relationship with his wife and daughter above everything. He never took any trips away, and gave everything he earned to his two girls. The robes he was wore daily were ragged and torn, with patches of different fabrics all over them. They were the same robes he had been wearing when I first met him. Once, when I had asked him why he didn't ask his wife to make something new for him, he turned red and said, "'With all respect, Master Judah, everything I earn goes towards my family, feeding and clothing them." I had walked away, embarrassed and frustrated that I could never live up to so high a standard of fatherhood.

I saw him sitting on a rock, his staff cast at his side, head buried in his hands. When I called his name, he sat up, startled. His eyes were blood red, and I could tell he had been crying. Uncomfortable, the two of us stood up, finding no words to fill the awkward space between us. Eventually, I asked him, "How are all the sheep, Sergad?"

"Just fine, Master Judah."

"And how is Niya doing? Is she still making clothes?"

"Yes, she is."

"Have you talked to Tamar recently?" I asked, finally finding the courage. Sergad looked back at me, his gaze as sharp as a piercing sword.

"No, Master Judah."

What had happened between Sergad and his daughter? I remembered the way he had looked at her when he took her to feed my camels during Er's birth. The look of pure love, of a father who would sacrifice his life to protect his daughter.

And how she had held his hand, unaware of any troubles and so secure in her father's presence. Why was he so upset?

"Keep up the good work, Sergad," I said as I walked away, with more questions than answers.

~~~

The next morning, as Reya and I were getting ready to begin our daily tasks, I asked, "Do you think Tamar is okay?"

Reya turned around, put her hands on my hips and said, "Judah, it's not your job to care. Er is her husband and she is his legal property now. Don't get involved."

There was an anger in her eyes I hadn't seen for months. What I saw was a mother defending her son at all costs. But from what? Reya was blind to what our sons were capable of. She still saw them as her baby boys, just as she had when they were children and they were allowed to do whatever they wanted. But I knew Er had a problem with drinking too much; once, I had seen him drunk in the middle of the day, yelling at one of my youngest servants, Belhan. The poor boy was crouched on the floor, Er towering above him, fist high in the air. I intervened before it was too late, but it made me question what kind of a man Er was and what he was capable of when he thought no-one was looking. He was only seventeen years old, but he was abnormally large, and very strong.

I wasn't convinced that everything was okay, but was this worth getting in a fight with Reya over? How had we drifted so far apart again? There was no way I could win if my wife was protecting my sons. Even as children, she never allowed me to discipline them. Plus, I didn't have any proof that there was something wrong, only a feeling. But if there was one thing I had learned from the past, it was that I couldn't trust my own judgment. If not for me, Joseph would have been safely back with Jacob, by now a grown man. The fact that I was an awful brother and son
~~~

didn't mean the same was true for my son. The last thing I wanted was to make an error of judgment that would ruin my relationship with my firstborn son or my wife. So, for the sake of unity, I said nothing.

~~~

I saw a black figure running towards me in the distance. As it got closer, I realized it was Tamar, and noticed that her black veil was spotted with dark blood. "He's dead, he's dead!" she yelled, her voice shrill.

My blood ran cold. The moment had arrived. My punishment was finally here. For years, I had been able to run from God's wrath, but no longer. Reya heard the screams and ran out of the tent, bewildered.

As Tamar stopped at our side, breathless, Reya screamed at her, "What did you do to him, you filthy peasant girl?" Tamar had fallen onto her hands and knees, panting and shaking, her veiled face raised towards us.

"He came home from his duties, drunk..." Clearly offended, Reya cleared her throat. "He was about to..." Tamar stopped. I could tell there was a lot she wasn't able or willing to say, at least for the moment.

"You evil woman," replied Reya, sobbing between words. "How dare you speak ill of my son."

"Please, just come and see him. And bring the healer."

I told one of my servants to call the village healer, then the three of us rushed towards the tents of Er. We saw Onan and Shelah along the way, shepherding the flocks.

"What has happened?" Onan asked with concern, seeing our haste and the blood covering Tamar.

"Come," I said to them, without stopping, and they followed behind us.
~~~

Before we even arrived at Er's settlement, I could smell the stench of blood. Inside his tent, Er lay lifeless, his face pressed into the dirt. Blood had dried all over what appeared to be his mouth and nose.

"Reya, go get some water, darling," I said to her as soon as she entered the tent. She could not look at this. It would scar her forever.

Her face drained of color, Reya retreated from the tent and Tamar and I sat there, staring at the stiffening body of my son. There was so much left unspoken. All I could think about was how God was punishing me. This life I had built for myself was finally crumbling around me.

As Tamar reached down to check Er's heartbeat, I saw bruises all over her arm. As I had feared, there was no longer any life within him. I saw the knife that was lying near his hand, and looked away as Tamar picked it up and wiped it clean.

The healer came rushing in, followed by Onan, who for the first time had nothing to say; then Shelah, who had never seen death before; and Reya, who didn't have any water. It was too late, and there was no prayer or charm which could bring my firstborn son back from the dead.

Chapter 11

Tamar

"Tell me what happened," said Dinah, with the look of a shepherdess protecting her sheep from a pack of wolves. She had come to visit me as soon as she heard about the death of her nephew. "Tamar, you don't need to protect him anymore."

I was not sure what I could and couldn't say. I had told my parents the truth about Er from the beginning, but this was his aunt, and I wasn't sure she would believe me.

"He came home, very drunk, hardly able to walk. He was about to... " I lost control and began to sob. The events of the past few months had been bottled up inside of me, and I couldn't hold it in anymore. I hadn't cried since my wedding night; it was too much effort, taking strength I didn't have.

"Go on, Tamar, I need to hear the truth."

"He was about to hit me. He would often beat me when he was drunk and force himself on me."

She stood up and began pacing around the tent. I remembered that she knew what it was like for a man to take something from you that you didn't want to give, so maybe I could trust her. I decided to take off the veil and show her, discarding the stained garment on the floor with disgust. Dinah gasped as she saw my bruised face. Then, reaching out, she ran her fingers through my hair. Or what was left of my hair: there were patches all over my scabbed scalp where all you could see was red skin from where Er had torn the hair out, caked with dried blood.

"Oh Tamar, why didn't you tell anyone?" Dinah asked. Maybe she didn't understand. Her brothers had massacred an entire village to protect her honor, but my own family had done nothing to help me at my hour of greatest need.

"I tried to tell my parents, and they offered to help me. But I was so scared because Er had threatened to kill me."

Dinah came over and held my hand, tears brimming in her eyes. Every word I confided in Dinah was a weight off my shoulders. Knowing someone else cared made the biggest difference in the world. I decided to tell her the rest.

"This time, though, he had a knife. You know the one he carried around in his pocket?" Dinah nodded. "He had been beating me, then when he knew me onto the ground, he was kicking me. When I tried to defend myself, he took out his knife. Er's last words to me were, 'Now you die'. Then…. " I stopped for a few deep breaths. "I don't know what happened, but suddenly blood began to gush out of his nose and mouth. His eyes rolled back and he fell down. I screamed. He fell with the knife still in his hands. The blood would not stop. I ran to tell Judah right away."

Dinah listened very carefully, and I could see she was holding her breath while I was speaking.

"Tamar, tell me the rest," Dinah urged.

"I still don't know why he died."

"Not that. There is something else. You can trust me."

How could she know?

"Er got me pregnant, and I hid it from him to protect the child. The day he found out, he made sure the baby wouldn't survive." I spoke each word softly, through sobs. "I was left with my little girl lifeless in my arms." Despite the pain of the memory, it felt good to speak these words out loud for the first time. "The next day, he returned home and saw that I had buried her. That's when he threatened to kill me, and died himself."

Dinah held me in her arms as I lamented, stroking my hair gently, avoiding the bruises. Part of me felt relief, as must a caged bird when it is set free. But another part, equally as strong, felt guilty for my happiness at my husband's death. All I could think about, as I drifted off to sleep in Dinah's arms, was how unfair my life was. Why me? Why Er? Worst of all, how could it be that the man I despised with every ounce of my strength would never answer for taking the life of my child?

Judah

After the time of mourning for Er had passed, I decided to take Onan and Shelah out to pasture the flocks with me. We used to make trips like this when the boys were little, but Reya and I learned that the farther apart we kept Er and Onan, the better for everyone's sanity. Maybe it wasn't too late with Onan and Shelah. At sixteen and fourteen, the boys were still unmarried and I thought through this trip I could encourage them to have a better life than their older brother. As we unpacked our sparse belongings and set up a temporary sleeping shelter, Onan asked with a smile, "So does this mean I am the first born now?"

Even though Onan and Er couldn't be in the same room for five minutes without fighting, I could tell Onan had not been acting like himself since Er's sudden death. Growing up, Onan always had something to say, a way to lighten the mood, more often than not at Er's expense. Yet with his older brother dead, his jokes had become uncouth, his humor out of control. His joyful nature had been replaced by arrogance. He would make fun of the servants and pick out people's flaws in the most obnoxious way. Er was not there to direct all his anger towards, so it spilled into every other area of his life.

It was our second day out in the wilderness, and Onan and I were sitting around the smoldering ashes of our fire. The remains of our dinner were laying around, none of us men being willing to clean them up. Shelah was already sleeping, the quiet boy appearing even more reserved than normal, and my son and I sat in silence, staring at the embers.

I kept glancing over at Onan; I had to tell him about Tamar. It was the honorable thing to do for him to marry her and give an heir to Er. I knew this would not go down well, but my integrity was worth the price. Otherwise, Tamar would have to be sent back to her father's house, and would remain a barren widow for the rest of her life. And then my name would be tarnished.

"Father, will you please stop looking at me like that? I am fine, really. It's easier without Er here. One less donkey in the herd," said Onan as he raised his wine glass towards me.

"Son, you must marry Tamar."

"What?!" He spit out his drink and stood up. "That will never happen."

"My son, it is the custom of all honorable people."

"When have you ever been honorable, father?"

I knew he was trying to provoke me, but I suppressed my rising anger and gave Onan a stern glance instead of what I felt like doing.

"Son..." I was about to give him the speech about the customs of our people, reminding him that every firstborn son needed to be left with an heir, but he interrupted me.

"Okay, I'll do it." He looked pleased at the look of shock passing over my face. "Er tried to make many things away from me, so now I'll marry Tamar just because I know it would annoy him to death. Oh wait..." He sniggered to himself, proud of his little joke. I was not amused.

I knew it was a lot to ask of him, but as a sixteen year old he was ready to be married. Eventually, he could take another wife if he wished, but right now he had to marry Tamar for his brother's sake.

"Onan, the first child that you and Tamar have will be Er's heir. He will carry on Er's family name, and receive the firstborn inheritance your brother should have received. But any children you have after that will be yours." I spoke with more assurance than I felt.

It appears that I sparked another fire. Onan smashed his drink onto the ground and shot up. He had grown so much over the last year, and now his face was level to mine. He grabbed my shoulders and shook me with all his strength. "I will do no such thing!" he bellowed. "I am not giving anything to my brother. He was an idiot who couldn't hold his drink and beat his wife!" I opened my mouth to protest, but he continued before I could protest.

"Father, everyone except you and my mother saw his cruelty. You said or did nothing, protecting your beloved firstborn who could do no wrong in your eyes, as always. Er was a despicable man; he doesn't deserve for his name to be remembered on the face of the earth, especially by the woman whom he treated worse than a slave treats a donkey. Mark my words, I will not give him an heir! I will not share the inheritance that is rightfully mine. The man is dead, and now I get his half of all you own as the firstborn son. Me, not Er. Finally, I am no longer second to him, and already you are trying to make me give him a son? And you say this is the custom of the land? Well, you've never followed any customs before, so you can't play this game now!"

Onan grabbed me by the shoulders and threw me onto the ground, ripping the edge of my robe in the process. My leg almost fell in the fire below our feet.

I was bewildered. I knew that Onan had a hot temper, but I had never seen it manifest like this. And something told me that this wasn't even the extent of his rage. I stood up, determined to do something I should have done a long time ago.

"Now you listen to me, boy. I am your father. How dare you disrespect me? You are only sixteen years old and don't have a clue about anything in the world. You will listen to me and do exactly as I say!" Onan was about to interject, so I raised my voice.

"If you do not do as I ask, you will never see a shekel of your inheritance, and I will expel you from my household," I threatened, striking him in my anger.

Onan, who had never been disciplined in his life, stood in shock with his mouth wide open.

He turned and ran towards the hills, as Shelah poked a sleepy head out of the tent. "Father, are you okay?" I said nothing, and sat back down near the fire. Shelah brought me a drink of water from the pail and said: "It's all going to be alright, father." He gave me a comforting squeeze of my shoulder and walked back into his tent.

I gazed up at the stars. Being a parent was no easy task. I thought of the way my brothers had acted towards Jacob. Although I still resented my father for the way he had ignored us, I realized I had a lot more in common with him than I thought. Had Onan felt about Er the way I felt about Joseph? I saw Onan's greed mirrored in my own. He didn't want to share his inheritance, but maybe he was only following his father's example. At least Onan hadn't sold his brother into slavery for a mere 20 shekels, I thought bitterly, gazing blankly into the dying embers of the fire.

Chapter 12

Tamar

There was no music at this marriage. No feast, no pretty robes, no sashes in the trees, and no candles lighting up the shadows. No-one felt much like celebrating. The only guests were our close family, as well as Judah's friend Hirah and his sister Dinah, who was covered in her black veil as usual. The food served was no different to any other day, and the wine supply was limited.

My first wedding, with Er, had passed in a moment, but every minute of this ceremony felt like a lifetime. As I looked around the table, I could see each person consumed by their thoughts. It has only been three months since the sudden death of Er, and Reya was a different person at the loss of her firstborn. She had no life in her eyes, and was little more than a walking corpse. She didn't even notice the other sons sitting beside her. Judah looked as if he had the weight of the world on his shoulders, his eyes focused on something far away. Shelah was his own quiet self, his eyes downcast. I was surprised that my parents had agreed to come at all, but they were hardly the life of the party, sitting quietly, not speaking to anyone, their brows furrowed. As Judah was my father's master, they had no way to refuse the invitation.

And me? Well, my anger was matched only by my bitterness at the way things had turned out. Er's death was supposed to be an escape, yet Judah's belief in custom and fear of dishonor left me as captive as before. I had heard the rumors that our firstborn was to be Er's heir, but I had no other option; as a widow, Onan was the only person I could marry without committing adultery and being burned to death. I wondered: would Onan be as cruel as his brother? I cast my eyes sideways and looked at him, and saw only the sorrow of the world hanging from his shoulders. He must be angry at being matched with me, when every virgin in the village would jump at the chance of marrying a man who stood to gain such a large inheritance. A few days before the wedding, I had walked to get water from the well and saw a group of young girls sitting together, pointing at me and whispering to each other.

After the meal, Judah stood up and murmured something, of which I didn't hear a word, and then, finally, the ordeal was over. People gathered around us as Onan led me off to the tent that would be our new home.

We were two strangers who were now husband and wife. Inside the tent, Onan took off his sandals and washed his face with the water from the pail.

"Today must have been a tough day for you," he said quietly, after drying his face.

They were such simple words, but I began to cry. I was shocked and unprepared for even so small a kindness; not once, in our entire marriage, had Er said something like this. Everything was about his needs, and he had never been sober enough to imagine what things were like for me.

Seeing my tears, Onan stepped back. "I am sorry, did I say something wrong?"

Those words: I am sorry. Something I had also never heard from Er's mouth. I began to sob even harder.

Slowly, obviously unsure of himself, Onan approached me and put his arm over my back. Sensing me relax, he sat down next to me and embraced me. I was weak and vulnerable, and welcomed the physical contact. I put my head on his shoulder, and he held me while I cried. After a few minutes, I looked up and saw the kohl and berry dye was running down my face and all over his wedding garment.

I was about to start apologizing for ruining his very expensive clothes, but then I looked up at him and saw that he hadn't even noticed. His gaze, fixed on me, was the way a father would look at his injured child. Seeing that I wasn't going to say anything, Onan collected his thoughts and began to speak.

"Tamar, I have no problem with this marriage, but I do have one condition." I listened attentively. "I will be a great husband to you. I will love you, and will not even look at any other women. I will provide everything you could ask or imagine. I will take care of you until you die, but I will never give my brother an inheritance. If we have children, the firstborn son has to belong to Er, as I am sure you have heard. And if that happens, then my brother's death had no significance, because his legacy will continue. Under no circumstances can I have that. I hated Er since the day I was born and I hate him still, even now he is dead. If you want children, I don't know what to suggest, because I am not giving Er anything of mine. I am glad he is dead, and I will love you in a way that will make him turn in his grave. I know how he treated you, and..." His voice heavy with desperation, and if Er had been in the room I couldn't imagine what Onan would have done to him. "All we need to do is to make it appear as if you cannot bear children."

"Onan," I began to say, astonished. Clearly, this was a good man. Younger than me, and even younger than Er, Onan seemed somehow more mature than both of us. Seeing him expressing his emotion, taking my feelings into consideration, made me ready to give up the idea of children without giving it another thought. I was starving and he was offering me sustenance. "That sounds wonderful. It will just be you and me, and we will come to know each other. I promise, I will never ask you for a child, and I'll make it appear to your father that I am unable to conceive. But I also have a condition."

"I'm listening," he said, looked amused.

"We never speak of Er again. He took so much away from me, and I refuse to let him take anything else that belongs to me, and now to us. I never want to hear his name again, to talk about what happened, or even remember him. And if I do remember, I need you to make me forget."

He opened his mouth and squinted his eyes like a child that just received a present. "Tamar, nothing would make me happier." He leaned in and kissed me. It was a gentle kiss, one that translated his empathy.

"Onan, wait…"

"What's wrong?"

"This is going to be my last mention of Er. But there's something you need to see." I began to undress, showing him the fading but still visible pattern of bruises and scars on my body.

He gasped at the sight of the patchwork of different colors - red, blue, and violet - and the rough, raised scar tissue. Then he kissed me again, drawing me close to him. This was a kiss of protection, making me feel like there was nothing in the world that could harm me.

That night, I experienced what relations between a man and woman were supposed to be like. There was no beating or pain, only raw passion. Onan wanted me and took his time to love me, allowing me to enjoy the process. Then, right before the climax, he abruptly pulled out and spilled his semen on the ground. That took me by surprise. He finished by himself, sighed with great relief, then wrapped me in his arms again.

Onan held me like I had never been held before. He was obviously very strong, but his touch was gentle. He showed me what it felt like to be a woman, and seemed to know that I wanted nothing more than to just be held.

I fell in love with my husband that night.

~~~

When I woke in the morning, I saw Onan's bare body stretched out beside me. I smiled as I remembered the night before, then stifled a giggle, embarrassed at how I had reacted in his arms. Onan stretched out his arms and said, "Good morning, Tamar, my wife." He gently kissed me, and we embraced again. What we had
~~~

discovered last night would become a familiar pattern as we made love, with Onan continuing to withdraw himself just in time.

At the back of my mind, I wondered if this life we were about to build for ourselves was tainted by the fact that it was grounded on common hatred of Er. But, over the next few weeks, our tent was filled with so much joy and laughter that I put my concern aside. Onan always knew how to turn any situation into something we could laugh about. We spent our evenings cuddling near the fire, and our mornings preparing for the day together. Onan commanded his servants graciously, and everything we needed was done for us. It was everything I had dreamed of as a little girl and so much more; my younger self couldn't have imagined having such feelings of passion. I was all consumed by Onan, and, bizarrely, I wanted to be. To me he was perfect: from his wit, to the way he treated the servants, to how he distanced himself from his mother. I loved his crooked smile and the way his soft hair curled up at the sides after a hard day's toil. He worked hard, and was the exact opposite of Er in every way. When he held me at night, it felt like that space between his arm and shoulder was made especially for me. It was my favorite place in the world.

~~~

Months of pure bliss passed in the blink of an eye. I had much time to myself while Onan was out working in the fields, with nothing to do and no one to fear. The servants still did most of the cleaning, but I told them I wanted to learn how to make the food myself. A cook from another village would come once a week and show me how to make breads, to season meats, and craft vegetables into beautiful dishes. I was amazed that my hands could make something so delicious. I lost myself in the food, spending hours trying different mixes of spices and flavors. After each successful new dish Onan would place his hands over his full belly and, with a
~~~

teasing tone and flashing grin, complain that he would soon be too fat to work if I kept this up.

We rarely saw Judah, Reya, or Shelah. I was glad that Onan didn't work for his father. When he told me what it had been like to grow up in someone else's shadow (without mentioning Er by name) I could understand why he had such a strained relationship with his parents.

Despite our happy household, as the days went by the realization that I would never be a mother began to sink in. I would never hold my own child in my arms, or have it nurse at my breast. And the more I got to know Onan, the more I wished, deep down, that I could bear his child. Onan would have been the perfect father, and I longed to meet the little person that the two of us would create together. Sometimes, I thought about telling Onan that we could get by without his inheritance, and that I wouldn't mind living a less extravagant lifestyle. But I had agreed to Onan's condition not to ask for children, just as he had never spoken of his dead brother. I comforted myself with the thought that I would rather be barren with Onan, one hundred times over, than have experienced motherhood with Er. Onan showed me everything I had been missing in my life, and managed to soothe the ache in my heart.

One day, Onan announced that he was leaving for Adullam to take care of some affairs, and would be gone for around a week. The time he was gone dragged on, and when the day before his return arrived, I was so excited to be reunited with him that I invited my mother over to paint my skin with a bridal pattern to surprise him. My bruises had slowly begun to heal and it seemed like the perfect time. There were still blemishes, reminders of the painful past, but I knew that Onan cherished my body and would be gentle with me.

My mother was very surprised at the invitation, but accepted gladly. After we had eaten together, I began, nervousness betrayed in my voice: "Mother, lets put the past behind us. Being married to Onan is even greater than I ever imagined.

He is a good man. Can you and I see each other once in awhile?" There was so much left unsaid, but I didn't want to talk about the past. I just wanted to move forward.

"Of course, daughter, but will you speak to your father as well?"

"Not right now..."

She looked disappointed, but then shook her head as if to get rid of the thoughts and smiled. She painted beautiful patterns on my skin. I hadn't had anything like this for my wedding night with Onan, and now I wanted to look beautiful as possible for him. Mother said nothing as she carefully painted around the slowly healing bruises and scars, then took her skin dyes and colored my eyes and lips. When she was done, she took a step back and said, "Oh Tamar, you are beaming! This is the happiest I have ever seen you. You look stunning!"

"I am happy, mother. Any girl would be lucky to marry Onan. He is a real man."

My mother paused, scrunching her lips to one side, a habit she had while she was thinking. "I heard some rumors that he threw Judah to the ground when he found out he had to produce an heir for Er..."

Why did people always have to bring up the past? I pulled my lips together, and reminded myself that mother obviously knew nothing of our plan to fake my barrenness.

"Maybe he just acted out of shock," I replied, smiling sweetly, trying to hide my discomfort.

"But..." Mother hesitated and then said nothing further. "You look beautiful, Tamar. Onan is a man blessed by the gods."

~~~

I could hear Onan's party approaching on their camels, and my heart leapt at the sound of his gentle voice telling the servants that they were free to go for the night.
~~~

There was a tension in my stomach at my husband's return, but one of longing rather than fear this time. Onan had managed to take all the horrors and sorrows of the past, and bury them deep in the ground. Anytime my memories would surface, I would push them away and focus on the present, and the fact that, by some miracle, my abuser had been replaced by my lover.

Before Onan could even pull back the tent flap, I ran outside, jumping into his arms. It felt so good to hold him again. "I missed you, my darling!" he whispered into my ear, gently kissing it. I felt the fire ignited afresh, and I began to kiss him back. He pulled away and laughed: "Let me get through the door, Tamar."

We ate the meal of roasted meat and bread I had prepared for us, in the light of flickering candles, and as I looked at Onan's face, red from the desert sun, I felt completely safe.

After we had finished, he began to undress me, and exclaimed as he saw the henna. He kissed my body and we began to make love as only two separated lovers can. I could feel him nearing the end, but as he climbed off me, he let out a hideous shriek and dropped to the ground. I screamed and ran to his side: "Onan, are you okay?" I yelled, shaking him. "Onan, please wake up! What happened?"

My hands were shaking as I checked his breathing. Everything Onan had helped me to forget came crashing back like a mighty river, with a weight I never knew I could feel. It was like a sudden, deadly frost in the middle of a hot summer. There was no life left in his eyes; no beating heart in his chest. My love was dead.

Chapter 13

Judah

"She probably has a disease!" yelled Reya through her tears, "and she's killing my sons! Two are dead. It is all her fault! I want *her* dead." I held my wife as she grieved the death of our second son, knowing that she had not yet recovered from the loss of our first. I wondered: can a mother's heart ever really heal after the death of her child?

"Judah, I do not care about custom or doing the right thing. There is no way that snake is going to marry Shelah. Stone her. Burn her at the stake. Or at the very least, exile her back home to her parent's house!" Reya hissed like a cornered animal about to strike.

As I looked at my wife, I saw the woman with whom I had fallen deeply in love all those years ago. I remembered the first time I saw her, how free and happy she was. Here we were, almost two decades later, and somehow I loved her even more. Now there were wrinkles scattered around her face, and her eyes were clouded with sadness. Oh, how she was hurting. I just wanted to protect her. I agonized about Onan's death, of course, but seeing my wife like this hurt me even more.

I felt her body stiffen in my arms. "Judah, if not for your stupid honor, Onan would have still been alive," she said. "Why did you force Onan to marry Tamar? He would have never chosen to marry her. And Tamar was your choice for Er, even though there were plenty of other women more beautiful, from better families, who would have been better suited for him! This is all your fault!"

I could sense this thought taking hold in her heart, and felt her becoming more and more distant from me.

"My sons are dead because you chose Tamar!" she yelled, and ran out of the tent, sobbing. I followed her outside in time to see her mounting a camel and setting off towards Adullam.

I stood alone, still in shock at what had happened. Everything I had done to my brother, Joseph, flooded back. There was no running away from my guilt, because now even my wife had declared me guilty. God's punishing hand was laid upon me, as my 'new beginning' finally merged with my sordid past.

There was silence all around my property, but for the calls of the animals. I had sent all my servants to search for Reya, and our tent felt so empty without her. The servants returned, empty handed, and I had to face the reality that Reya was gone, possibly for good. That night, alone in our bed, Reya's words haunted me. My bad decisions had caused my own wife to desert me.

~~~

A few days later, as I struggled to cook myself a meal, Reya returned. The place was a mess, with flour scattered everywhere. Cooking was a lot harder than it looked. One of my servants had offered to help, but I refused; I was determined to do something right for a change. Reya approached me from behind as I pulled the bread, dark as her skin, out of the oven. I spun around at the sound of her laughter, to see her biting her bottom lip, clearly amused at my failed attempt at housekeeping.

"Judah, I am sorry. I never should have blamed you for the death of Er and Onan. It just seemed like you didn't even care that they were...gone!" Her eyes were filled with so much pain and the tears hung in her eyes.

I dropped the bread and it landed in a pile of dusty flour on the ground.

"Reya, my love, of course I care. I was hurting deeply, but I was just trying to keep myself together so I could support you."
~~~

She took my head in her hands and drew me in for a kiss, and I allowed myself to feel the pain of my sons' death. Reya didn't need me to be strong; she needed me to grieve with her. The sorrow was all-consuming, and I was surprised at the depths into which I could feel it dragging me. The heart of a father was not designed to cope with such pain, but at the same time it felt like a relief to finally let myself feel my loss over Er's and Onan's death.

The sun had set and we were getting ready to go to sleep when Reya suddenly said: "I want Tamar gone, Judah. I don't want her in this household anymore. If it was up to me, I would have her burned alive. I really meant that, about her having some sort of disease. Maybe she wasn't a virgin when she first married Er, and passed on some deadly condition; or maybe she poisoned both of them... Either way, I don't care, I just want her gone. Please, Judah, send her back, in honor of Er and Onan."

Perhaps I was feeling emotionally spent, but at that moment I didn't care about Tamar or the 'right thing', or even my own reputation anymore. I was just glad to have Reya back in my arms. I knew that by sending Tamar back to her father, I would ruin her life, disgrace her, condemn her to life as a childless widow. But maybe, I tried to tell myself, this was her all her fault. I had to think about Reya now.

~~~

As I made my way towards Onan's settlement, on the edge of my property, opposite Er's holdings, my head was clouded with memories of my two boys. It hurt me that they had never made up with each other. I had always believed that they would outgrow their adolescent rivalry, but in the end they had taken their hatred for each other to their graves. Pushing away the whirlwind of thoughts, I focused on the familiar path in front of me. Suddenly, it occurred to me that Tamar had been left alone for the last few weeks, and that nobody had checked on her.
~~~

As I walked into the tent, I immediately smelt the stink of human waste. Tamar was laying on the ground, her short hair mixed with the dust and dirt. I cleared my throat, but she didn't move. There was no sign or smell of alcohol, but she had the look of the vagrant beggars I so often saw along the roads.

Before my courage completely deserted me, I said: "Tamar, go back to your parents' home and remain a widow until my son Shelah is old enough to marry you."

In truth, Shelah was already old enough to wed, but the boy was all we had left, and Reya was still against his union with Tamar. There was no way she would recover if Shelah was to suffer the same fate as his older brothers. I knew that, in sending Tamar away, I was declaring to the world that she was 'cursed' and unwanted. But, in honesty, I treasured my wife's sanity over Tamar's reputation and my integrity.

Tamar looked up slowly, saying nothing. I could see caked saliva on the sides of her mouth, and there was some sort of paint smeared all over her body. Trying hard not to inhale the stench inside the tent, I continued.

"I'll send word for my servants to come and help you. Goodbye, Tamar."

I began to turn around, then remembered the widow's garments. I reached down to hand her the black garment Reya had made, whose purpose was to fully cover the entire body and face.

"Put them on," I said, and waited outside the tent until she was ready. I had never seen a widow personify sorrow as much as Tamar in her mourning outfit: a coarse burlap material dyed black. "Wear this, and never take it off in public, until Shelah is old enough to marry you," I said, then turned around and left before I could change my mind.

~~~

Dinah came storming into our tent while Reya and I were brewing beer.
~~~

"You sent her back? How dare you disgrace that poor girl like this!" she yelled.

I rolled my eyes as Dinah went on and on about how we had ruined Tamar's life, leaving her with no husband or children, and no means to support herself. At first, Reya ignored the tirade; she had always looked up to Dinah and aspired to be like her. Finally, though, she could contain her anger no longer, stood up, and threw a handful of barley in Dinah's face.

"Shut your mouth! She killed them, Dinah! It is her fault my sons are dead! She is cursed, and there is no way she will kill my youngest son as well!" Reya screamed.

"Your precious firstborn died because he couldn't keep the wine cup away from his mouth! How much alcohol do you think one body can take before it just gives up?" Dinah retorted, her eyes burning. "Er drank himself into his own grave, and almost dragged Tamar down with him!"

"How dare you!" Reya roared, seizing the jar of unfermented beer and pouring it over Dinah's head. "You are only saying that because you are a whore yourself! Were you even raped by Prince Shechem, or did he pay you?"

I could tell that Dinah was hurt. Her next words were spoken quietly, through clenched teeth. "He beat her, Reya! She was pregnant, and he beat her until she lost the baby! Haven't you ever wondered why she began to wear a full body veil like mine? Her entire little body was covered in bruises!"

Reya looked at me, searching for an answer in my eyes, and seeing only as much shock as she felt. I had suspected Er of being abusive to Tamar, but I never believed he could go so far as to kill his own child. True or not, Reya would not be able to process this, and Dinah had to be silenced.

"Dinah, how dare you come here into our home, while we are grieving the death of our sons, and tell such blatant lies," I said. "My brothers and I gave up our father's respect to defend you after your rape, and here you are, lying to our face, defending the girl who caused your nephews' deaths. I invited you into my life, even though I haven't spoken to the rest of my family for many years! I treated you as my precious sister..."

"Just as you treated Joseph?" Dinah broke in, savoring each word.

Seeing Reya's anger change to confusion, Dinah redirected her rage.

"Oh, you didn't know, Reya? Your perfect husband, who loves you so much, beat and sold his younger brother to slave traders. The only reason he came to Adullam in the first place was to escape his guilt."

"Stop, Dinah," I barely managed to mutter. There was no good moment for Reya to discover my long-buried secret, but she was at her most vulnerable right now, and I feared how she would react.

"Judah and the others kidnapped their brother, Joseph, threw him into a cistern, then sold him to a band of Egyptians. He's long dead now. If not for your husband, my oldest brother, Reuben, would have rescued Joseph."

"Judah," said Reya, tears forming in her eyes, "please tell me the snake is lying."

What could I say? I had done everything to please my wife, but it had never been enough. And now she knew the truth about the crime I had spent my life running away from.

"And now, sister," hissed Dinah, "God is punishing Judah by killing your sons."

Chapter 14

Tamar

Judah's servants wasted no time in helping me gather my belongings, and by late afternoon the camels were ready to transport what was left of my life, packed into sacks, back to my parents' household. As I helped load the camels, I kept tripping over the long hem of my widow's garment. The rough material felt like bark on my bruised skin, and I struggled to breathe through the veil that covered my head. I kept flinching when little strands of my tousled hair caught in the fabric. Regardless, when I saw my reflection in my polished stone mirror, I was pleased to see that my appearance for the outside world reflected how I felt inside.

I thought back to my very earliest memory, of the time Reya was giving birth to Er. My mother was rushing to get to Judah's property, and my father was left behind to take care of me. I had just learned to walk, but I remembered the feeling in the air that something incredible was happening. Even though I was scared when I heard the screams of labor, when my father brought me back to my mother, she had looked very pleased with herself. She explained that now there was a new baby in the world, one whose life held a million possibilities.

The sweetness of my memory turned to bitterness as I contemplated the fact that I would never experience giving birth to a healthy child. Two husbands were dead, one having left me broken in body, the other leaving me broken inside. I had no husband, no children, no possessions: no future. Judah had told me that he would arrange my marriage to Shelah, but I strongly doubted he would do so. All I could do now was fall on my parents' mercy.

I was so lost in my thoughts, I didn't even realize we had entered my home village. More memories from my childhood came flooding back as I inhaled the all too familiar scent of the date palms surrounding my father's property, which only served to compound my grief. That innocent little girl had no idea of her fate. As I rode closer to my father's tent, I could see the villagers whispering to each other and pointing. How they must all be relishing my downfall. Those girls that had been so jealous of me when I had married Er were now looking at me with pity, even as they mocked me and laughed at the return of 'the unwanted one'.

As a widow, I belonged nowhere. I had no legal rights, and could never get married again, unless by some miracle Judah changed his mind and allowed me to marry Shelah. Even then, the thought of being back in Judah's household, surrounded by reminders of all I had lost with Onan, seemed even worse than the fate I was rapidly approaching. Every option for my future seemed grim.

In the distance, I saw my mother and father, standing silently like sentinels outside their tent, waiting for me. I guess my outfit of black burlap made me pretty hard to miss. The last time I saw my father was in Er's tent when I accused him and blamed all my tribulation on him. My stomach churned at the words I had spoken to him. I knew I had hurt him immensely, and now I was about to face him again, after all this time.

Even from afar, I could see the hard lines on his face, his wrinkles set deep in his eyes and near his mouth. The man before me had aged decades in just a few years. When I was little, to my great enjoyment, I used to fasten ribbons into his hair. He patiently sat on the floor while I did my best to fit as many colorful fabrics, even scraps from my mother's sewing, around his black curls. He would proudly wear my creations until the end of the day, telling me what a great job I did. Only when I grew up did I realize not every papa did this. It made me feel that much more loved. But now, most of the hair on his head had fallen out, leaving a big shiny open space at the top. Whatever hair was left was almost white. His hair, much like my own, suffered the consequences of life's misfortunes. Even though we stood in the same vicinity, we were a chasm apart.

Suddenly, while I was still some distance away, I saw him pick up his robes and start running as fast as he could towards me, kicking up clouds of sand into the air. As I dismounted my camel, I felt a wind stirring behind me, as if pushing me towards home. I could do nothing but stand there, my head bowed in shame and pain, as he ran towards me and fell at my feet.

"Daughter, please forgive me," he said, beginning to weep. "I am so sorry. It is all my fault. I never should have chosen Er as your husband."

"Oh, father," was all I could meekly reply as I knelt down towards him.

He raised his head to look at me, then gently pulled the veil away from my face, and cast it to one side. The way he gazed into my eyes, it was as if he didn't even see the scars.

"You don't need this veil, Tamar. You are safe in my home - *your* home."

My mother had reached us, and knelt down and enveloped us both in her arms. For the first time in years, my family was whole.

That night, as I lay in my childhood bed, I had an overwhelming feeling of a familiar presence. I knew without a doubt that He had come into the room; the One whose voice I had heard after my nightmares. I hadn't felt him since the day my dead daughter had lain in my arms.

I stood up, unsure of what to do, and slowly bowed my head. Even while my hands started to shake, my heart soared, and a sense of peace washed over me like a river. How was this possible? I had been rejected and shamed by the world, and had lost everything. This feeling of calm made no sense, but I welcomed it with open arms.

Through my eyelids I could see the outline of a figure, shining brighter than the sun. Somehow, even though my eyes were closed, He looked through me and His gaze pierced my heart.

Daughter, forgive him.

It was nothing more than a whisper, as gentle as a feather.

Er. He wanted me to forgive Er.

I saw myself surrounded by a dark wall, which I knew was made up of my bitterness, self-pity, and rage. I heard His voice on the other side, repeating those words: *Forgive him, for I have taken away your shame.*

At the sound of His voice, the wall came tumbling down and I felt my anger and resentment melting away. What had seemed impossible just hours ago was becoming a reality: I was prepared to forgive the man who had trampled my body and soul.

With the barrier no longer between us, I looked at Him and felt His eyes, full of love, boring straight into my being. I had never felt love like that before, more than an emotion or feeling. His very being was radiating this love. He was love itself.

He was beautiful; I was made clean. He was holy; I was made complete. He held my life in his hands, and I never wanted to leave His presence again.

Daughter, praise me!

I looked down at the broken pieces of the wall, and they twisted into instruments of praise. I had never seen these kinds of instruments before, but I picked them up and began to play, singing and dancing with the music before the One who had saved my soul. There was no darkness, only light as far as my eyes could see.

As I danced, I looked down to see that my widow's raiment had changed into a red dress of silk. My hair was long again, flowing free. The love I had experienced with Onan, and the love I felt for my daughter, seemed like water to the wine of His love for me.

Look down again. As I followed the command, I saw my red dress turn to a gleaming white, more pure than I had ever seen before. For the first time in my life, I was clean. I was truly free.

Suddenly, my eyes opened. It was still nighttime. I was kneeling on my childhood sleeping mat, my hands covered in dirt. I looked over at the black burlap laying next to me. My widow's clothes had not changed, but I knew I would never be the same again.

Chapter 15

Judah

It had been two years since Onan's death, and Reya had still not recovered. The argument with Dinah had triggered something within her, and it was as if she had completely shut down emotionally. She showed neither gladness nor sorrow, and slept most days until the sun was high in the sky. Her loom was untouched, and our servants had to take on her role of running the household. She ate little, but reached for her wine cup as soon as she woke up, and kept it topped up throughout the day. Each day, I struggled to persuade her to eat at least one meal, which she would usually do begrudgingly.

Seeing sorrow taking hold of the woman I loved was terrifying. Her hair, of which she had been so proud, fell out in large clumps, and the whites of her eyes became dull and grey. At the beginning, I had hoped she would return to the carefree woman I had fallen in love with, but with each passing day, I began to fear that that day would never come.

I tried everything I could think of: I talked; I cried; I even tried tickling her, but she gave no reaction whatsoever. Her gaze was focused somewhere far away, in the past, I guessed. The only time she would show emotion was when she was drunk, which was more often than I could have ever imagined. After enough wine, she would start sobbing and talking to Er as if he was still alive. I tried to protect her by making sure the servants never saw her one-sided conversations, as they would surely think she had lost her mind. I would never say so out loud, but sometimes I wished to myself that I could just walk away; it seemed so much easier than loving someone with no hope.

~~~
~~~

One day, one of Hirah's servants arrived with an invitation to join him for dinner. I declined at first; there was no way I could leave Reya for that long. But, as servant after servant arrived the same request, I gave in and accepted my friend's invitation. When I told Reya where I was going, she just stared at me blankly, saying nothing.

By the time I reached Hirah, I knew that we couldn't go on like this. I feared that Reya's behavior would make me lose my mind, and I was so angry with everyone: with Tamar, with Dinah, but especially with my wife. She was just like my father, unable to deal with the sorrow of losing a child. We still had Shelah, but it was as if he had never existed. Why couldn't she just pick herself up and move on?

"Welcome, Judah. I am glad...," Hirah began to say, but I interrupted him. Like a dam, holding back a torrent of water, I exploded. I confided in him about the argument between Reya and Dinah, and about Reya's descent into sorrow. My friend sat me down and listened as I spoke, every so often refilling my cup of wine. In each word I could hear my rage, my anguish, and very little hope.

"Have you thought about contacting Tamar's mother?" asked Hirah.

I froze. This was not a bad idea; Niya was probably the only person that Reya would listen to. But how could I ask her for help after how I had treated her daughter? I had to try, and determined that as soon as I got back to my tents, I would send a servant to ask Niya to come and talk to her daughter.

After too many cups of wine, I gladly accepted Hirah's invitation to spend the night. What harm could one night away do? Reya wouldn't even notice I was missing. I slept soundly, and woke in the morning with a pounding headache, but a little more hope that I could still save my wife.

Embracing Hirah, I said, "My friend, you were always there for me. From the time I came to Adullam as a man with no home, to now, you have helped me so much. Thank you. If there is ever anything I can do for you to show my gratitude, let me know."

On that morning, as I set off towards my settlement, I felt more hopeful than at any point in the past two years. Things could change - they *would* change. Niya would help Reya claw her way out of the darkness she was in. Maybe I could even mend things with Tamar and give her a sum of money that would allow her to live comfortably. There was a way out; a way to get my wife and my honor back.

Before I had even reached the boundary of my property, I saw Belhan running towards me, panic in his eyes.

Instantly, I knew what he was going to say. My biggest fear was about to come true.

Chapter 16

Tamar

I look down and see myself holding Judah's walking staff, his cord, and his seal of identification. My hands begin to shake, soon followed by the rest of my body. As my whole being trembles, I watch in amazement as the wooden staff and the seal change before my eyes, taking the form of mewling twin baby boys. As I look into their eyes, I feel completely restored. A longing I have suppressed for years now fights to the surface of my mind. We are a family.

I woke up, gasping for air, already feeling the dream falling away from me, slipping out of my grasp. The light of the rising sun was creeping through the little hole at the top of my tent, and I knew it was time to start the day. There were loaves to bake, animals to feed, a water jug to be filled.

The day passed as every other one had for the past two years, with its blessings and its burdens. At least the rumors had finally stopped, and the villagers had found someone other poor fool to mock. After two years, no-one seemed to care about my exile anymore. The villagers returned to their ordinary lives. Most even greeted me as I passed them in the market.

And there was something else: that encounter with Him had changed the way I saw the world, and there was a love that thread its way through my day. I still didn't know who He was, but I was very eager to spend time in the peace He brought. Most of the time it happened at night, or sometimes even during the day, where I dropped my things and just soaked in that unforgettable feeling. Sometimes, bitterness and resentment were still my companions, but for the most part my life was good. My relationship with my parents was better than ever, and we experienced the ups and downs of life together as a family.

~~~

My parents had retired to bed, and I was left sitting at the fire by myself.

Tamar.

I smiled as I heard His voice, inaudible but as sure as the stars in the sky. He was always there, even if I sometimes didn't feel it. Suddenly I remembered my dream.

A staff, a cord, and a seal. "What does it mean?" I asked out loud. It felt a little odd, speaking into the darkness, but I knew I could confide in Him. He was more real to me than the rest of the world I could see or touch.

Go to Judah.

I looked back down at the fire, noticing the flames swaying from side to side, dancing mischievously. I must have misheard. Go to Judah? What did that mean? And what was the significance of the staff, cord, and seal in my dream? I recalled the twin boys I had held in my dream, and I longed to hold them, even though I knew they weren't real.

Go to Judah. It was a simple command, but left me with more questions. His request ignited a tiny spark of hope, an ember burning brighter and brighter, catching fire in my mind. Maybe there was something more for me than the way my life was now. I was content, but deep down I still longed for more. I desired to be a mother, even though I knew it was impossible. It was very clear that Shelah had reached maturity, but it was just as clear that Judah - or Reya - was not going to allow him to marry me. Legally, there was only one other man who could give me a legitimate child.

I remembered the night Er brought home a prostitute. Whenever Er had fallen asleep, the poor woman crawled out of the tent on her hands and knees, unable to even get up. I saw her before she saw me. I knew that feeling much too
~~~

well. When she finally saw me sitting outside, her face went white. Startled, she asked, looking at me intently, "Who are you?"

"His wife."

Horror spread through her lovely face. I exhaled and helped her up, gave her some nourishment, and a very large sum of Er's money. She protested, but I insisted.

As she left, she had told me, "Thank you for your kindness. If there is ever anything I can do for you, please, come find me."

It was time. I needed to find Rahab, the prostitute.

Chapter 17

Judah

Who am I?

I am not a husband anymore, because my wife is dead. I am not a good father, because I raised two sons who hated each other to the grave. I am not a good brother, or a good son. I have failed in everything that means something. I am a coward, who runs away from his actions instead of dealing with them. I am a murderer. I cost my younger brother his life. Surely he is dead by now, his body left decaying under the unyielding desert sun, in the manner of slaves. I am a liar. I never told my wife the truth about who I was, and in the end it was my lie that killed her.

God of my fathers, why didn't you punish me instead? Why did you make my sons and wife pay for my sins? That is even worse than receiving the punishment myself.

I was just a restless soul in a body that was little more than a corpse. I held myself together for Shelah, whom I hardly saw anymore, but I was hardly good company. He did what was required of him, but otherwise kept to himself as much as he could. Whenever I asked him to have dinner with me, he would eat silently and return to his tent as soon as his plate was empty. I wondered what life was like for him now, having to deal with the death of his mother and brothers, and now seeing my apathy towards life. I knew that I was failing him, and that I could not possibly go on with the way things were now. Every breath felt strenuous, and the simple task of getting up in the morning left me exhausted. Sleep wouldn't come. I would happily accept countless nightmares if only I could rest and forget about the shattered pieces of my existence.

I thought about asking Hirah if Shelah and I could move onto the same property again, but as I lay awake at night I realized that our entire friendship had always been about me. I never asked about the latest children Hirah was sheltering, or about his flocks and land. I knew almost nothing about his past, while he knew everything about mine. Yet, somehow, he was still there for me. One day, I would make it up to him.

One day, I saw Hirah approaching across the sands on his camel. As we embraced, he said, "Judah, let's go to the sheep shearing festival. We can have some fun again, just like it was in the old days. We can forget, and drink away the sadness in our hearts." Then he pointed towards the sacks on his camel; I could see they were full of wineskins, jugs of beer, and fresh fruit. "But for now, I brought something to entertain us," he said, smiling.

How could I say no? He was trying so hard to be a good friend. And, to be honest, the prospect of drowning my sorrows, even for one night, was too attractive to refuse. I took one of the jugs from the sack, held it to my lips, and began to drink.

~~~

We left for the festival in Timnah. Our servants were taking care of all of our animals, and we walked behind them, trying our best to appear carefree. Even my best was not good enough, however, and Hirah was beginning to get frustrated with me.

"Judah, don't be so downcast! Look, even our herdsmen and women are enjoying themselves along the way. Can you stop looking like someone has died?" His face was immediately filled with regret. "I didn't mean... you know... I'm sorry, Judah, that was not what I meant."
~~~

Since when had I become someone people had to tiptoe around, watching their every word? I wondered if Hirah was looking at me in the same pitying way I had looked at Reya before her death.

Hirah stopped walking, waved our herdsmen ahead of us, and turned towards me. He just stared at me, his head tilted to one side, and put his hands on my shoulders.

"I know what's wrong."

Didn't everybody? I thought.

"When was the last time you felt the joys of a woman?"

"Hirah, please."

"Tell me! When?" he demanded.

"Not since Onan died," I replied, feeling my face burning.

"Judah, that was many years ago!"

When I didn't reply, he continued. "You were faithful to your wife until the end. You never used prostitutes. Truly, you never so much as looked at another woman while you were married. Look, I don't understand that, but I respect it. If I was a woman, I would want a man like you."

I laughed and shook my head.

"Judah, she's gone now. You don't have to be faithful anymore. You are a free man. I can't imagine what it must feel like for you to lose your wife and sons. What I've been running away from my whole life has happened to you."

"What do you mean, running away from?" I asked.

Hirah rubbed his temples as if he had a sudden headache. "My mother died giving birth to me. My father loved her so deeply that he took his own life that very same day. They were buried together and I was left to die near the road."

He hesitated, and I could see how much it took for him to share this with me.

"An old man found me and took me in. He raised me himself as his own son, providing for me out of the goodness of his heart, requiring nothing in return. Then, when I was nine, he died. Alone again, I survived by stealing the food people left out for their animals and sitting in the market to beg for food. I didn't find out what had happened to my real parents until my first trip to Adullam. A villager recognized me and told me everything. I have made many bad choices in my life, but I have never forgotten who I was. The orphans and strangers I take in are my way of thanking the heavens for sending me that old man. But I will never love anyone like my father loved my mother; it just causes too much pain. And now you know this, you owe me. In fact, you already owed me, one hundred times over!"

That was so typical of Hirah. Even as he bared his greatest sorrow, he was still thinking of me, trying to cheer me up.

"Next prostitute you see," he said, winking at me.

"Hirah, I don't think..."

"No, Judah, it is time. You must do this, for the sake of my sanity at least! You win her over and make her the luckiest woman alive."

The man had just made a joke about my dead wife, yet something about his disarming manner meant that I couldn't help but smile. I was already feeling better.

~~~

We walked along the road, and in the distance saw the village of Enaim through which we had to pass to get to Timnah. Standing at the entrance of the village, at the shrine, was a prostitute. I hadn't allowed myself to look at any other woman this way for many years, and doing so now ignited a fire in me. I stood up straighter, admiring her curves and breasts from a distance. She was like the first rays of daylight after years of night.
~~~

Hirah saw how I was looking at the girl and was soon doubled-over, laughing. His mirth may have also have had something to do with the empty wineskins we had discarded along the road. "You don't need much convincing now, do you, Judah?" he asked with a smirk.

She looked over at us, and I slapped Hirah. "Stop it, she's going to think we are lunatics and my chances will disappear down the well. And you are right, I need this. Now leave me to it! I will see you soon."

"Hopefully not too soon," replied Hirah as he staggered off, still laughing.

As I approached the girl, I realized that I had no idea how to ask for what I wanted. Hirah always charmed his prostitutes before bringing up the subject. I felt so awkward.

When I was right in front of her, I opened my mouth and said: "Let me have sex with you." Instantly, I felt my face burn, and cursed myself inwardly. Was this really the best I could do?

"How much will you pay?" the girl replied, discreetly.

I hadn't thought about that! I was such an idiot. Of course you have to pay! All my money was with the servants, but it was too late to back out now.

"I'll send you a young goat from my flock."

"But what will you give me to guarantee that you will send the goat?" she asked.

She was smart, this girl, and spoke with dignity and assurance. Wasn't she supposed to be trying to seduce me?

"What kind of guarantee do you want?" I asked.

I was trying to look at her face, which was hidden beneath her veil. She smelled so good, like a mix of exotic perfumes and baked bread. Why did that blend smell familiar? I couldn't help but look at her exposed breasts. She was beautiful, and I felt like I was about to explode with all the desire that had lain dormant in me for so long. I needed her, and I knew I would give her anything she asked for.

"Leave me your identification seal, its cord, and the walking stick you are carrying."

I hesitated; she was asking me to give away the signs of my status as a rich landowner. But I had to have her. Looking around to make sure no-one saw me, I handed over exactly what she had asked for.

She took me by the hand and led me through the streets to a small leather tent. I didn't know what I expected, the simple tent she led me into with a sleeping mat just big enough for two people was not it. It was over within minutes. She made no sounds of enjoyment; in fact, she never even took off her veil. When it was over, she got up and left the tent, leaving me alone with my emptiness.

What had I done? The pleasure was not worth the price I had paid. My mouth had watered for some incredible feast, but instead I had been given hard bread and dirty water. I felt so ashamed. All I could think about was Reya and the way we used to spend hours in each other's arms. What happened today so was shallow compared to what Reya and I had shared during our marriage. I hadn't allowed myself to cry since Reya died, but there in that tent, with my clothes lying scattered on the ground, I wept.

Chapter 18

Tamar

I ran home as fast as I could, Rahab's clothing in my bag and my thick widow's garment catching on my feet. The perfume Onan had given me had such a sweet scent, which only made me feel more nauseated the faster I ran. I lost my balance a few times, just managing to catch myself before I fell.

Did that really happen?

I hadn't thought about how I would carry Judah's objects home. Anyone who saw me in my widow's attire and carrying a man's staff would know something was wrong. No woman was allowed to carry such a symbol of male status. I had tried tying it to my body underneath my veil, but it kept hitting the back of my legs as I ran; I would have bruises tomorrow. At least Judah's seal was hidden safely in my bag, wrapped up in Rahab's clothes.

God of Jacob, please help me.

Sweat poured off my body as I ran through the desert towards Kezib. When I saw a caravan approaching me on the small path, I slowed down, aware of the danger. My heart beat faster. Any trader worth their salt could easily take me and sell me as a slave. I was easy pickings: a woman, in a widow's veil, alone in the desert. Suddenly, I was clear of the caravan, and I started running again. Somehow, the faster I ran, the less tired I became. I felt the breath in my lungs like I never had before. It was exhilarating.

Finally, my father's house was in sight. Relieved, I let out a long sigh and closed my eyes.

Now, all I could do was wait.

Judah

"I'm telling you, Judah, you get what you pay for. From what you are saying, it seems like the girl had no experience at all. Maybe you were her first" Hirah teased.

The festival for celebrating this year's herds and crops was the biggest I had seen. As soon as I had left the prostitute's tent, I went to search for Hirah. He was not difficult to find, standing right next to the wine stall. The sheep had already been sheared and the celebration was in full swing. People were gathered together from many different towns and villages, trading everything from food to slaves. Most of the men had come alone with their servants, leaving their families behind, and were spending most of their money on wine. All the different tribes and nationalities danced together, the marketplace a swirl of robes and prints of many different colors. The women that were here were mostly dancers or prostitutes, and some dressed in long veils stood at the stalls selling food.

I looked like a beggar without my staff, no-one would sell to me without my seal. But Hirah took care of everything for me. His favorite dish was lamb served with fresh bread, and we ate it several times a day, washing it down with more wine than I had ever drank in my life. In fact, every time I went to one of these festivals I would get more carried away than before.

On the way back home we both had headaches like storm clouds. We took a different route, avoiding Enaim, and soon settled back into normal life. The only difference was that I had moved back to Hirah's property, as we had decided during the festival. It was really the best option, as Shelah had gone away to live in another village, and I didn't want to be alone.

One day, soon after the festival, we were both sitting down on a nearby hill, watching our flocks.

"Hirah, you tried to make me feel better, and for a few moments, you succeeded," I said. "But that girl took my staff and seal, and without it, I can't do anything. I can't even make any purchases because she took my identity!" I slowed down, choosing my next words carefully. "This was your idea, so you need to find her and take my property back."

There was no way I could deal with the shame of seeing that girl again, and I was desperate. Hirah was my only option. I tried to think of something which might be more convincing.

"Try her out for yourself, and if you aren't disappointed, then I'll admit ..."

I hadn't even finished my thought before Hirah interrupted me: "Just be a man and go yourself!"

As he spoke, two of our rams charged at each other, their curved horns cracking as they came together. Normally, we would quickly separate them, but neither of us moved.

"Okay, Hirah. Maybe this was just one bad experience. Please, go give her the goat I promised, and get my staff and seal back." I stared at him with raised eyebrows. "Hirah. I can't see her again."

"Fine, give me the goat! But you ... "

"Yes, I know, I owe you. Thank you, my friend."

"Actually, I was going to say, guess who is doing *all* the work when I am gone?"

~~~

The air was pregnant with heat, the cool and pleasant breezes of spring by now a distant memory. It was morning, but I was already drenched with sweat. I wiped my forehead with my sleeve as I looked up at the rocky, mountainous terrain in the distance, then back to the trees and bushes around my tents. The green leaves were already starting to shrivel and fade into a lifeless yellow, crushed by the desert sun. I looked around me, strangely conscious of my surroundings. I looked at my hands. Somehow, I hadn't noticed that my nails were cracked and tinted yellow, a
~~~

thick crust of dirt underneath them. I smiled to myself as I remembered how Reya would scold me for not cleaning my hands before our evening meals.

"No clean hands, no food," she would always say. Now, it looked as if I couldn't make them clean even if I tried. The rough callouses on my fingers and palms told the story of years of working in the fields. I took another look around to check that I was alone, then slowly, unsurely, lay down on the ground, feeling the dirt warming my back.

When was the last time I took a moment for myself, setting my worries aside? A goat approached me nervously, bleating loudly, clearly confused by my behavior. It walked back and forth, and then settled over my legs. We lay there comfortably until the sun filled the sky with bright orange. Eventually, when it was time to get up, I shook my foot and the startled goat bleated again and got up reluctantly. As I stood up, I saw that I had been lying on the goat's droppings, which were now smudged onto my cloak. For the first time in a long time, I laughed. Not just a chortle, but deep laughter that came from the pit of my stomach and resounded through the surrounding hills. The sound was foreign, as if it was being made by someone else. The goat looked at me with wild eyes, and I felt one hundred years younger.

~~~

A few days later, Hirah returned from his search and found me in the fields.

"I couldn't find her anywhere," he said, still out of breath from his journey, "and the men of the village claim they've never had a shrine prostitute there."

I dropped the bale of hay from my hands.

"What? But what about my staff and seal?"

"I'm sorry, Judah, she was nowhere to be found."

Normally, I would be overcome by anger at the way I had been taken for a fool. But that morning in the field had changed something in me. Hirah was still
~~~

standing there with his lips pursed together, waiting for me to respond, but I was done. I was tired of worrying, of doubts and fears. I was exhausted.

"Let her keep the things I gave to her," I said, quietly. "I sent the young goat as we agreed, but she is nowhere to be found. There is nothing more I can do."

I had no more capacity to care, and my apathy felt as sweet as honey. There was no way I was going to let anyone know I had been outwitted by a prostitute, however. I engaged the services of the local craftsman, who tried his best to mask his surprise at my having lost such precious objects as my staff and seal. *Lost*, being the story I was sticking to. In a few days I had a new staff, but with none of the markings from all the way back to my adolescence in the house of Jacob. My new seal had none of the significance of the old. To have both objects replaced cost me a small fortune. Oh, the price I was paying for a few minutes of pleasure.

~~~

The next month passed in a blur. I sent my servants to reach out to Shelah, but he refused to come and visit me. So I determined to move on with my life. Living with Hirah, just as I had when I first moved to Adullam, was easy. The first time, I had been running away from the chaos of Jacob's house; this time, it was my own household which had fallen apart.

I would never admit it, but in the back of my mind I was glad to be living with Hirah again. There were no noisy children, no warring sons, no wife who always wanted something I couldn't give. There was no pressure for me to act as head of the household; all I had to do was take care of my flocks, eat, and sleep. Of course, I would never have chosen to lose my family, but now I had, part of me was relieved. I felt awful even admitting that. But I was not willing to let my feelings of guilt overcome my ability to breathe again. I was free.
~~~

Chapter 19

Tamar

The punishment for a woman who got pregnant out of wedlock was death. I had seen it happen before: a young girl begging for mercy, surrounded by the angry mob, burned to a crisp in front of the whole village.

I awaited the day my menstrual blood was supposed to come, not wanting to get my hopes too high. The day passed, then the next, and the one after that. I imagined every possible scenario in my head: the one where I was not pregnant, and had made that trip to Enaim for nothing; the one where I was pregnant and Judah found out, and my child and I were burned together; the one where I ran away to Egypt with my child, offering myself as a slave to protect my baby's life; one where my mother pretended it was her baby, or I gave it away to the temple to be raised in exchange for my life.

The answer was already in my body, so how could I still not know?

One week later, my monthly bleeding had still not come. Gradually, the thought seeped into my mind like a fall of rain on the parched desert sands. I was going to be a mother!

I told my mother right away, who rejoiced with me. "My baby is going to have a baby!" she repeated over and over again, struggling to contain her excitement.

The next day, I worked up the courage to tell my father. After I had given him the news, his eyes widened and he stood completely still.

"But Tamar, this could mean..." He didn't have to say any more; we both knew what it could mean.

Somehow, knowing was even harder than not knowing. According to the law, I had done nothing wrong. I had been married into Judah's household, and since my husbands had died, the law allowed me to produce an heir with someone else from the same family. Morally, however, I knew there were those who would not accept what I had done, and I could not blame them. I had heard the voice of the God of Jacob telling me to go to Judah, but the rest of it - disguising myself as a prostitute and tricking my father-in-law into sleeping with me - had been all my own idea. Had I made a mistake which would cost me my life? If Judah denied that he was the father, his word was worth far more than mine, and my death would be certain. No-one else, apart from my parents, knew whose child I was carrying. The fear grew and grew in my mind: was another of my children going to die because I was unable to protect it? The image of my tiny baby girl, lifeless in my arms, had never left me, but now it was the only thing I could see.

I wasn't afraid for myself, because my life didn't mean that much to me anymore. When I had that first encounter with the God of Jacob, I was filled in a way I could not imagine. But my child… I had to do everything I could to protect it.

Lord, please, I beg you, please allow this child to live. Let this child love you, know you, and yearn for you. If I have heard your voice in the wrong way, please forgive me. I do not have the words to express my plea, but you know my heart. Please, God of Jacob, turn this situation for your good, your glory.

And so I waited, but there was only so long I could hide my pregnancy. My fate was about to unfold, there was nothing I could do now to stop it. If I lost this baby, the village would not need to kill me; the last bit of life and hope within me would die with it. I could not lose this baby and survive.

~~~

As I walked through the village, the angry faces and whispered threats told me that my worst nightmare had come true. Everyone knew. As I ran home, wild with fear, I
~~~

tried to understand how this could have happened. I was sure that no-one could see the bump on my stomach under my widow's garment, and the only people who knew already were my parents and Rahab.

The only possibility was that someone I trusted had betrayed me.

Judah

"Your daughter-in-law has acted like a prostitute, and now, because of this, she's pregnant."

I looked up in astonishment at Belhan, the servant who had grown up in my household, and who had replaced Sergad after Onan's death.

"Pregnant?" I asked as my new staff tumbled out of my hands and thudded to the ground.

"I went to the marketplace near Sergad's house to buy some mandrakes, and the women who was selling them asked who my master was. When I said it was you, master, she was outraged. She told me that she would not have anything to do with such a disgraceful family. I asked her what she was talking about, and she said: 'Your master's daughter-in-law is pregnant from playing the prostitute! The whole village knows!' Then she threw a mandrake at me and told me to get out of her sight."

I could not believe my ears. The feeling of serenity I had felt lying in that field were long gone.

"How dare she disgrace my name like this! That girl has brought shame upon me, and upon my sons and wife, whose deaths she is responsible for! I told her very clearly not to take off her widow's veil in public, and now she is acting like a whore!"

Belhan looked down, saying nothing. He was the only one of my servants who had followed me back to Hirah's house, perhaps because he had nowhere else to go. He had been loyal to me and I knew he would do anything I asked of him.

I knew what I had to do. This was the rightful punishment. This girl was the cause of all my problems. I had stood up for her after Er's death, even when it cost me my relationship with Onan. And after his death, I did everything I could to send her quietly and peacefully back to her father's house. After all that, she had still chosen to disgrace me in this way. I was sure that, had she not married my sons, my life would not have fallen apart.

I wanted to see her die.

"Bring Tamar out of her father's house, and let her be burned in front of the entire village, just as our law requires!"

Chapter 20

Tamar

The wait was over. The sun was setting, and I could see Belhan approaching in the distance. With him were the people from my village, swinging ropes in their hands and wielding flaming torches.

I could hide no longer. They were here to take me to my death.

I placed my hand on my belly. It was only slightly larger than normal, yet inside there was a being whose life depended on my actions in the next few minutes. How was it possible to love somebody you had never met so deeply? I knew I would give every ounce of myself for this baby, and right now I had to fight for my life, for my child's survival depended on mine.

As the mob closed in around my tent, I stepped outside. All I could do was have faith.

Daughter.

His voice gave me all the strength I needed. Whether it was my mistake or His command which had led me to this moment, wasn't important. All that mattered now was that He was with me.

I feel scared, but I will not be afraid. Please help me.

As I sent my silent plea to Him, I took a deep breath, and somehow there were words in my mouth.

"You won't need those ropes. I'll go with you."

A murmur of shock spread through the mob. It was hard for me to believe that these were the people and faces I had grown up with. The women from the market who would touch my shoulder as I walked by. The men who would give me a sweet fruit when their wives weren't looking. The faces I had seen as a child, tugging my parents' hands, impatient to get back home. The other children who had searched for stones with me, and to whom I had proudly showed my baby camel. What had become of these people? I didn't feel any anger towards them. They were just doing what they thought was righteous.

I turned to Belhan. "But first, may I talk with you alone?"

Belhan had grown into a tall man with the body and tanned skin of someone who worked outside all day. Even as a youth, when I had first moved to Judah's household, he had always treated me with great respect. It seemed like the years had been kind to him. He stood tall with his shoulders high, but there was a gentleness in his manner.

"Careful! She just wants to corrupt one more man before her death!" yelled someone from the crowd.

Belhan hesitated, looking downcast. We didn't know each other well, but I knew he could relate to me. He had taken orders from Er and Onan for years, and had borne more than his fair share of abuse. If Judah had not intervened, Er would have killed Belhan on more than one occasion.

"Trust me," I whispered, my eyes pleading with him.

It would have been so easy to shame Judah and save myself. In one moment I could have produced his seal, tied to the back of my garment, and my name would have been cleared, my child's life secured. I pushed away those thoughts: I needed to do this the right way.

The moments in which Belhan was deciding whether to trust me felt like the rock I had once thrown into the well once. It kept falling and falling, as if frozen in time, drawing deeper and deeper into the darkness.

Finally, the rock landed with a splash, and Belhan nodded his head quickly towards the tent. "Be quick, Tamar," he said, his voice cracking with the strain of his responsibility.

The crowd howled in outrage. One man threw their torch to the ground, and the dry desert grass sparked with fire. We hurried into the tent, and I wasted no time in reaching for the sack that was hanging on my back. Belhan's eyes widened as I pulled out Judah's identification seal and its cord, and held them in my palm. Then, with my other hand, I reached behind me for the staff I had placed there for precisely this moment.

His mouth opened as he recognized the object he saw every day as Judah gave him orders.

"Tamar, why do you have this?"

Did he really not understand? I had no time to explain. I could already hear the crackling of the fire as it spread around the tent.

"Belhan, I need you to listen very carefully. Run back to Judah and give him these three things. Then give him this exact message: 'The man who owns these things made me pregnant. Look closely. Whose seal, cord, and staff are these?' Will you do this for me, Belhan?"

He gasped. It all made sense now.

"But, Tamar," he started to say, a new sense of urgency in his voice, "what if I don't get to Judah in time? My master's reputation is not worth your life!"

There was no time for this. I could hear the crowd getting more and more restless outside.

Grabbing his shoulders, I said: "Belhan, do you know what my name means?"

He shook his head, like a little child trying to escape a scolding.

"It meals 'palm tree'. I stand tall, no matter what heat comes in the middle of the day. Now run!"

Chapter 21

Judah

My heart began to race inside my chest as I saw Belhan approaching in the distance. Had something happened to Shelah? Too many times, I had seen a servant run towards me with news of death. My son was all I had left. I tried to tell myself to relax. It was most likely news of Tamar's death, not Shelah's, that Belhan was bringing to me.

Tamar the prostitute: who could have known?

I shuddered to think that the woman who once lived under my roof, and had married my two eldest sons, had sold her body like a common whore. How grotesque. How shameful. Reya was right all along: Tamar probably did have a disease she picked up from some stranger, and she killed my sons with it. After I sent her back to her father's house, she had obviously returned to her old ways.

I had to admit that there was more to my decision to have Tamar killed than simply her chosen profession. I had to protect my youngest son - my only son - from her, and Belhan's discovery at the market had provided the perfect opportunity. This was an easy way out.

As Belhan struggled to get his breath back, I imagined the relief which his words would give me.

"Master...Judah," he began, his working tunic drenched with sweat.

My brow furrowed. There was a look of panic on his face that I knew too well.

"What's wrong, Belhan?"

"I'm sorry, master, but..."

"Just spit it out, Belhan! Has Shelah been hurt?"

"Shelah? No, master, he is safe. But I...I have a message for you," he stuttered.

My son was safe. I could breathe normally again. Surely nothing Belhan could say now would be worse than what I had imagined.

Slowly, the servant took out a large black sack and untied the twine that was holding it closed. His hands shook as he took out the contents and held them before me.

I grabbed them out of his hands, running towards the fire to examine them in the light. I felt like I had been kicked in the stomach by one of the camels.

"Tamar told to me to give you this message: 'The man who owns these things made me pregnant. Look closely. Whose seal and cord and walking stick are these?'

My head spinning, I sat down on the dirt floor, not caring whether my robe was stained. It was Tamar. Everything made sense now; the broken pieces of the puzzle were falling together.

It was another of those moments where I had a choice of great significance to make. Just like when Joseph had approached my brothers and I for the last time. A moment in which I had made the wrong choice so many times before, blinded by my anger and pride. All those wrong choices had led me here, and I knew I was not going to fail again.

"She is more righteous than I am," I muttered. "She could have chosen to humiliate me after refusing to allow her to marry Shelah."

"Master Judah," Belhan interrupted, "with respect, if you don't send orders to spare her right now, it won't matter that Tamar did what was right."

Picking up our robes, we both took off running into the night.

~~~
~~~

Tamar was stripped naked, tied to a bare tree trunk. Her stomach looked unusually large for her stage of pregnancy. Her bald scalp shimmered in the light of the moon and stars; the villagers had cut off all her hair, as prostitutes would do to mark themselves in public. A few people had thrown rotten vegetables and animal manure at her. Others had spat on her or thrown dirt, and there were clumps of it stuck all over her naked body. I saw all this from the light of the torches carried by the mob as they prowled around her. She was looking down at her belly, yet I could see from her countenance that she was not afraid. She looked up, then straight at Belhan and I as we pushed our way through the crowd. By now everyone but the sick and elderly had come to see the execution. The voices, filled with curses and threats, fell silent we approached Tamar.

It was too late for Joseph, but I knew I could still save Tamar and my child. I whispered in Belhan's ear.

"Gather around, everybody," commanded Belhan, his voice booming in the night air. "There will be no need for that." He looked over at the men sitting around Tamar's tied body, preparing the kindling for the fire that would bring her death. "Come now, gather around. Judah has an announcement to make." As the people gathered closer, Belhan nodded his approval.

I looked at the faces staring at me. Some were intrigued, while others were obviously upset that their evening's entertainment was being disrupted. Tamar's eyes locked with mine, and there was no bitterness or anger in the smile she gave me.

For the first time in my life, I began to make the right choice.

"The man you see before you had everything. Three sons, a wealth unlike any this village has seen, and a beautiful wife that I love..." I trailed off, then cleared my throat. "That I loved. Most of you also know that the hand of God has taken my family from me," I continued, feeling my eyes grow hot with tears, "but what you don't know is that the man before you is also a fraud. My firstborn son was a bully, who got Tamar pregnant and then took the life of their child, leaving Tamar barely alive." The crowd began to whisper among themselves. I had never heard anyone talking about abuse in marriage before, and I wondered how many people listening to me had their own bitter knowledge of what I was saying.

"My second son refused to fulfill the customs of my people and give an heir to his older brother. In truth, my two sons hated each other from birth until death. And as for my wife: well, I lied to her for our entire marriage. I ran away from my family and came to you, not as a victim, but as a criminal. The real truth is that I helped sell my young brother into slavery."

I heard someone in the crowd gasp. Another yelled, "Get to the point, Judah! This woman is pregnant out of wedlock."

"Then let's burn her!" shouted another.

"But it is I who am the child's father."

Silence fell across the valley, the only sound being the gentle wind sweeping the sand through the village streets.

"By the customs of my land, it is perfectly lawful for Tamar to carry descendants for my dead sons."

Belhan knelt at Tamar's feet, untied her bonds, and she fell to the ground. Swiftly, he took off his robes and covered her. She stood up, breathing hard and sharply, her hands instinctively protecting the life within her belly. I approached her, and took her hand.

"Tamar, with the God of my forefathers - Abraham, Isaac, and Jacob - as my witness, I repent for the way I have wronged you. I had no right to discard you after my family mistreated you. You are clearly a woman of deep integrity, and unshakable strength. And if there are any of you here who are beating your wives, daughters, or servants, as one of the leading men in this region, you will answer directly to me."

Strictly, even a married man and woman should not have any physical contact in public. But no-one protested as Tamar threw her arms around my neck.

I felt hope in my heart again, and as I held the mother of my child, the wound that had been growing within me for decades began to heal. How beautiful was repentance and forgiveness!

The crowd began to disperse, some clearly disappointed they hadn't seen the spectacle they had hoped for. I noticed a few of the women in the crowd beaming with pride, feeling worthy and dignified for what may have been the first time in their lives.

As Tamar released me from her embrace, I turned to Belhan. "Thank you, faithful servant. You have served me well." The young boy smiled, and I knew it was time to do what I had wanted to for a long time. I took a rolled piece of papyrus out of my pocket and handed it to Belhan. The boy raised one eyebrow in confusion.

"Your freedom, Belhan."

His jaw dropped. Since his birth, he had been a servant in my household, and not once had he dishonored me or complained. He had been faithful.

"Master, I don't..."

"Belhan, I am no longer your master. You are free to go."

The look of shock was still on his face as I smiled and walked towards Sergad and Niya. Niya's face was red from sorrow, streaked black from the ash around her eyes. Sergad had ripped his tunic in grief when he saw Tamar being taken to her death. They held each other as I said: "Please forgive me for the way I allowed your daughter to be treated, and the way I treated her. I was wrong for not noticing her sorrow, and for blocking her marriage to Shelah."

Sergad stepped closer to me, putting his hand on my shoulder. "Judah, you are brave like a lion. I have never seen anyone do that before. I don't know your God, but after hearing everything Tamar has told me, and seeing you today, I think I want to know Him."

And there, in the middle of a dispersing crowd, as the torches lit our faces, turned towards the stars shining in the heavens, we all knelt and praised God.

"God of my Fathers, you are righteous and you are just. You have seen our sins and transgressions, and you have chosen to forgive us, love us, and inspire of all our failures. You remove our guilt and shame, and give us commands that bring us life." I gently lay my hand on Tamar's belly. "My God, I praise you for this miracle. Its conception was untimely and full of darkness, but I pray that this child grows up to know you, obey you, and love you. You are a God of miracles, and a hope in impossible circumstances. We give our lives to you. We choose to listen to you, obey your words, and walk in faith. You promised my great grandfather, Abraham, descendants as numerous as the stars in the sky, and here under this bright firmament we stand, descendants of hope."

Chapter 22

Tamar

When I opened my eyes in the morning, all I could see was the massive bump where my stomach used to be. I was as round as a full moon and as heavy as a boulder at nine months (and two very long days) pregnant.

Everything that most women complained about during pregnancy felt so beautiful to me, for these were the things I had never been able to experience with Davida. I didn't care that I struggled to pick things up from the floor, or that I had no husband to support me through the pregnancy. It didn't matter that everything inside of me felt squashed together, or that I hadn't seen my feet in months. I cherished the pain in my back from the extra weight I was carrying, and I was consumed by the prospect that, at last, I was going to be a mother! There was a tiny person inside of me who could emerge any minute; a son or daughter whom I could take care of for the rest of my life. How was it possible to love somebody you had never met this much?

My mother and Dinah had become close friends, bonding over their shared excitement about the baby. They fussed around me like worker bees protecting their queen. Was I drinking enough water? Was I comfortable in my sleep? Of course the answer was no, but which other woman at my stage of pregnancy enjoyed a full night of rest?

It was only when Dinah heard how Judah had defended and apologized to me that she had returned to the village. "My only problem with my brother's apology is that he delivered it to you while you were still tied up!" she had told me, laughing. She then informed my mother, with no hint of a request, that she would be moving in with us for the next few weeks to help with the birth. How could we say no when Dinah's energy and presence brought so much joy to our home?

My father was also overjoyed about the baby and took up carpentry so that he could build a crib. I often saw him running frantically here and there with an axe searching for more wood, frightening the goats and sheep in the fields in the process. He was determined to finish the crib before I gave birth, which could now be any minute.

Judah had brought over a camel-load of the fabric that had belonged to Reya, and asked my mother to make clothes for the baby with it. "Fit for a king," he would say; "or a queen!" when Dinah nudged him in the ribs. He didn't visit often, but when he did he brought rare foods like oranges, honey, and the spices I craved - cinnamon and coriander. He would hand me the presents, make small talk with my father, then leave. I could tell he didn't really know how to act around me: as a father, grandfather, or father-in-law?

Even Hirah had eventually paid me a visit. He arrived while Dinah was massaging my swollen hands; entering the tent he stopped dead, then looked from me to her, and back again. He swallowed hard, then continued to stare at Dinah with his mouth hanging open. Since her return, Dinah had exchanged her black veil for ordinary robes, and I realized that this was Hirah's first glimpse of the woman behind the veil.

"It's okay, Hirah, come in," I said, trying hard not to laugh out loud.

"I forgot...I forgot my...," he stuttered before backing out of the tent.

We giggled for a long time after Hirah left. I didn't blame him; his reaction was one I had become used to whenever anyone saw Dinah's beauty for the first time.

Mother, father, Judah, Hirah, and Dinah: they were like any other family expecting their first grandchild. It seemed like everyone was trying their best to put the mess of the last few years behind us. This baby felt like a new beginning.

~~~

The midwife burst into the birthing tent Judah had prepared for me and ran straight towards me. She looked disheveled, her hair sticking up as if she had just woken up, and she was still wearing her sleeping tunic. Without so much as a greeting, she began to massage my stomach. Her gaze was intense, and after another contraction had passed, she finally smiled and said, "Okay, let's get these twins out of here!"

"Twins?" exclaimed my mother and Dinah at the same time. The midwife looked at us like we were stupid.

"You didn't know? Why else did you think she was this large?"

The three women looked at me. I couldn't believe I hadn't known there were two babies inside me. Even though the labor was already causing me great pain, I was overjoyed. I didn't have long to savor the feeling before another, even stronger, wave of pain hit.

"Get these babies out of me!" I yelled, spurring the women into action. My mother held my hand and patted my head with a wet towel as I screamed at the top of my lungs.

"Push, Tamar, you can do it! Push! Good girl!" Dinah urged.

I could feel my teeth grinding together as I clenched my jaw. We were at a standstill. I could sense the midwife's concern as she massaged my belly, trying to get the babies to shift into the right position. The pain grew worse with each contraction, but still the little bodies inside me refused to budge.

Hours had passed when the midwife finally shouted, "The first baby is about to come out!" I felt something tear, and the sheets under me were suddenly wet with blood. Too much blood. Everyone began to panic as I slipped in and out of consciousness, picking up only fragments of the frightened conversation happening around me.

"I see a hand!"
~~~

"This isn't the correct position!"

"Quick, tie a thread around the arm so we know who came first."

More noise, more agony. When would this be over?

"Get ready to push the first one out!"

"Wait, look! It's pulling its hand back."

More tearing. Something cracking. More blood. The most intense pain I had ever felt.

"Here comes a head!"

In my lucid moments I felt as if I was being ripped open from the inside. With strength that came from somewhere deep within me I pushed, clenching my teeth, and felt the first baby come out.

"What? How did he break out first? This isn't the one with the thread!"

"One more to go, Tamar!"

I felt the second baby slither out, with much less effort than before. That was fortunate, because I had nothing left to give. I closed my eyes and everything faded into darkness.

~~~

"Nothing short of a miracle!"

That was the first thing I heard when I opened my eyes. My mother was hovering above me, with a smile so wide the corners of her mouth looked as if they were about to burst. I could tell from the rays of light creeping into the tent that the night was finally over.

"The miracle was that we didn't need to cut you open!" said the midwife. "Those babies were completely in the wrong position!"

My body was still too tender to move, but through my half-open lips I whispered, "My babies."
~~~

My mother wasted no time bringing them to me. "Tamar, meet your two sons."

"Sons," I muttered.

The two boys were washed and tightly wrapped in their swaddling clothes. My mother swiftly lifted my gown, undressed the twins and placed them at my breasts.

I had no words. The birth already felt like a distant memory, and all I could feel was an overpowering love for these two babies. I couldn't take my eyes off their perfect little noses, their tiny fingernails, their wrinkly necks.

One of the babies let go of me and began to wail. The other one opened his eyes at the shrill sound and joined in. It was the most beautiful sound I had ever heard. Once they had satisfied their hunger, they drifted off to sleep in my arms, their mouths still half open.

My father, Judah, and Hirah were let into the tent once the boys were asleep and the mess of the birth had been cleared up. They all looked terrified, unsure of how to act around the babies they had been obsessing over for the past few months.

"Their names are Perez and Zerah," I declared. "The first will be Perez, and the one with the scarlet string will be Zerah.

Dinah came and took the sleeping infants out of my arms and placed them in Judah's.

"Your sons, Judah," she said.

Hirah's brow furrowed in surprise as he inspected the twins closely. He gently nudged Judah and whispered, "Look, actual babies!"

"Yes, Hirah, I had noticed," replied Judah, beaming, as the rest of us tried not to laugh.

Soon, everyone had left, leaving Judah and me alone. As he held our sons, I saw tears in his eyes. I couldn't imagine what was going through his head, after losing two sons and suddenly being presented with two more. Here were his double portion, his blessing, his heirs.

Judah was not going to be my husband, but I had my family around me to help: aunts, uncles, grandparents. They would not let me fall. Even as an unmarried widow, I would not be raising these children alone.

The One who had given me life and saved me was right here in this dirty tent. I could feel Him in this miracle of life, in the gentle whistling of the spring wind outside. I felt Him in the heat on my shoulders, as if two hands were resting there.

My beloved daughter, I will protect your sons and walk with them all the days of my life. They will become great nations.

I was at peace.

Chapter 23

Judah

A few weeks after I became a father again, I decided to take my flocks and head out into the wilderness alone, leaving my household in Belhan's safe hands. So much had changed over the last few months. I felt as if I had been running down a mountain side, unable to stop, going faster and faster. Now that things had settled down, it was time to stop running, even if only for a few days.

Once I had passed the last familiar landmark, I sat down on a rock and took off my sandals, sinking my feet deep into the sand to cool them. The day had been hot and dry, with no breeze to bring relief. My back was soaked with sweat and my mouth was dry. I took out my water jug, but just before the cold water touched my lips I heard a gentle whisper.

My son.

The voice so familiar it made my heart ache. Familiar, yet somehow foreign at the same time.

I am here.

The desert seemed to freeze around me, and I knew I was not alone. He was here, just like He had been when my father set my brothers and me around the fire and told us stories and dreams about his God.

The feeling of peace I had experienced before in my solitude had returned in an instant.

'God of Abraham, Isaac, and Jacob, is that you?' I said out loud. My camel looked at me with curiosity. The wind began to blow harder, lifting the sand and forming beautiful patterns on the ground. I dropped to my knees. It was time to begin again.

"God of Abraham, Isaac, and Jacob, please forgive me. I am sorry for the hatred and jealousy I felt toward Joseph, and for running away from my family, your people. I was wrong not to discipline my sons and for letting my wife worship her gods in our house. We both mistreated Tamar. My guilt is overwhelming, and your blessings, even in my darkness, were abundant."

I knew what I had to do. It was something I had seen my father and grandfather doing many times before. Finding some loose stones in the caves nearby, I built an altar, then sacrificed the young goat I had brought from my flock to sustain me in the wilderness. As I plunged my knife into its throat, tears filled my eyes as I remembered how I had used the blood of another innocent animal to stain Joseph's coat of many colors. As the flesh burned in the flames, a weight I had been carrying for years was lifted from my shoulders.

My son, I am your God, the God of Judah. Take Tamar and your three sons and go back to the land that I have given your father.

Go back? Was that really what God wanted from me now? I was petrified to face my father, mother, and brothers after all these years. Would Tamar trust me enough to move to my father's land with me? In spite of all my doubts and questions, I took out my flute and worshipped the God of my fathers - my God - until the sun rose over the hills. I knew that if the same God who had restored my family was asking me to go back, then that was what I must do.

I was scared, but I would not be afraid.

Dreams

Viktoriya

I am so fascinated that the people filling the pages of the Bible, specifically Genesis, have dreams just like people today have. God approaches people at night, and speaks to them: some in a clear way, other much more vaguely. God intervened in the lives of Abraham, Isaac and Jacob through dreams, and one of the sparks that set of this story was the dreams God gave to Joseph, which he clearly didn't know how to deal with. Some of the dreams in this story are actually recorded in the Bible, while others are purely fictional.

Just like I'm sure some people in the Bible had trouble sleeping, many people today struggle to rest during their time of sleep. Whether its nightmares or just restless nights, I want to take this opportunity to pray over your sleep. First of all, I want to command any nightmares, terrors, or sleepless nights to cease right now in Jesus name. They have no right to disturb your rest. And then I want to speak God's dreams over you. I ask God on your behalf to speak to you in your dreams, and to show you the great plans He has for you, your family, your city. I ask that He speak specifically into situations you are encountering, that He gives you divine insights into problems you are facing- at home, at work, or at church. I believe that for some of you, God will give you ideas in your dreams that are the solution for breakthrough in your field of work. To others, that He will give you dreams about other people that you are to pray for and encourage. And for some of you, God just wants to spend time with you in your dreams. Prepare your heart to encounter Him during your sleep. Not all dreams are from God, but the ones that are bring hope.

Part 3

Chapter 24

Judah

The cows refused to take any more steps, mooing loudly in protest, and the sheep lay down peacefully on our path instead of shuffling forward. One of the camels walked over to the cart carrying our possessions and began to chew my tent. I exhaled loudly, wiping the sweat off my forehead. The task of moving my family and all my possessions back to my father's land, accompanied by an eighteen-year-old son and a woman breastfeeding her twins was turning out to be much harder than I had thought.

I looked over at Tamar, who was sitting on the camel, holding our sons in her arms, and saw that her robe was drenched with sweat from the powerful midday sun. A fly was swirling around her nose, and she sneezed. Disturbed, one of the boys began to wail. The sound of a crying infant felt so eerie in the desert land we were crossing. Not to be outdone by his brother, Perez joined in, screaming at the top of his tiny lungs. Tamar looked up at me, the bags appearing heavy under her eyes. Shelah came over to Tamar, took Perez, and gently rocked him from side to side, which helped to calm him down.

I smiled as I saw Shelah rocking his brother. I had been overjoyed when he had accepted my proposal to move back to my father's house with me. He still hadn't spoken much, especially to Tamar, but I had to admit he had an incredible talent of taking care of his new brothers. Shelah had arrived from Egypt as soon as he had heard about the birth. I suspected his return had a lot to do with him not having to marry Tamar anymore, but I could see he was genuinely excited to meet his new brothers. He brought them expensive presents he had acquired from traders on the way to Egypt.

When I had told him about hearing God's call, he had listened quietly and said nothing. After sitting in silence for a few minutes, he asked if he was still part of my household. Did he really not know the answer to that question? His face lit up as I replied: "Of course, my son!"

The trip that took just a few days on my own was going to take a few weeks at the pace we were going. It was all too much: the sun was hot, the animals unruly, and our food supply too small. I was constantly thirsty, and knowing we had a limited supply of water made my throat even drier. With every new obstacle, I kept asking my God the same question: *Am I really doing the right thing?*

That evening, as we sat down to the scraps making up our meal, we were all exhausted. Shelah was holding the twins, giving Tamar a chance to eat. Shelah gently stroked Zerah's cheek as he slept. He got my attention, then nodded in the direction of Tamar, who had already fallen asleep with her head in her hands. We both smiled as she began to snore lightly. I looked up at the starry sky. These boys were a symbol of hope.

I remembered how we had said goodbye to all our friends in Kezib just a few days ago, at the wedding feast of Hirah and Dinah. Nobody had been more surprised than Hirah when Dinah had accepted his marriage proposal. He had fallen in love with her from the first time he saw her, but never imagined that she would actually feel the same way. Since our father wasn't here, Hirah had asked me for Dinah's hand in marriage. The calm, assured man who could find humor in any situation, was nervous and lost for words as he presented his request. I had said yes straight away. There was no-one better I could have picked for my little sister than my very best friend. Their wedding was a small, yet luxurious and intimate feast.

Saying goodbye felt so right at the time. As hard as it had been to say goodbye to my friend, I could leave with peace in my heart, knowing that he now had Dinah to take care of. The excitement of the journey ahead was all that had been on my mind; the thought of seeing my mother made me want to run home as fast as I could. But now, here alone, fighting the animals and the elements, I was regretting my decision.

God, did I hear you right? Maybe it was too soon; maybe we should just go back. I thought you asked me to make this this trip, but I hope you know that two babies in the desert is not a good idea! At this rate, all our food and water will be done by the time we reach the middle of the journey! Help us!

Trust me, my son.

Lord, are you sure you don't want us to just go back? We could wait until the boys are older and hire a few servants to help us move?

Do not be afraid.

I smiled and shook my head. Of course He knew what the real problem was.

Okay, God, but if we die here in the desert…

Before I could finish my prayer, Tamar suddenly awoke from her sleep and jumped up, searching for her boys.

"They are with Shelah. He has put them into the wagon to sleep."

She nodded, visibly relaxing.

"Thank you Judah, I needed that rest."

The next morning, as we packed up our tents to continue our journey, I saw a group of camels approaching across the empty desert landscape. Immediately, I began to panic. Were they robbers? Was my family in danger? Was I going to lose all my possessions before I even got to my father's house? There was no place to hide. No caves, no hills, just empty, sandy space, dotted with a few thorn branches. Why had I given my all servants their freedom? I should have waited until after we had crossed safely to the land of my father. The best we could do was to keep going and hope that, by some miracle, whoever was approaching us didn't mean us harm. We were absolutely defenseless.

I didn't tell Tamar or Shelah about the caravan, and they were too preoccupied with the boys to notice. We kept walking, and the caravan got closer and closer. I tried not to look back, not to panic. But soon enough, I heard the wagons rolling and the sound of their animals.

Suddenly, Tamar looked back and exclaimed.

I grimaced, preparing for the worst.

"It's Hirah, Dinah, and Belhan!" she yelled.

Shocked, I squinted my eyes, and saw my friend and sister waving back. Could it really be true? Surprised and relieved, I ran towards their caravan.

"Aren't you supposed to be having your wedding week?" I asked after a long embrace, still catching my breath. Hirah and Dinah smiled at each other.

"We have the rest of our lives together. Right now, our friends need help. Last night a man came to me in my dream and told me to take my new wife and Belhan and move with you to Dinah's father's house. When I told Dinah about this dream, we decided it was time to follow the God of her father. We've been travelling through the night to find you."

I was dumbfounded. At the same time God had been speaking to me, He had been moving on my behalf.

"Hi, Judah!" exclaimed Belhan, quick to embrace me. He was nineteen years old, but could have passed for twelve. Even after gaining his freedom, he refused to leave my side.

"Judah," said Dinah said with pride, "Belhan is part of my family now."

I couldn't have been happier in that moment. *God, you are truly a God of miracles.*

"Okay now, let's get this procession into shape!" said Hirah. He took out a long rope and tied the animals together. "It makes them feel more secure in a new place," he explained.

The rest of the journey was more than just manageable. Strained silence had been replaced by laughter (often at Hirah's expense). Dinah helped out with the boys, while Belhan and Shelah took charge of the herds and wagons.

Thank you for the help, my God. You are so faithful.

Now that my mind was not focused on survival, it finally hit me that, after almost two decades, I was going to have to face everything I had run away from.

~~~

A few days later, we approached the familiar valley of Hebron. When I left this place I had only been twenty-five years old, with the weight of the world on my shoulders. Now, I was returning having seen grief and death, but having also encountered the One who had given me true life. I had been faithful to my wife well till the very end. My sons had died, and I would always grieve for them, but God had been gracious enough to bless me again.

I told my family to wait on the outskirts of the valley while I went on alone. I knew Hirah would keep them safe. As I walked deeper into the valley, I remembered running all over these hills with my brothers as a boy. We would make weapons out of just about anything, playing and fighting like little boys should. I saw people going about their duties, just as my brothers and I had in my father's household. No-one seemed to notice as I approached the circle of tents at the bottom of the valley, Everything looked smaller and older than I remembered.

There, beside the bread-making stove in the middle of the tents, was an old white-haired woman in colorful robes. I would recognize her anywhere. My heart burned in my chest as I thought about all the time we had lost.

"Mother," I whispered, restraining the sob rising in my throat.

She froze and dropped what she was holding, spinning around. The flour in the bowl rose in a white cloud that covered her colorful robe and the surrounding ground.
~~~

"Judah!" she exclaimed, throwing her shaking arms around me. "My son has returned, he has returned!" She kept shouting my name, as if that would somehow keep me here longer.

"Don't worry, mother, I am not going anywhere," I whispered into her ear. The commotion soon attracted the attention of the rest of the camp. The little children came running, unsure of this strange man and the ruckus he was causing. Then, as I dusted myself down, I saw the aged faces of my brothers among the crowd. They looked as if they had seen a dead man come to life. They all had thick, dark beards, and their heads were covered. Simeon and Levi ran up and lifted me in their embrace. Reuben nodded towards me approvingly. The rest just continued to stare in silence. Many of them had women standing next to them. My little brothers were now married with children!

Then I saw Benjamin. The frail little boy I had left now towered above me, with a body like a carved tree trunk and hair like a lion's mane. He was very handsome, as Joseph had been. His hair was just as curly, but black as night instead of Joseph's bright red. Benjamin smiled at me: his face was so familiar, like looking at the ghost of Joseph.

"Where is father?" I asked my mother, nervously.

She looked down to the floor and began drawing lines in the sand with her feet; I had forgotten I had picked up that habit from her.

"He's resting," she replied, not making eye contact.

"Is he sick?"

She didn't answer, but took my hand and led me to a tent set apart from the rest and covered in dark material. "This is your father's tent," she whispered. "He doesn't leave his bed much, or let many people see him. He never...recovered from Joseph's death."

The feelings I had tried to leave in this valley came rushing back like a raging torrent. Mother went into the tent and I heard her gentle voice say, "Jacob, my love, Judah has returned."

"Joseph has returned!" I could hear the rustling of blankets, then my father emerged from the tent. The smile drained from his face in an instant.

"No, Jacob, it is Judah who has returned," said mother, resting a hand on his shoulder.

"So I see. I'm glad to have you home, my son."

He didn't ask where I had been, or why I had returned. I embraced him, masking my disappointment. I couldn't tell him about the rest of my party yet. His eyes reminded me of Reya's in the last two years before she died: anxious and hopeless. I had spent so much time imagining my reunion with my father. Now, I knew it was not as bad as I had feared, or as good as I had hoped for.

~~~

"Here is the tent for you and Tamar, my son," said my mother proudly as she led us through the crowded camp. When I left, there had been no more than ten tents. Now there were dozens and dozens, scattered around my father's property. There were children of all ages, many wives to each brother, and enough animals to outlast even a famine.

"Oh, mother," I said awkwardly, "Tamar and I aren't husband and wife."

Mother looked confused. "It looks like we have a lot to catch up on," she said, quickly beginning to prepare a separate tent for Tamar.

Everyone was smitten by Perez and Zerah, especially Leah. "I never thought I'd see Judah again and now I am holding his sons!" she said, putting her arm around Tamar. "Thank you for being the mother of my grandchildren."

Tamar beamed with pride. Then mother turned her attention towards me. "Son, tonight we feast in your honor. I will start the preparations." She ran her
~~~

fingers through my hair, like she used to when I was young, then went about her work, almost bouncing with joy. That night, we feasted like never before.

Over the next few weeks, I gradually related the events of my life since leaving the valley. Some were shocked by the story of Tamar's pregnancy, others appalled, but mostly everyone was happy to have us back.

Eventually, my brothers and I escaped from the business of the camp went to tend our flocks (now more numerous than we could have imagined) at Shechem. Benjamin had wanted to go with us, but father protested. "Benjamin stays," was his final word, and none of us had objected.

It felt so surreal to return to this place of such significance and sorrow. We talked about everything: from our wives, children, and livestock; to Joseph, and how every single one of us was still impacted by what we did that day. Reuben was not slow to gloat, and Simeon and Levi soon grew tired of his criticism. I spent much of my time trying to keep the peace. We were all grown men, but I couldn't help but smile at how some things never seemed to change.

And then there was the one unavoidable discussion: father.

"He's done nothing since you left, Judah, except wallow in sorrow," said Naphtali.

"Most of his days were spent in mourning, or talking about the days when Rachel and Joseph were alive," added Issachar. "Eventually everyone began to ignore him, and he retreated to his tent."

"If not for us running his household - so well that it flourished, I must say - he would have lost everything," boasted Asher.

Levi spat on the ground. "I think that's despicable. What kind of a man is he?"

"It's our fault he is this way, Levi," replied Dan. "We've tried so many times to talk to him, to shake him out of his sorrow, but he just repeats his favorite phrase: 'I will go to my grave mourning for my son.' "

"Judah, why don't you try getting through to him?" asked Simeon. All the brothers looked at me.

"What would I be able to say that you, my brothers, haven't already?" I replied, hesitantly.

"Judah, you ran away from this, leaving us to deal with father and the aftermath of your idea to sell Joseph. We all know Reuben would have rescued him if not for your 'brilliant' plan!" yelled Levi, clearly frustrated. "Now that you are back, do your bit of being part of this family and talk to him. It's the very least you can do."

I could not believe my ears; my brothers blamed me for what happened. I knew I had blamed myself, but hearing it coming from their lips was worse than I could have ever imagined. Defeated, there was nothing I could do but agree to talk to Jacob.

The rest of the trip was soured and strained. Whereas on the way up we had been full of laughter, on the way back we walked in silence. Things that were left unspoken for decades had finally been said, and the words blazed like fire.

As soon as we returned to Jacob's property, I went to go see Perez and Zerah. The little boys had just learned to crawl, and babbled excitedly when I walked through the door. They raced each other, battling to be the first one to be picked up. I smiled at their chubby little arms and legs, picking them up, one in each hand. As they babbled and tugged at my beard, I felt immensely better. I held them close as they relaxed in my arms.

"How was the trip?" asked Tamar, smiling at the boys trying to pull off my head covering.

"Not at all what I expected," I confessed.

She didn't pry, but gave me a sympathetic smile. "It's all going to work out, Judah. No family is without complications, but I can see without any doubt that you are loved here."

She was right. It was time to talk to father. I set the boys down and headed towards Jacob's tent. Inside, there was a strong stench of mud.

"Hello, father," I began, hesitantly.

"What do you need, Judah?"

My hands were clammy, and all I could do was stare at the floor. What was I doing here? I had no right to talk to father after what I did to Joseph. This was my fault. My own father had lost years of his life because of my hatred and greed.

"Well?" He sat up and stared at me, ashes smeared all over his face.

For my brothers, I thought. They all needed their father back. With every last bit of fleeting courage, I explained to the old man why he needed to stop grieving and return to overseeing his household. The more I said, the deeper Jacob furrowed his brow. Finally, when I had finished, he sat silently and stared at me.

"You don't know what it's like to lose your beloved wife and son, Judah. You have no right to disrespect me with those words."

I gasped. Had he not heard that my life was marked by the same tragedies as his? There was so much I wanted to tell him. But without another word, I left the old man to his ashes.

Chapter 25

Tamar

Being a part of Judah's family fascinated me. Everything was different, and a lot more complicated. Somehow, all of Jacob's sons, with their wives and children, functioned as one big family. It was a lot of mouths to feed. When I was growing up, my mother would bake the bread to fill us in less than an hour, but these women spent the majority of their days cooking. Each meal was as large and luxurious as a wedding feast, with wealth and prestige laid out on the tables. It was no easy task to feed the masses, and the women were constantly complaining. It was in the kitchen that I got to know the other the wives and concubines of Judah's brothers.

They did everything loudly: talking, laughing, but mostly fighting about small things, such as the best way to spice meats or the exact procedure for baking bread. Leah, who was in charge of the entire operation, gave orders and tried to maintain the peace. I tried to keep to myself and did what I was told. Luckily, I had learned how to make basic dishes when Onan was alive, which saved me from embarrassment in front of the other experienced cooks.

The two women who argued the most were Cayla and Jenna, Simeon's wife and Canaanite concubine. Kayla acted as the superior and found ways to degrade Jenna whenever she could. When Jenna was in charge of making the bread, Kayla even went so far as putting more wood into the fire, burning the dough to a crisp. At dinner time, when everyone complained about not having enough to eat, Kayla made it very clear whose fault it had been. Later, I came into Jenna's tent and found her crying, nursing the hand she had burned in trying to save her loaves. As I comforted her, I remembered the tension between my mother and

Reya, and wondered what kind of things my mother's status had forced her to endure.

Jenna and I bonded quickly, being both foreigners and unmarried. Jacob believed his sons should only marry women from his homeland, and forbade Naphtali from taking in another Canaanite concubine after a fight with his wife. Gathering the whole camp together, he declared:

"My own grandfather, Abraham, didn't want my father, Isaac, to marry any of the local women. He sent his servant all the way to his distant homeland of Aram-nahariam to find my father a wife. We must follow in his example. There will be no more Canaanites in this family."

Jenna and I looked at each other, feeling more than a little uncomfortable.

I often missed my homeland. There were so many laws and customs which Jacob demanded that everyone observe. It was all so foreign to me. I wondered how my parents were; I would have given anything to have a quiet meal with them under our palm tree, rather than this ostentatious feast with a family that wasn't my own. Whenever I saw Perez and Zerah, however, playing happily among the large crowd of cousins, I smiled and reminded myself how much better my life was compared to what it was with Er.

Judah's mother, Leah, taught me all about the God whom I already loved. She taught me how He had created the world; about the lofty tower of Babel and the great Flood; about the promises God had made to Abraham, Isaac, and now Jacob. She explained to me that we were God's chosen people, and that one day our descendants would be as numerous as stars in the sky.

"Your sons get to be a part of that promise," she said. "I know it must be hard for you to be suddenly part of such a large and loud family. I felt the same way when Jacob first moved us away from my family. But it will get better, Tamar, I promise."

Talking to Leah lifted my spirits, and whenever the women cooking began to argue, Jenna and I would go to work quietly next to her.

Months passed, and I grew more accustomed to the new routine. Despite the arguments and complaining, our days were mostly filled with good things. So good, in fact, that nobody really noticed that the crops were failing: the rich platters of food grew steadily smaller and smaller; the milk in the pitchers fell lower and lower; the land gave us less and less vegetation. The land was dying, and famine stalked us like a lion.

Judah

The entire family was ravenous. Hunger affected everyone, from our frail father, to little Perez and Zerah. The best of what could be scraped together was given to the children, while the adults made do with stale bread and stew made from plant scraps. We had been utterly unprepared for this disaster. The market where people traded food and goods fell into disuse, as there was nothing to sell. Every evening, the families wandered into what used to be the tent used for food storage and preparations, their stomachs howling for food, only to find disappointment.

The famine shocked Jacob, and he started asking to be carried out of his tent more and more. He was already weak from mourning, and there was little else to give him strength. He wore his burlap less and less, but instead of focusing on running his household, he gave all the energy he had to Benjamin. "He is the only remaining son of Rachel. He must have the very best," Jacob would announce to us frequently.

Benjamin, meanwhile, did not appreciate his father's attention. As we worked in the fields one day, he confided in me: "For my entire life, Jacob blamed me for the death of his beloved Rachel. And now I have taken Joseph's place. I thought he hated me! He has ignored me for as long as I can remember, and now I am the very air he breathes."

It was actually a little comical to see a grown man be spoiled like a little child. Benjamin, with his athlete's physique and deep husky voice, spent the majority of his days tending to Jacob instead of working in the fields. At mealtimes, Jacob demanded that Benjamin always sit at his right hand. Less amusing was the fact that Benjamin was always awarded a double portion of food, which he would eat guiltily while the children looked on with hungry eyes. The favoritism made Benjamin very angry; whenever he could, he would sneak as much food as he could to the youngest children in the camp.

Jacob's behavior was even worse than it had been with Joseph, except no-one was jealous this time. My brothers and I sniggered at the sight of Benjamin's discomfort. Jacob's wives chose to ignore what they saw; they were just glad to see Jacob obsessed instead of depressed.

With every passing sunset, the famine became more severe. We killed off our animals one by one, just to keep the family alive. Eventually, even Jacob had had enough. He ordered the servants to summon the sons of Leah, Bilhah, and Zilpah.

"Why are you standing around, staring at each other, while your wives and children are slowly dying? I have heard from the people in our village that there are mountains of grain in Egypt. Take the donkeys, and go buy enough grain to keep us alive. Otherwise we will die. Go tomorrow at dawn. Your brother Benjamin will remain here with me. Reuben, get enough grain for your own family and Benjamin's."

Reuben looked very displeased. "Father, why should I? The boy does nothing to contribute to this family. Why should I get food for the family that will receive my firstborn inheritance?"

Suddenly, Benjamin bust into the tent, looking furious. "Jacob, I am a grown man, with a wife and children. I am perfectly capable to go to Egypt with my older brothers. Let me go! I need to do more than just sit around waiting on you. I am not Joseph."

It was the first time Benjamin had complained openly about Jacob's smothering affection. The contrast with the way Joseph had yearned for Jacob's attention was stark. Benjamin wanted nothing more than to be with his older brothers.

At the mention of Joseph's name, Jacob's whole body seemed to collapse.

"Benjamin, my son, if something were to happen to you, I would lose the last shred of hope. Then who would act as my firstborn?"

Reuben stood up, his hands clenched in fists. I quickly went to his side to hold him back.

"What about them?" he shouted, pointing at his brothers. "They are your sons as well! Don't you care if anything happens to them?"

Jacob eyes flashed with anger. "Benjamin, you will stay here, where it is safe. As for the rest of you, when the sun rises tomorrow you should already be on your way."

Our father limped out of the tent, leaving eleven brothers standing in silence.

Chapter 26

Judah

Dawn arrived, and the first streaks of light filtered through the dark sky. The ground was slightly damp from the morning dew and I could see the breath of the sleepy children gathered to say their farewells coming out in little clouds. The women rushed to get everything ready for our journey, having labored all through the night. All my brothers, except Benjamin, were scattered out around the camp with their wives and children surrounding them.

I looked at the loving faces around me and took the twins into my arms. "Boys, make sure you take good care of her, okay?" I whispered to them. The boys nodded enthusiastically.

Shelah came over to us and took the twins from me, and said, "Please be safe, father." We were not a traditional family, but I knew how blessed I was to have every single one of them.

~~~

The journey to Egypt took around a week. Without our herds and families with us, we covered a lot of ground during the day. The first day was spent mostly in silence, but soon our curiosity about what lay ahead of us in Egypt overcame our rivalry. All we knew of the mysterious land were rumors and stories from traders and migrants. None of us had ever been there. None, that is, except perhaps our brother, Joseph, before his death.

Each of us seemed to have heard different things about the land of Egypt and its people. One heard that the people lived in buildings of clay and brick instead
~~~

of tents; another, that there were many slaves there, who were forced to build things for the Pharaoh.

"I heard that the Pharaoh is like a god, the most powerful man of all," said Simeon.

"Don't let Father hear you saying that; you know he believes our God is the only God," warned Reuben.

"I didn't say he was god, Reuben, but that he was treated like one," replied Simeon, his frustration showing in his tone.

"Has anyone heard anything about the man Pharaoh appointed as his chief advisor?" I asked, trying to distract them from the argument that was clearly about to break out.

"I heard the Pharaoh gave him his own signet ring!" said Naphtali.

"Well I heard that everyone is required to bow before him or else they are beheaded!" added Dan.

The discussions continued as we got closer and closer to Egypt. By the time we saw the great pyramids and tall statues in the distance, our skin was burnt and withered from the strong sun and desert winds. The very little food we had brought with us had run out three days before. As we approached the massive brick gate marking the entrance to the city, our eyes grew wide at the sheer scale of the monuments and homes made out of brick and cement. Our tents suddenly seemed meager in comparison.

The people had much darker skin than I had seen, and I noticed that their eyes were painted black and their cheeks painted red. The men wore white clothes that covered their hips, while the women had a shawl for their chest and another for their hips. Some weren't wearing any clothes at all, and I guessed they were the slaves. Alongside the Egyptians were people from all over the world. I heard languages and accents I had never heard before. Some of the people I saw had skin lighter than ours, others skin as black as the night sky. The entire city was brimming with noise, color, and life.

After being inspected by the guards at the gates, we entered the city marketplace, where everything from clothes, to cotton, to different jewels, to fruits, were being sold at extortionate prices. My brothers scattered, all fascinated by what seemed like a new world. I began to look for somewhere we could buy food. I was just as intrigued by this place, but the hungry faces of my family were ingrained into my mind.

Eventually, I found the long line of people queuing to buy food. I joined the throng, and my brothers soon found me, leading their donkeys. Levi had managed to steal something from one of the vendors. Like a little boy, the grown man laughed with pleasure at having deceived an Egyptian. After what seemed like hours, it was finally our turn to buy the grain.

"Look, there's the Pharaoh's deputy!" exclaimed Simeon. We all stared at the man, whose name we found out was Zaphenath-paneah. He was adorned with jewels from head to toe, with skin lighter than the other Egyptians, and a cold look in his eyes. Not wanting to cause any trouble, we practically threw ourselves to the ground before him as he passed.

"Men of Canaan, rise," said a voice in our Hebrew tongue. We rose to our feet and saw the Ruler towering above us, his Hebrew interpreter at his side.

The Ruler said something in the language of the Egyptians, and we waited for the interpreter to translate: "Where are you from?"

"From the land of Canaan," I replied. "We have come to buy food."

As the interpreter relayed my words, the Ruler's face grew red with fury and he began to shout something we did not understand.

Our hearts sank as the interpreter addressed us again: "You are spies! You have come to see how vulnerable our land has become. You are not here for food, you want to see Egypt destroyed!"

All the crowd around us fell silent, shocked at the accusation. This man was so powerful that he could someone killed for no reason at all, and now he was accusing us of being spies, a crime which would mean certain death. With all eyes on us, my brothers and I attempted to defend ourselves.

"No, my lord!"

"This is not true."

"We are honest men!"

"All we want is to feed our families!"

The Ruler remained silent. In desperation, I continued: "Your servants have simply come to buy food to save our families. We are all brothers, members of the same family. I swear on my very life that we are honest men, lord! We are not spies!"

"Yes, you are!" declared Zaphenath-paneah through his translator. "You have come to find our weakness."

I looked at Reuben for help. "Lord," he pleaded, "I am the oldest of my brothers here. There are twelve of us, but one of our brothers is no longer with us, and our youngest brother is still with our father in the land of Canaan."

"As I said, you are spies! This is how I will test if your words are true. I swear by the life of Pharaoh, the most powerful of all, that you will never leave Egypt unless your youngest brother stands before me! One of you must bring your brother to me while my guards keep the rest of you here in prison. If it transpires that you have been lying, then I'll know your story is not true and that you are spies."

As the Ruler gave his judgment, the faces of my three sons flashed before my eyes.

"Guards, tie these men up and place them in prison!"

~~~
~~~

"We are truly being punished for what we did to Joseph," declared Asher.

"Reuben, why did you tell him about Joseph? What possessed you to say that there are twelve of us?" screamed Simeon.

"Even worse, why would you tell him about Benjamin?" Gad added, angrily.

"Brothers, stop attacking Reuben," I interjected. "None of us were expecting this."

"I admit, I was wrong to put our lives in danger. But what are we going to do now?" Ruben's quiet voice echoed against the prison walls. As the words left his mouth, a rat the size of a loaf of bread ran across the cold floor.

"This place is awful," said Zebulun, waving his hand in front of his face. "I don't think those are animal droppings I stepped on."

My eyes were open, yet there was not a single ray of light in the small, cement, underground cell. It reminded me of the cistern we had thrown Joseph into. Every breath was a struggle, like we were running out of air.

"How long will he keep us in here?" whispered Naphtali. Nobody answered.

~~~

We couldn't tell whether it was day or night, if a day or a week had passed. Time crawled so slowly. We took turns sitting down as there was so little space, and all we could hear were footsteps in the entrance above us and each other's stifled breathing.

Eventually, we heard the chains on the door clanking, and the heavy metal door being slowly pulled ajar. We all averted our eyes from the light we hadn't seen in days, and as our eyes adjusted, we saw the Ruler peering at us from above in silence. The guards surrounding him quietly murmured among themselves.
~~~

The first thing that came into my head was execution. Why else would the man who was second only to Pharaoh personally come to our prison cell? Would we be thrown into the Nile to be torn apart by crocodiles? Would we be hanged or stoned? What if I never saw my sons again?

"Three days in here can feel like a lifetime," said the Ruler finally, through his Hebrew interpreter.

How would he know? I thought. *Had it only been three days?*

"I am a God-fearing man. If you do exactly what I am about to tell you, you will live. If you really are honest men, choose one of your brothers to remain in prison. The rest of you may go home with grain for your starving families. But you must bring your youngest brother back to me. This will prove that you are telling the truth, and you will not die."

We all looked at each other in the gloom.

"Reuben, you stay, because it is your fault he knows about Benjamin."

"No, let Judah stay, it was his idea to sell Joseph in the first place."

"Didn't I tell you all not to sin against the boy?" said Reuben through gritted teeth. "But you wouldn't listen. And now we all have to answer for his blood!"

"Can we please discuss this later?" I hissed.

We all looked at the Ruler, who was still gazing at us intently. All of a sudden, he murmured something in the language of Egypt, and before we knew it, the prison door was slammed shut above our faces.

Darkness. Silence. Stench. I clenched my teeth: "Why would you fight in front of the Ruler? He must have changed his mind. Who knows how long we'll be stuck in here now?"

Had we really lost our only chance for survival? Silently, I pleaded with my God. *Please help us! Don't let us all die here in this ghastly cell while our families waste away from the famine. Please save us!*

I knew what I had to do. "Brothers, let's all ask the God of our father to deliver us. If we are ever going to get out of this cell alive, every single one of us needs to Him."

I got down on my knees, not caring about the filth scattered everywhere on the prison floor. One by one, my brothers joined me. Somehow, there was enough space for us all. Together, we cried out to the God who had kept his promises to our forefathers.

In that dark prison cell, something changed.

Just moments after we finished praying, the cell door began to open again. I smiled as I saw the shock on my brothers' faces. They would soon know without a shadow of a doubt the faithfulness of the God they had only heard stories about until now.

The Ruler had returned, but his face was now covered by a veil. He issued some order to his servants, then one by one, from youngest to oldest, we were pulled out onto the ground. Then he pointed to Simeon, whose arms and legs were tied by the guards, and his mouth gagged. The guards threw Simeon back into the dank prison cell once again.

"The rest of you, leave my presence at once! Bring your youngest brother to me!"

I could see our donkeys just behind the Ruler. We ran to them as fast as we could, our legs still stiff from our captivity. We barely had time to think of poor Simeon, still stuck in that awful cell.

Once we exited the city, we slowed down to catch our breath and noticed the size of the load our donkeys were carrying. On each animal were sacks of grain large enough to feed a family for almost a year. The thought of freshly baked bread made my stomach churn. Surely, this was more than we had paid for.

~~~
~~~

We walked as fast as we could during that first day and night. By dawn, we were exhausted, man and animal alike. I couldn't even imagine the last time my stomach had been full, and the constant hunger cramps were only getting worse. I looked over at Levi, walking next to me, and could tell he was missing Simeon. He was licking his dry lips, trying to moisten them even a little bit. I looked at him knowingly. Our mouths were as parched as the desert we were crossing.

Somehow, we kept going until dusk. When we finally stopped, I looked down at my feet. They were covered in the slime of the prison cell, encrusted with a layer of desert sand on top.

"Can we please stop for the night?" pleaded Manassah.

We all agreed that we needed a few hours of sleep. We tried to make a fire to warm ourselves, but had to abandon our efforts because of the strength of the sand being blown in our faces. Eventually, we ended up just lying huddled together, trying our best to escape the bitter cold for a few hours.

In the gloom, I thought I saw a shadow approaching the sacks of grain. I got to my feet and saw it was Zebulun.

"We are almost home, brother, hold on just a little longer," I told him, but he only made a whimpering sound and opened the sack of grain. We both peered in. Instead of golden grains, what we saw made our blood run cold: shiny silver coins reflecting in the moonlight.

"Judah, look! My shekels have been returned; they are here in my sack!"

A few of my other brothers gathered around while Zebulun lifted out some of the money with shaking hands. Sure enough, all the money we had paid was right there on top of the grain. One by one, each brother looked into their sacks, only to find the same glittering surprise. All of us were thinking the same thing: once Pharaoh found out we had left with the grain *and* our money, Simeon was done for, and so were we.

"What has God done to us?" asked Dan softly, sinking to his knees. The little seed of faith that began to sprout in our prison cell had just been crushed by the fear now filling our hearts.

Chapter 27

Tamar

The famine was biting deeper and deeper with every passing day. With no word from the men who had gone to Egypt, the sons of Judah's brothers tried to step into their fathers' shoes. When the well nearest our house dried up, the young men tried to dig new ones. It was strenuous work which only left them even more ravenous. It took three attempts before they found a small supply of water. At the end of each day, the hungry faces of the children appeared in the women's cooking tent. The sight of their swollen bellies was heartbreaking. Everyone was too tired to fight, and we longed for the good old days when we had the strength to argue.

One night, when I was putting my sons to sleep, they couldn't stop crying. "I am hungry, mother," whimpered Perez through his tears.

"Me too, can we please have something to eat before bed?"

I could see bones protruding above their little stomachs. My heart felt like it was being torn in two.

"Maybe your father will come back tomorrow. As soon as he does, you'll be able to have some food, okay?"

"But I am hungry now!" said Perez, his stomach gurgling loudly in agreement.

What could I tell them?

"Lets pray to God that He helps your father and his brothers come back quickly, okay?"

They nodded sadly. We prayed to God and then I patted their backs until they fell asleep. After their breathing steadied, I went outside of the tent, hugged my knees towards my chest, and cried.

Why is this happening, God? My children are slowly dying and there is nothing I can do to feed them. Why, God, Why?

Only silence.

"Tamar, Tamar!" I heard Jenna's stifled voice. I sat up quickly and wiped my tears away. "There is somebody here to see you."

A short distance away, I saw an unfamiliar figure kneeling on the ground. When I approached her, I saw that it was the handmaid who had served Reya before her death.

"Anna! What are you doing here?"

The old woman was gasping for breath. She was as thin as a tree branch, her eyes sunken into her head.

"Tamar, it's your parents. They are dead."

My head started to spin. I knew the famine was bad, but nobody in our camp had died yet. We had found a way to make broths from different plants, and once every couple of weeks we slaughtered an animal to keep us fed. But my poor parents! They didn't have a herd of animals to systematically slaughter. I began to weep. I wasn't even there for them at the end. Their deaths must have been slow and painful. As my sobs grew louder, the women and children of Jacob's clan came out to see what the commotion was about.

Anna embraced me. "I am so sorry, my dear," the old women uttered, then started to cough heavily and heave.

"Somebody get her some water!" I yelled. Nobody moved; the water was too scarce to waste on a stranger. "This old woman is dying! Have some compassion!" I screamed through my tears. Then I saw Jenna running off towards the well.

Anna's frail body was so light, yet I was so weak I could hardly hold her up as her body convulsed with coughs. I lowered her gently to the floor. Finally, Jenna returned with a small goatskin of water and I began to lower the water towards her cracked lips. She took a small sip, and her coughing subsided just enough for her to talk.

"I have done my duty. Tamar, your parents loved you. Keep the rest of the water," she said, then slowly closed her eyes and took a last few shallow breaths.

I threw my arms around the old handmaid, my whole body shaking from grief. Slowly, those surrounding us drifted back to their duties. From that day, we all feared that we would soon share Anna's fate.

~~~

"They are back! They are back!" yelled Shelah, running frantically around the entire camp. "Our men are back!"

The camp went crazy with excitement. A few ran out to greet the men who were approaching from the barren hills, while others continued with the preparations for dinner with new energy.

"Slaughter a cow!" Leah commanded. "Tonight we feast!"

I expected to see the men's faces filled with joy at having saved us. Yet, as they approached, I saw that they looked only grim and weary. Something was terribly wrong. I quickly scanned their faces, and noticed that there were only nine. I wasn't the only one to make the calculation.

"Where is my husband? Where is my Simeon?" yelled Cayla, panicked, as she circled the brothers, searching for the father of her children. I looked over at Jenna, who had every right to panic about Simeon, but she was only staring intently into the distance.

A murmur of discontent spread throughout the camp. Straightening his shoulders, and after a deep breath, Judah said, "We will explain everything. But first, let's eat together."

~~~

Never in my life had I seen food prepared more quickly. As we sat around the feast that evening, every bite of food was cherished. We hadn't seen that amount of grain since before the famine started. The children grabbed the fresh baked bread and squished it into little balls, so more could fit in their mouth. I looked over at my sons. They were beaming at the sight of the food before them. Nothing else seemed to matter; it was all a mother could ask for.

After everyone had their fill, Jacob stood up and led his entire family in a prayer of thanks to the God who had provided for them. After he finished, he looked over at a sorrowful Cayla and Simeon's six sons, who had barely eaten anything, then at Judah. It was time to explain what had happened to Simeon.

"We were standing in the line to buy grain, just like everyone else who had come from different countries," Judah began. "When we approached the front of the line, the man who is governor of the land spoke very harshly to us. I do not know why, but he accused us of being spies scouting the land. But we protested, trying to convince him that we were honest men. We explained that we were twelve brothers, sons of one father, that one brother was no longer with us, and that our youngest brother was at home in the land of Canaan."

Judah held everyone's attention. When he paused, the only sound was made by the children still chewing their last scraps of food. After he had told the whole story of the captivity, and the conditions for their release, Judah looked over at Jacob. "Father, if we are going to survive this famine, you are going to have to let Benjamin return to Egypt with us."

Benjamin jumped to his feet and exclaimed, much too loudly, "I will go!"

Jacob slowly lifted himself off his stretcher, then erupted: "You are robbing me of my children! Joseph is gone! Simeon is gone! And now you want to take Benjamin, too. Everything is going against me!"

Cayla ran towards Jacob and fell at his feet. "Please, let Benjamin go!" She reached out towards him, but Jacob backed away with no reply.

Reuben ran over towards his father, a dark intensity filling his eyes. "Let Benjamin go. You may kill my two sons if I don't return him safely to you. I'll be responsible for him. Let him go, and I promise to bring him back."

Reuben's wife gasped loudly and covered her sons' ears, too late. The young men were trembling like branches in the wind. Their mother ran to Reuben's side and fell at his feet.

"You will not take my sons from me!" she cried in desperation.

"Be quiet, woman! Do you want to die?" Reuben barked, shoving her away from him.

"That's enough!" Jacob shook his head in disgust. "Why would you say that in front of your children, Reuben? Under no circumstances will my son go to that land with you. His brother Joseph is dead, and he is all I have left. If anything should happen to him in Egypt, you would send me to hell."

No one spoke. It was clear that no-one would change Jacob's mind. I looked over at the bags of grain. Was this going to be the last we would ever see?

"There's more," said Dan. "The money we paid for the grain was put back in our sacks. We do not know what this means or who is responsible." Dan went to one of the unopened sacks and took out the silver coins. "I think the Ruler will try to blame us for stealing the money. If we don't return to Egypt and explain, we will condemn Simeon to death!"

Judah

Months passed, and the famine continued to consume the land of Canaan. It was a famine like none the land had ever seen before. Most days, we heard of one or two people who had perished from the villages around us. Those who had not died were weak, weary, and very thin. Even the land seemed hungry. There was no greenery anywhere, just an ever-increasing desert. The hills that had been filled with trees and wildflowers were now bare.

The grain my brothers and I had brought back from Egypt was running out quickly. With over a hundred mouths to feed, everyone knew that the food would not last much longer.

Tamar came to me one day and said, "Judah, there's only enough grain for a few more weeks." I sighed and looked at her. I knew she was right. I had to try to convince my father; it wouldn't be easy, but I knew I had to keep trying or else his stubbornness would lead us all into the grave.

I thought of Simeon. When we left Egypt my brother had been tied so tight and discarded in a cell unfit for a cockroach. I needed to do something, for his sake, and for the sake of Tamar and my sons. Every attempt at convincing father in the last few months, however, had only left him more upset.

I lifted my eyes towards the sky. *God, please help. Please change my father's mind.* There was no answer from above. God's silence felt as real as our hunger.

~~~

After the scraps which had passed for our evening meal, Jacob approached me and my brothers.

"Go back and buy us a little more food," he said with a guilty smile.

"Finally! We will take Benjamin and leave at dawn," said Levi, overjoyed at the possibility of being reunited with Simeon.

"No. Go without Benjamin."

What a stubborn old man! I tried to suppress my anger as I replied: "The Ruler was clear that he wouldn't admit us unless Benjamin is with us."

"Judah is right, father. We will not receive any more grain without Benjamin going with us. Anything else would only put the rest of us in danger. If you
~~~

send Benjamin with us, we will go down and buy more food. Otherwise, we all stay here," said Dan.

"Why are you so cruel to me?" moaned Jacob. "Why did you tell him you had another brother? Do you want to see me dead?"

I could see that all of my brothers were becoming as enraged as I was.

"The man kept asking us questions about our family," said Reuben, trying to defend himself. "We answered his questions truthfully. How could we know he would demand to see Benjamin?"

Jacob pulled on his hair, clearly agitated, and bent down on his knees.

I was about to walk away when, crystal clear, I heard the voice of God in my heart in a way I hadn't since the famine began.

Honor your Father.

He is going to get us all killed!

Forgive, as I have forgiven you.

"Father, send the boy with me, and we will be on our way," I said, mustering my last bit of respect for the old man, "otherwise we will all die of starvation. I personally guarantee his safety, and you may hold me responsible if I don't bring him back to you. Then let me bear the blame forever. We could have gone and returned twice by now. Think of Benjamin, of his sons, of Rachel's young grandchildren."

Jacob exhaled and rubbed his temples. After months of persuasion, he could resist no longer.

"If it can't be avoided, then at least do this. Pack your bags with the best of our produce. Take them down to Egypt as gifts: balm, honey, gum, aromatic resin, pistachio nuts, and almonds. You will take double the money that was put back in your sacks, to pay back the Ruler for what we already bought. Take Benjamin and leave at once. May God Almighty soften this man's heart, so that he will release Simeon and let Benjamin return."

Jacob paused and lowered his head. "If I must lose my children, so be it."

My mouth dropped open in shock. The change in my father could only have been made by God Himself.

Thank you, I thought, my heart rejoicing.

We set off early the next morning as the first streaks of orange light appeared over the peaks of the mountains.

"Do you think Simeon is still alive?" asked Levi when we left the valley.

Although it was hard for all of us to leave our brother behind, Levi had suffered the most. I looked around at the men travelling beside me. Somehow, this experience of fighting together for Benjamin and Simeon was bringing us closer. Yes, we had all made our fair share of mistakes, but the famine had changed. Even so, the lying and betrayal of the past would never be forgotten. Only if Joseph rose from the dead would our hearts ever be complete again.

Chapter 28

Judah

For the first day of our journey, Benjamin skipped ahead of us with his black curls bouncing up and down, clearly enjoying his freedom. He asked many questions about Egypt, and kept shouting things into the desert, enjoying the way the sound dissipated into the empty space. We walked all through the heat of the day, not stopping for rest When we decided to continue walking through the night, Benjamin was not slow to show his disappointment. He protested and complained, showing us his blistered feet.

Reuben had no patience. "Benjamin, stop acting like a foolish child. We are not stopping tonight."

"You are not in charge, Reuben. Judah must make the final decision," Benjamin replied, showing his anger.

"What are you doing to do, run to your father like a little boy?" replied Reuben in a mocking tone.

"At least I'm not going to sleep with his wife," said Benjamin, grinning.

Reuben growled, then ran up to Benjamin, grabbing him by the shoulders. The two brothers were standing face to face: one, the rightful firstborn who had that lost his birthright; the other much younger, but taller and more muscular, and favored by their father.

"What are you going to do, hurt me like you hurt Joseph?"

"I did nothing like that!" Reuben yelled back, his face red with anger and the heat of the sun.

"I don't believe you. I know you had something to do with it. Joseph clearly wasn't mauled by a wild animal. Why else would you hate me so much?"

Reuben stood still, his nostrils flaring like a raging bull before it charged. I looked down at the floor. Benjamin still didn't know.

Reuben was still holding Benjamin's shoulders as he kicked him hard in the stomach. Benjamin groaned and bent over, looking upwards at his assailant.

"At least I didn't kill my own mother," said Reuben through clenched teeth. When he saw Benjamin gasp as if in pain, knowing he had voiced his brother's deepest insecurity, Reuben relaxed and turned to me. "Tell him."

There was silence. Benjamin looked at me, his weathered face full of questions.

"Judah? Tell me what?"

Maybe it was time. But, just as I was about to speak, Levi stopped me.

"Sit down for a minute, Benjamin," he said. Nervously, our youngest brother sat down on the sand.

"Ugh, I'm not doing this again!" yelled Reuben. "I'll meet you in Egypt." He kicked the ground, throwing up a large cloud of dust, and disappeared.

"Benjamin, don't mind Reuben, he is just trying to get to Simeon as quickly as possible," I said, trying to diffuse the tension. But Benjamin wasn't going to be distracted.

"What did Reuben mean? Tell me what?"

Levi, his head held high, looked at us and nodded.

Over the next few hours, Benjamin learned what his brothers had done to Joseph. His face gave nothing away as we told him every detail we could remember.

"Did you really just sit down and eat after betraying your own brother?" Benjamin asked with horror in his voice. Nobody answered. "It's just that...I was so young when it happened. I don't even remember what Joseph looked like. I think about him every day."

When all the questions had been asked, we slept for a few hours, then set off in the light of the full moon. Benjamin walked all day and into the night without another complaint. Half-way through the night, as we walked in the silence of the desert, he began to lag behind.

"Where's Benjamin?" I asked, and sent Dan and Asher to search for him. Then we saw him, lying face down on the ground. I gasped and knelt beside him, putting my ear to his chest. As we checked his breathing and pulse, Reuben appeared out of the darkness, took one look at the prone body before him and said, "The boy is sound asleep."

I looked at Benjamin again. He looked serene, and his breathing was steady and calm. I looked over at Naphtali, who coughed while trying to hold in a chuckle. We gathered in a circle around Benjamin under the night's sky, I couldn't help but think how much had changed since the last time we had circled round our younger brother's body on the ground. For a moment, I almost saw Joseph's red curly head at my feet instead of Benjamin's black locks. Issachar helped me to pick up Benjamin's large frame and we placed him on top of our donkey. We kept walking.

On the third day, we reached the border with Egypt just beyond the desert. Our pace quickened. As soon as we entered the great city, several guards approached us, as if they had been waiting for us. They said that the Ruler had given direct orders to bring us to him immediately. Without further explanation, the guards surrounded us and led us through the busy streets, crowded with Egyptians and slaves, towards the gates of the Ruler's palace. All eyes were on us as we passed. Did they think we were criminals or friends of the Ruler?

The smell of baking bread filled the air, mixed with sweat from the naked bodies of the slave workers, and the strong odor of wet bricks. I took a deep breath; Egypt smelled just like I remembered. Just off the path we were led on, in a large pit, I saw one of the slaves being whipped. His Egyptian guard towered over him, yelling in his native language. The slave was crying out in Hebrew. I looked over at Benjamin, who winced every time the whip cracked against the slave's shredded skin.

"Come on, Benjamin, let's keep walking," I said quietly.

The guards went straight to the front of the long line of people waiting to buy food. When we were still some distance away, we saw the Ruler, dressed as splendidly as ever, his precious jewels reflecting in the sun. Before we even had the chance to bow low at his feet, another guard ran up to the men with us and said something we did not understand. The guards surrounding us changed course and led us out of the marketplace.

"Where are they taking us?" asked Benjamin.

We would find out soon enough.

~~~

The iron gates were closed, and the guards opened them hastily before us. The white palace that gleamed behind them was majestic. The light reflecting off the River Nile blinded us as we entered the building, its beauty only adding to our trepidation.

"Are we all going to die?" asked Benjamin.

"We are going to be okay," I said, with more assurance than I felt, as the guards led us into the palace.

Benjamin wasn't the only one who was afraid. From oldest to youngest, every one of us was trembling, for we knew that our fates could be determined at any moment. At one word from the Ruler, we would never return home or see our families again; nor would we be able to provide the food they needed for their survival. All the promises our father told given us about our descendants being as numerous as the stars in the sky depended on what happened next.
~~~

We whispered among ourselves, speculating about what our detour meant.

"Why can't we just line up to wait for our food like everyone else?" asked Naphtali.

"It's because of the money someone put in our sacks last time we were here. He plans to pretend that we stole it, just wait and see. Then he will seize us and make us slaves," offered Asher.

"Or we will be cast into the dungeon to rot," added Levi.

In the courtyard outside the palace, the guards asked us to sit down and wait. After they left, we absorbed the majestic scene surrounding us. The courtyard was enclosed with a tall brick wall, so nobody outside could see. At one end was the river, and at the other, the palace. In between there were pools of clear water along with colorful flowers and large trees in pots large enough for a person to sit in, adorned with gold and silver. Just one pot was probably worth more all the wealth my father owned, and there were hundreds of them decorating the courtyard.

I was becoming restless. We needed to explain to someone that we didn't steal the money from the Ruler. I decided to approach the manager of the household, whom I had seen standing just outside the courtyard. Hesitantly, I got up and began walking towards the palace. The manager saw me approaching and stepped outside. I thought he might speak some Hebrew, so I addressed him in my own tongue:

"Sir, we came to Egypt once before to buy food. But on our journey home, we stopped for the night and opened our sacks. Then we discovered that each man's money - the exact amount paid - was on top of the grain! We have brought the same amount back with us; here it is." I held out the large sack of coins. "We also have additional money to buy more food. We have no idea who put our money in our sacks. Please, let us live."

Looking at our bag of money, the manager laughed.

"Do not be afraid," he told us. "Your God, the God of your father, must have put this treasure into your sacks. I am certain I received your payment. And here is something else you might be missing."

At that moment, approaching from inside the palace halls, we saw our brother.

"Simeon!" we exclaimed in unison, and ran over to him, embracing our lost brother.

"We thought you were dead!" said Levi, finally reunited with his best friend.

The questions poured out of us at once:

"Why are you in the Ruler's palace?"

"How did you survive that prison?"

"How long have you been here?"

Simeon looked like he had been eating well and was dressed in a gleaming white, expensive cloak. Before we could ask any more questions, the manager of Zaphenath-paneah's palace held up his hands, smiling at our joyful reunion, his white teeth shining against his dark skin.

"You will soon dine with the Governor himself. Come inside and prepare yourselves." He led us through spacious corridors lined with columns and into a room near the entrance to the palace.

What a way to live! There were curtains made of purple velvet, benches made out of the most expensive looking material, and marble floors. Everything was oversized, and there were golden trinkets and statues everywhere. In every corner there were slaves from many different countries waving large palm branches to keep the room cool.

We must have looked amazed, because the manager began to laugh. "That was my first reaction when I saw this palace as well. Here is some water to wash your feet, and here is food for your donkeys. You will be eating with Lord

Zaphenath-paneah shortly, but at the moment you may just relax from your journey."

We did everything asked of us, except relaxing. Simeon and Levi, overjoyed to be reunited, went to feed the donkeys together. The rest of us began to unpack all the presents we had brought for the Ruler. We hadn't eaten since leaving the land of Canaan, and our bellies began to grumble as we laid out the pistachios, honey, and almonds. We hadn't tasted such delicacies in months, but we knew better than to eat them ourselves.

Before we knew it, the manager returned. "Your feast awaits, men of Canaan."

We entered the room where we would be feasting. My nostrils savored every exotic scent pervading the air. Slaves, holding large trays of food I had never seen before, were scattered near the Ruler's throne. I breathed deeply, my mouth watering. Just after us, the Ruler entered. We turned around and fell to our knees before him, bowing our heads to the ground. We presented him with our gifts, but he did not seem impressed by them. He could not take his eyes off Benjamin.

"How is your father, the old man you spoke about? Is he still alive?" he asked, all the while gazing intently at Benjamin.

"Yes," replied Reuben, "our father, your servant, is alive and well." We bowed low again, but he seemed not to notice.

"Is this your youngest brother, the one you told me about?" We nodded in unison. "May God be gracious to you, my son." His voice cracked as he spoke and he cleared his throat. After staring at Benjamin in silence for a few moments, the Ruler picked up his royal robe and ran out of the room. The doors slammed shut behind him. I looked around at the faces of all the servants. Everybody was confused. We stood there awkwardly, unsure of what we should do. A few of the Egyptians looked at us with hatred; everyone knew they despised Hebrews.

God of my fathers, please deliver us.

The Ruler soon returned, his face covered with the veil again. He shouted something in Egyptian at the servants, who rushed out into another room and quickly returned with even more food: dozens of silver trays, overflowing with meats, breads, cheeses, and delicacies.

The Ruler told each of us where to sit through his translator; to our amazement, he seated us according to age, from oldest to youngest. How did he know? Something strange was going on here. I felt a familiar sensation, but could not place it exactly. The Ruler then sat down at his own table, and was served separately.

The food was all placed at the Ruler's table. Then the servants filled our plates with food, starting with the oldest. At Benjamin's turn, he was given five large plates instead of the one offered to the rest of us. Benjamin started eating immediately, like a hungry animal, seemingly unaware of the special attention. But the rest of my brothers certainly noticed. What was happening? But the food was too appealing to our empty bellies, so we laid aside our doubts for the moment.

We feasted that day like never before. There was plenty of wine to go around, and by the end of the feast, everybody was relaxed. The Ruler, who had had slightly too much to drink, put his arm around Benjamin's shoulders. The Egyptians left their separate table and joined us. Everyone danced and sang late into the night.

~~~

The next morning, at dawn, we all woke up when a few palace guards came into the room we were sleeping in. One of the guards came over to me and rang a cymbal. I jumped up, forgetting where I was. My head ached and my mouth was parched. I had not had this much to drink since Hirah's parties. The noise of the cymbal just kept ringing and ringing in my head.

"What's wrong?" I asked sleepily.
~~~

"Lord Zaphenath-paneah has given us orders to send you on your way. Your donkeys are packed with the grain you bought, and you are ready for your journey."

I suddenly remembered the feast. Quickly scrambling to my feet, I tried to rouse my brothers, who swatted me away sleepily. I ran over to the Egyptian guard, who was clearly amused at my frantic efforts. I looked longingly at his cymbal and he smiled and handed it over.

Curses filled the air as I struck the cymbal as hard as I could. We were all sleepy and groggy. That amount of wine on an empty belly hadn't done anyone any good, and I saw I wasn't the only one having trouble keeping the food down. Clothes were put on quickly and hair smoothed down. As I handed the cymbal back to the guard, I saw him looking down at my beard with disgust. Running my fingers through the tangled mess beneath my face, they caught on some bits of food from the night before. At least the beard covered the redness of my face as the guard smiled and walked away.

Soon we were on our way. As we were exiting the city gates, I looked over at Benjamin, then at Simeon. The second trip had been much better than the first. Even though our stomachs ached from too much food and our heads still rang from the loud music and wine, we would soon be home with enough food to last us another year. We were given so much that our donkeys couldn't have carried more. I couldn't wait to tell my family of the incredible palace we had seen, and how we had dined with the second most powerful man in the world. There was much joy and chatter as we set out for home.

I looked over my shoulder to get one last glance of Egypt. Instead of a vision of the sparkling city, however, I saw a group of Egyptians running in our direction.

"Look!" I shouted. My brothers all turned around. The closer the men came, the more we were afraid, especially when we saw a very angry manager of the palace among the party. We stopped dead in our tracks.

The manager began to yell: "This is what the Ruler of Egypt says to you: 'Why have you repaid my kindness with such evil?' Why have you stolen my master's silver cup, which he uses to predict the future? What a wicked thing you have done!'"

I looked around at my brothers. The shock and fear on their faces told me everything I needed to know.

"What are you talking about?" I replied, my voice trembling. "We are servants of your master! We would never do such a thing!"

Levi joined in: "Didn't we return the money we found in our sacks? We brought it back all the way from the land of Canaan. Why would we steal silver or gold from your master's house?" The strange feeling I had had at the feast had returned, and my full belly was doing turns.

"If you find his cup with any one of us, let that man die. And all the rest of us, my lord, will forever be your slaves," said Reuben.

Why did he keep offering for people to be killed? First his sons, now us!

The manager nodded. "That *is* fair, but we will only take the one who stole the cup into slavery. The rest of you may return home. Take out your sacks for inspection!"

We had no choice but to obey. The palace manager started with Reuben's sack of wheat. He inspected it thoroughly, spilling some of the precious grains onto the dirt. Then he inspected Simeon's and Levi's sacks. When it was my turn, I held my breath as the sack was opened and thoroughly searched by the other guards. I exhaled, a little too loudly, as they moved on. It was the same for each of my brothers until, at last, it was Benjamin's turn.

God, please help us. Don't let it be found with Benjamin.

Suddenly, all the extra attention given to Benjamin made sense. The unrelenting demand for the youngest brother to come; the award of more food than everyone else; the way the Ruler had been transfixed by Benjamin; it all began to fit together in a reprehensible way. I had an awful feeling that the final sack was not going to be clean.

I was never so sorry to be right as I saw the silver rim of a cup shining among the grain.

"Here it is!" yelled one of the guards as he held the extravagant silver cup aloft. It was so large that the guard had to hold it with two hands. I had seen this cup before, at the party. The Ruler had been drinking wine out of it. Benjamin dropped his sack in shock, and the priceless grains spilled out onto the sand, some of them being picked up and carried away by the breeze.

"No, it can't be..." whispered Benjamin, his teeth chattering despite the dreadful heat.

"What did you do, Benjamin?" hissed Reuben.

"I didn't do anything! Please don't kill me!" He fell face down on the ground and began to weep, his teeth still chattering together. I could not believe this was happening! The guards pulled him up, matching his strength as he squirmed and struggled in protest. Once he was firmly tied, one of the bigger guards threw him over his shoulders and they all set off towards the city.

Benjamin turned his head, hanging upside-down on the guard's back, and yelled, "Judah, help me!" It was an all-too-familiar sight. I dropped to my knees and grabbed my head covering, letting out a deep cry of anguish that echoed from the barren land in front of us.

God, why do you continue to punish us?

No reply.

We were standing in our tunics, our clothes lying torn on the floor. We were vulnerable, exposed. We had ten sacks of grain with us, and our freedom.

There was no one to stop us from returning to our starving wives and children. But decades ago, we hadn't fought for our brother. He was dead, and we were being punished for it by the all powerful God. I looked at my brothers, and I saw that there was no question in their minds about what we were to do. We loaded our donkeys, picked up as much of Benjamin's grain as we could, and headed back to the city to fight for our brother.

~~~

We knew exactly where to find the Ruler. We ran past the guards and through the city. The palace gates were still open, so we rushed through the courtyard and found the room we had feasted in the night before. Bursting through the large doors to his throne room, ignoring the protests of the guards, we saw the Ruler slumped on his throne, drinking wine out of his retrieved silver cup, resting his head on his hand. My eyes searched for Benjamin, but he was not in the room.

Seeing us enter, the Ruler dropped his silver cup on the white marble floor, splashing red liquid everywhere. We threw ourselves to the floor, not just kneeling before him, but fully prostrating ourselves in surrender. He spoke and was instantly translated by the Hebrew beside him.

"What have you done? Is this how you repay my kindness to you? Don't you know that a man like me can predict the future?"

It was time to fight for our little brother. I didn't care that my life was at stake. For the first time since I had betrayed Joseph, I felt I was doing something right. I wouldn't let my brother suffer an injustice like this. We would not abandon him; I had to rescue him at ay cost. With the faces of my sons flashing before my eyes, I made what could have been my last attempt at doing the right thing.

"Oh, my lord, what can we say to you? How can we explain this? How can we prove our innocence? I know that God is punishing us for our sins. My lord, we have returned to be your slaves; all of us, not just our brother who had your cup
~~~

in his sack." If the Ruler wouldn't let Benjamin go, we would all become slaves like Joseph.

"No," he replied calmly. "I would never do such a thing! Only the man who stole the cup will be my slave. The rest of you may go back to your father in peace." He looked intently at us. With one word, this man could have had us all killed or thrown into prison. But I wasn't going to back down. Not this time.

My hands were sweating and my legs were wobbling, but I stepped forward and spoke again: "Please, my lord, let your servant say just one word to you. Please, do not be angry with me, even though you are as powerful as Pharaoh himself. Previously, you asked us if we had a father or brother. And we told you we had a father who is an old man, and his youngest son was born to him in his old age. We explained that his full brother is dead, and that he alone is left of his mother's children, and that his father loves him very much. And you told us to bring him here so that you could see him with your own eyes. So we returned to your servant, our father, and told him what you had said." I paused, finding that I commanded not only the attention of the Ruler, but also that of his servants, who were whispering to each other around the room.

"Later, when our father asked us to buy us more food, we explained that we could not return to Egypt unless Benjamin was with us. Then my father said to us: 'As you know, my wife had two sons, and one of them went away and never returned. Doubtless he was torn to pieces by some wild animal. I have never seen him since. If you take his brother away from me, and any harm comes to him, you will send this white-haired man to his grave.' " The Ruler covered his eyes, tilting his head to his side until his face was not visible.

"And now, my lord, I cannot go back to my father without the boy. If he sees that the boy is not with us, our father will die. We, your servants, will be responsible for our father's death."

I took a few steps towards the throne. Two of the guards rushed towards me but the Ruler held up his hand, indicating that they should let me continue. "My lord, I promised my father that I would take care of the boy." I came even closer to the Ruler, and lay my face at his feet, kissing them. I looked up at the face of the man who would determine my destiny. "So please, my lord, let me stay here as a slave instead of the boy, and let the boy return with his brothers." I held out my hands, ready to be chained forever.

There was silence. The Ruler wasn't even looking at me. From this angle, I saw that his eyes were closed and his lips were pursed tightly together. Every eye in the room was on him; the tension built like waiting for a flash of lightning after a rumble of thunder.

The Ruler opened his eyes. Then he turned to his Egyptian attendants, guards, and slaves, yelling harshly in their language. Our fate was sealed; the promises of God were shattered.

Chapter 29

Judah

As the guards sprinted out of the room, we all looked at each other, trembling and confused. The Ruler stood up, and we watched as he fell to his knees. To our great confusion, he began to weep. For a few long moments, he stood there below us. Sobs wracked his entire body, echoing out past the columns overlooking the plains of Egypt. Each sob was heavy, carrying a weight of emotion I could not understand. Finally, without saying anything, he went over to the fountain of flowing water and washed all the Egyptian makeup off his face.

Barefaced, blotchy, and sniffling, this man of vast wealth and honor opened his mouth: "I am Joseph! Is my father still alive?"

We stood there, stunned. The Ruler took off his head covering, revealing curly red hair, streaked with the silver of age.

"Please, come closer," he said in the Hebrew language. Immediately, despite a heavy accent from years of disuse, I recognized his voice to be Joseph's.

We slowly inched closer.

"I am Joseph, your brother, whom you sold into slavery in Egypt. Do not be angry with yourselves for bringing me to this place. It was God who sent me here ahead of you to preserve your lives." He raised his hands towards the sky, the way a drowning person would reach for the hands of their rescuer. "I was a slave. I was in prison. I suffered greatly there, but God led me through the prison into this palace. It was His plan all along." Joseph spread his arms out towards the plains outside his window. "This famine that has ravaged the land for two years will last five more years, and there will be neither plowing nor harvesting. God has sent me ahead of you to keep you and your families alive and to preserve many survivors from among our nation." Our mouths were still hung open in shock, so he smiled and repeated, ". was God who sent me here, not you, my brothers!" He laughed, even as tears flowed from his eyes. "He has blessed me with a wife and two sons, whom I love more than life itself. He is the one who made me an advisor to Pharaoh, the manager of his entire palace, and the governor of all Egypt."

My brothers and I stood frozen to the spot, staring at this man who had come back from the dead. I was still too shocked to speak. He looked exactly like Joseph, only older. His skin was darkened from the sun and there were creases all over his face. I could not stop looking at his eyes, the same green ones which had often looked at me, naively and mischievously, in my youth. Now they were older, wiser, and greyer around the edges. The only things radiating from those eyes were love and forgiveness. He was looking at us the way a mother looks at her newborn, not a hint of hatred in his gaze.

Joseph ran towards the doors connecting the room to the rest of his palace. I couldn't help but gasp when I saw him running the same way he had done as a child, with his arms tight to his sides, like the wings of a bird. We had always teased him for it. This man really was our brother. He poked his head out and shouted something at the guards. At his command, Benjamin was brought in. At first, Benjamin looked annoyed to be handled so roughly by the guards. As soon as the door closed, however, his mouth hung open as he saw the mirror image of himself standing in front of him, only with redder hair and darker skin.

"What is...I am..." Benjamin babbled like a child, his eyebrows raised so high they were hidden beneath his curls.

"My brother!" cried Joseph, and tackled him to the ground. Benjamin landed with a thud, with Joseph on top of him. Startled, Benjamin rolled the stranger over until he had Joseph pinned down. He stared at the face beneath, still babbling nonsense, then looked up at me.

I nodded. "It's true, Benjamin!"

"J... J...Joseph?"

"Yes, its me, your brother!" Joseph was laughing, then he began to cry again. Benjamin quickly jumped up, as though he were on fire, then lay down on the ground next to Joseph, speechless.

After a few moments, the two brothers sat up. The two sons of Rachel were sitting on the polished floor of the palace, cross-legged and teary-eyed, with the rest of us circled around them. No one spoke; it was too beautiful for words.

After a while the guards knocked on the door and entered cautiously. Joseph stood up quickly, composing himself. After confirming that he was not in danger, he turned to us and said in Hebrew: "Now hurry back to my father and tell him, 'This is what your son, Joseph, says: God has made me master over all the land of Egypt. So come down to me immediately! You can live in the region of Goshen, where you can be near me with all your children and grandchildren, your flocks and herds, and everything you own. I will take care of you there, for there are still five years of famine ahead of us. Otherwise you, your household, and all your animals will starve.'"

We nodded our assent.

Then Joseph approached Benjamin, swinging his arm over the shoulder of his younger, but taller, brother. "Look! You can see for yourselves that I really am Joseph! We look so similar!" The two boys were undeniably of the same blood. The shape of their face and the little dimples in their cheeks looked nearly identical.

"I am definitely taller, though!" said Benjamin proudly. Joseph laughed. Looking at his brother, he said, "Go tell my father of my honored position here in Egypt. Describe for him everything you have seen, and then bring him here as quickly as you can."

Then Joseph ordered his servants to prepare another feast for us. As we laughed and spoke freely over the food and wine, I could almost hear our God laughing with us. Here we were, twelve brothers, united for the first time in our lives.

~~~

Joseph was standing inside the gates of the city in his royal robes, accompanied by his wife and two sons, ready to send us off. His sons were very handsome young men. They had their mother's smooth dark skin, and had an auburn shade to their curly hair. Their eyes were just like Joseph's. Seeing his sons made me miss Perez and Zerah. I was filled with joy knowing that we would soon be reunited. I couldn't wait to tell them about the miracle that had taken place.

I quickly refocused my attention on my long-lost brother. Standing behind Joseph were his household manager and translator, who had been almost as shocked by the revelation as we were, as well as the guards and crowds of people of all nationalities, who had come to watch the Ruler of Egypt present gifts to his brothers. At Joseph's signal, his guards brought out eleven carts filled with more than enough grain for our families, as well as supplies for our journey home. I stared in awe as sacks upon sacks of grain were loaded onto the donkeys. Then Joseph himself brought out beautiful violet bags, handing them over to us in order from oldest to youngest. We opened the gifts in amazement, pulling out shiny gold coins and an exquisite change of clothes. I felt the soft fabric in my hands. Reya would have been overjoyed to hold material like this. In pairs, we retreated to a private room to change into the garments, while the other brothers hitched the carts to the donkeys.

With our Egyptian clothes and the look of starvation gone from our eyes, we no longer looked like men of Canaan. As we were saying our goodbyes, I saw Joseph leave Benjamin's side. He soon returned with five more sacks.

"Benjamin, I have another present for you," Joseph said, his face radiant. Each sack contained another change of clothes and sixty pieces of silver. The boy's eyes widened as he did the sums in his head. The rest of us gathered around. It
~~~

was more money than anyone in our family had owned at any one time. Benjamin was now the richest one in our family, second only to Joseph.

"But Joseph…" Benjamin began, unable to find any more words.

Joseph quieted him and looked at his older brothers, and seeing our shock, winked at us: "Don't quarrel about all this along the way!" I chuckled. Joseph knew we had learned our lesson. Many years ago, a gift like this would have only made us jealous. Today, we were happy to receive what we had been given, and even happier that our Joseph was alive. We had fought for our youngest brother, and I knew that from now on, none of us would ever be left behind. Our bond was unshakable.

Tamar

Leah was dead. Her one hundred-year-old body just could not handle the lack of food. We mourned her death, but we could not do much more to show our sorrow because life was already so painful. Jacob, who had retreated to his tent of mourning when Benjamin left, seemed unalarmed at the news of his wife's death. He was carried out on his stretcher to bury her but his eyes hardly opened, and when they did, they looked distant and glazed. The mothers ushered their children away from him.

The funeral was nothing more than the dead burying the dead. Like a ravenous wolf, the famine had consumed everything in its path, leaving no life behind. There was nothing to eat. The trees produced no fruit, the fields no vegetables or grain. The soil was as dry as our parched mouths. Jenna and I would go and collect leaves and weeds, cooking them into a broth over the fire. My stomach growled as I sipped the same foul concoction day after day. How I longed for freshly baked bread and juicy tender meat.

That said, I would gladly have eaten this stew for the rest of my life to allow my sons to have just one proper meal. Zerah and Perez had caught a fever and were hardly able to speak, let alone get out of bed. But that was no different to the majority of children at the camp; even those who hadn't fallen sick were too weak to move. Without their joyful chatter, there was very little sound in the camp. Most of the animals had either been killed for food or had died of starvation. A few lucky goats that produced a little bit of milk were still alive, but they spent their time lying in the shade, ribs clearly protruding from their thin bodies.

As I looked around at Jacob's household, I remembered what it was like when Judah and I had first moved here. Our children were young and I was in awe of the large wooden table that hosted our gatherings, filled with food and faces of family. Even though the table was large, there was no way all of us could have fitted around it at the same time, so we took turns: first the youngest, then the older, until finally the women making the food sat down at the very end to eat the leftovers. Even those scraps seemed glorious now, and the table stood empty and desolate. There was a large crack in the wood right down the middle, and the once smooth surface was rough and splintered, as if hungry for nourishment like the rest of us. I sighed and looked away. Everyone ate in their tents now, the sounds of laughter that had once echoed in this place now replaced with an eerie silence.

Our men were still gone. We were all alone. I couldn't watch my children die! *God, why did you let this famine happen to us?* This morning, we ate the very last meal we could scramble together. There weren't even any more weeds to make into stew. If Judah and his brothers didn't return today or tomorrow, they would return to a valley of corpses instead of their families. *Oh God, why have you forsaken us?*

I couldn't shake off these thoughts as I summoned my remaining strength to make my daily trip to the well. I remembered the time when I was only fourteen years old, when getting married was all that I had wanted to do. So much time had passed since then. I smiled weakly as I thought about the silly things that had filled my mind back then, and how extremely important they had seemed. Approaching the well, I was so lost in my own thoughts that I almost didn't see the caravan approaching our valley in the distance. When I finally did look up, I dropped my clay jar. By the time it landed, shattering into little pieces, I was already gone.

Breathless, I burst into Dinah's tent. The woman's beautiful features had all sunk into her face, and most of her hair had fallen out. "They are back! Dinah, come look outside. There is a caravan coming." I squinted my eyes and without a doubt, could see that Judah and his brothers had returned! Everyone who could walk filed out to greet the men.

"He's alive!" The cries of the crowd filled the space between us. They must be talking about Simeon! Two of Reuben's older sons carried Jacob out on his litter to greet the men. We waited. As the brothers descended into the valley, the reunion was put on hold for a moment while everyone stood in silence. The men stared at our land, at the starving, sullen faces of the people; we stared at the men who looked just like Egyptians, their clothing made out of the finest material and their carts loaded with grain and other foods. Each party looked as if they had come from another world.

Only a few weeks had passed since the men had left, but the chasm between us seemed infinite. Then, finally, I heard the sounds of loved ones being reunited. Abundance replaced desolation. We hurried to bring out the children from their dark tents. Some had to be carried, while others crawled in the dirt. Jacob sat up in his stretcher and demanded to be brought straight to Benjamin. At the sight of her husband, Jenna collapsed to the floor. Kayla ran into the arms of Simeon, who spun her around and kissed her. Then he came running over to Jenna, embracing her. Both were weeping. Soon, their five sons between them joined in as well. It was beautiful to see a father reunited with his family.

Trying to gather everyone's attention, Judah clapped his hands loudly. When no one seemed to notice, he yelled, "Everybody listen! Joseph is alive!" Everyone fell silent.

I looked over at Jacob, who shot up in his stretcher. "Joseph?" The name sounded painful coming out of his lips.

"Yes! And he is governor of all the land of Egypt! He is the man who put us in prison, who gave us our money back, who kept Simeon with him in Egypt, and who wanted to see Benjamin. It was Joseph the entire time! He is alive, and because of him, we will all live! My brother requests that we all move to Egypt and live in it's finest lands. We won't want for anything ever again."

I could not believe my ears. Did we hear Judah correctly? All eyes were on Jacob. How would he take this news? He got up out of his stretcher and the crowd parted as he approached Judah. With tears running down his cheeks, he spoke, shaking his head, "I don't believe it. Don't lie to an old man like me, it will put me in my grave." But as Judah and his brothers kept repeating to Jacob everything Joseph had told them, and when Jacob saw the carts of food Joseph had sent, proof of their words, the frail man's spirits revived. He fell at Judah's feet and sobbed. The whole family stood still, not moving or speaking. Eventually, Jacob stood up, looking fifty years younger. A man who was no longer able to walk began to dance. "It must be true! My son Joseph is alive! I must go and see him before I die."

At that moment I remembered Davida, my little girl who had never seen a day on this earth. The pure exhilaration Jacob showed was exactly the way I would have reacted had Davida been standing before my eyes, alive and well. It was the joy of a parent who had lost their child, a pain too great for the human heart to bear, being handed hope again.

~~~

Judah ran up to Perez and Zerah, embracing them. "My boys, well done on keeping this place running while I was away!" The toddlers beamed at his praise. Smiling, I soaked up this beautiful sight. Everything seemed exactly the way it should be. My
~~~

sons were alive and seeing Judah was like being reunited with a really good friend. I let out my breath, which I hadn't even realized I was holding.

After the boys showed him some of the little rocks and pieces of glass they had found in the sand, Judah approached me. "Tamar, where is my mother? I brought her a present from Egypt."

He hadn't heard yet? Oh no, I didn't want to be the one to tell him. Everyone knew how much Judah loved his mother. "Judah, I am so very sorry, but Leah didn't make it." He gasped and walked slowly out of the tent.

The twins looked at me. "Mother, is papa going to be okay?"

"Yes boys, we are all going to be just fine," I replied, hugging them tight. "We are saved."

Chapter 30

Tamar

We spend the next few days eating our fill and gathering our things. The children, who wanted to eat as much as they could fill their bellies with, had to be restrained. Slowly, we reintroduced them back to a normal diet. With their returned strength, they quickly went back to playing games and making a mess of the things we were packing for the journey to Egypt, preparing to leave the land of Canaan for good. Everyone was rushing around, packing their possessions into the carts sent to us by Pharaoh.

Even though we had lost a lot in the famine, Jacob's family was still one of the most prosperous in the entire region. The few animals which had survived the famine were slowly recovering, as were the sick and feeble children. *God of Jacob, you are so kind to us*. Other than Leah, nobody had perished. Compared to the death toll in other villages, we felt extremely blessed.

I remembered my nightmares as a child, and how I would hear God's voice right after them. He brought me peace. He was there in those moments with my mother and father when everything seemed right in the world. He was there in the tent with me when Er was beating me. He was there when I lost my first child, that lifeless little body in my arms. He was there when my heart died with Onan, and when I lost all hope. He was there when I crawled back to my parents' house. The eyes of my heart were opened. He never left. He spoke to me through nature, through my dreams, and through the love of my sons. I was forgiven; I was set free from my bitterness. I was part of His family.

Perez raced into my arms, distracting me from my thoughts. After I scooped him up, his little brother wobbled behind him. "Mama, look!" said Zerah, pointing to a piece of fruit that his father had brought for him, grinning happily with the few teeth he had. I smiled at these little men. The color had all returned to their cheeks, their olive skin glowing as bright as their few toothed smiles. I didn't know it was possible to love anyone this much, but these adventurous little boys had captured my heart in so many different ways. I never thought I would have children after Davida, but here I was, holding my two healthy boys.

I lay my sons down on their sleeping mats for the very last time in the valley of Hebron. That night, as I drifted off to sleep, all I could think about was God's faithfulness. He is like water on a parched tongue, like a breeze on a hot summer's day. He is like a feast in famine, like the shade of a palm tree in the humid heat. The palm tree. I finally understood the true meaning. The tree swayed in the wind, but it didn't break. It produced fruit even though it was attacked by hot and cold. My life had been the same in the wonderful hands of my Father, my Master, my Redeemer. My eyelids closed and I drifted off to sleep.

I see a man I know to be Abraham standing on top of a mountain. There is a cloud above him, and God's presence is all around. Suddenly, the cloud lifts and I can see Abraham's face; it is shining like the midday sun. Next to him is his wife, Sarah. She is gleaming as well. There are more people on the mountain, all the way to the bottom. I see Isaac and Rebecca, and a little lower, Jacob and Leah. One by one, the light is cast on each of them, permeating them. Then I see myself, with Judah standing next to me. He smiles at me, and suddenly the light fills us as well. What I feel is indescribable. We shine brighter than the stars in the sky. Just below us, Perez is standing next to a woman. There are hundreds and hundreds more people all standing together down the mountain. The light flows down through them like a waterfall.

As the light reaches the bottom of the mountain, a beautiful explosion of color showers the entire mountain, circling like raindrops in the wind. Every single person bows low, and the light swirls all around the mountain. We are surrounded by it. The light is Love.

Judah

We set out for Egypt with all our possessions packed onto the carts Pharaoh gifted us, each brother filling his with the things precious to him. Perez was in my cart, sitting on top of my folded tent, pretending to lead the donkey. He concentrated, taking his role seriously. I looked at Tamar, who was walking beside the cart with Zerah on her hips. The little boy was trying to pull of her head covering, smiling and laughing. The journey was pleasant, everyone full and excited for what was to come.

We stopped at Beersheba for the night. After another, much too extravagant, meal, Jacob called the entire clan together, explaining that we were to sacrifice to God, thanking Him for our deliverance. As my father began to speak, his voice carried so much weight.

"Last night, God came to speak to me in a dream. He called me by name and told me not to be afraid." The old man paused, tears falling silently down his face. "He told me that in Egypt he would make this family into a great nation, and that He Himself would go there with us." As he spoke, a strong wind began to blow. My father's wrinkled face creased in a smile. "I know now I will die in Egypt, with my son, Joseph, at my side." He got down on his knees, his frail body cracking as he did so, and raised his arms towards Heaven.

Tears brimmed in my eyes at the thought of all my father had been through.

"To the God of my father, Isaac, and his father, Abraham. He is the God of all of us. We are His chosen people. He promised Abraham that his descendants would fill the land and would be as numerous as the stars in the sky, yet he promised this when Abraham and Sarah still didn't have any children. And now here we are, children of that promise."

The entire family watched as we offered sacrifices to God that evening.

We left Beersheba and set off towards God's promises in Egypt

~~~

As we approached Egypt, Jacob called to me, and I ran over to his cart. "Judah, I want you to go ahead of us and get directions to the region of Goshen," he said, smiling. Did he really want me to go first? Was this his way of securing my firstborn status? He nodded, as if he had heard my thoughts.

As I turned around to follow his request, he called to me: "My son, thank you for returning Benjamin to me. He told me how you put your own life on the line for his."

I had no words, just nodded and swiftly turned around so my father could not see the tears rolling down my face. I could not stop smiling. Even as a grown man, his words meant more to me than he would ever know.

Bubbling with emotion, I kissed my sons goodbye and headed off towards Egypt, my camel racing ahead of the caravan. I rode through the entire day and long into the night. At dawn, I saw the outline of the city appearing in the distance. Seeing my new home before me, I reflected on my past. I had spent my whole life being afraid of God, questioning His existence, running away from Him, or waiting for His punishment. What I hadn't known was that I had always been part of His family. That had never changed, no matter where I had been. God wanted me to turn to Him so He could restore me. I was broken and I hadn't even known it. Like a little bird, fluttering around its cage, I had been afraid any time God had come close enough to set me free. He didn't hate me. He wanted me to return to His family. He wanted me to turn away from my sin, from what was hurting and blinding me, and He wanted to set me free.
~~~

I didn't know what would happen here in Egypt, but this would be the place where my sons, and their descendants, would grow up. This land, now foreign, would soon be home, the final new start. The famine would end, and we would live again as family: the family of my father; God's family. Our lives were in His hands.

~~~

There had never been a more joyful reunion. Old man and long-lost son embraced each other for a long time. Jacob and Joseph laughed and wept, shedding joyful tears. After decades of much sorrow, they were together again at last.

It was only then, watching their embrace, that I realized something: had my brothers and I not sold Joseph into slavery, our entire family would have died from this famine. Not just our family, but thousands upon thousands more from all over Egypt, Canaan, and beyond. The thought was too much to bear. I fell to my knees. I would never have made the same mistake again, but somehow God took my betrayal, my choice of hatred and anger, and turned it into good, bringing about the salvation of thousands, and millions of those who were yet to be born. My entire body shook, overcome by God's goodness, oversight, and mercy to one so unworthy.

I don't know how long I lay there, but eventually I felt a tap on my shoulder. Slowly, I sat up, wiping the tears away from my eyes. Above me was Joseph. I was still on my knees, looking up at him. In that one moment, I remembered the dream that Joseph had had as a young boy, where our entire family had bowed down to him; it was this dream which had filled my young heart with such anger and jealousy, somehow leading us to this very moment.

"Joseph!" I cried, jumping to my feet. He raised his eyebrows, waiting.

"Your dream!" My mouth hung open as I struggled to take it all in.

My brother smiled.
~~~

The Biblical Narrative

Now it is time to read the real story that God authored. While I really hope you enjoyed reading my fictional story, what matters most to me is that you get to know the God of Judah and Tamar for yourself. Reading these chapters can be a great start, so I have included the majority of the Bible verses used. As you read, you will see little symbols next to some of the verses. These symbols mean that there is a note for that verse at the end of the chapter. In these little symbols and the notes beside them, I hope to show you some of the depth of beauty hidden in this Biblical narrative.

Symbols and Meanings

Questions: The point of asking yourself these questions is not just to find an answer, but is more about discovering the passage on a deeper level. Sometimes asking ourselves questions about a Bible passage can lead us to discover hidden truths, whether about God's heart or our own thinking and understanding

Cross References: Think of the cross references like clues on a treasure map. One Bible verse can show such insight and significance into another.

Observations: These are just my own thoughts: the things that stand out to me, fascinate or even confuse me. As you read my scrutiny, I hope it inspires you to find the things that interest you. Whenever something grabs your attention, ask God what He is trying to tell you.

Discovery: Instead of telling you facts, I would rather ask you questions, so you can discover the details for yourself. Google, Biblehub.com, Jewish encyclopedias, and commentaries are a great place to start.

My Notes

These notes that I wrote are just the tip of the iceberg. There is so much more hidden in every chapter. I hope that even after reading the notes provided, you want to know more and have observations you'd like to record. Feel free to use the section 'My Notes' at the end of each chapter to write these thoughts down.

A great way to discover more is to ask yourself questions about the text, look up the original words used and the significance of them, and look for patterns and themes. And at the end of every chapter, ask the Holy Spirit, "What do you want to show me?" He knows exactly where to lead us to show us what we need to see and hear. The Holy Spirit is the one who reveals these scriptures to us, the very best Bible reading partner and friend. Without Him, this is just a story of people long ago, but with Him these chapters can be life changing.

Jacob: From Trickster to Israel

So much of this story revolves around Judah's father Jacob, also called Israel. Jacob was God's chosen, the man His beloved nation is named after, one of the most favored men in all of the Bible. He showed great faith and is one of the founding fathers of the Jewish nation. It is his twelve sons that father the tribes of Israel.

Yet I want you to see for yourself how the Bible describes his struggle with anxiety, maybe even what we know as depression, after Joseph's departure. It's safe to say Jacob was an unfair parent, maybe even a failure as a husband to three of his wives. Jacob was a man who wrestled with God, saw Him face to face and knew Him as a friend, but also who went into a deep period of sorrow for more than ten years. What a paradox!

As you read the start of Jacob's story, keep in mind what he said at the end of his life.

'...May the God before whom my grandfather Abraham and my father, Isaac, walked- the God who has been my shepherd all my life, to this very day, the Angel who has redeemed me from all harm- may he bless these boys.' (Genesis 48:16)

I love that Jacob says he was redeemed from all harm. He isn't saying the harm did not come, but that his God, the Redeemer of all, turned all things into good. What a mark of a true man of faith.

Genesis 27

One day when Isaac was old and turning blind, he called for Esau, his older son, and said, "My son." "Yes, Father?" Esau replied. ₂"I am an old man now,"

Isaac said, "and I don't know when I may die. ₃Take your bow and a quiver full of arrows, and go out into the open country to hunt some wild game for me. ₄ Prepare my favorite dish, and bring it here for me to eat. Then I will pronounce the blessing that belongs to you, my firstborn son, before I die." ₅ But Rebekah overheard what Isaac had said to his son Esau. So when Esau left to hunt for the wild game, ₆she said to her son Jacob, "Listen. I overheard your father say to Esau, ₇'Bring me some wild game and prepare me a delicious meal. Then I will bless you in the LORD's presence before I die.' ₈Now, my son, listen to me. Do exactly as I tell you. ₉Go out to the flocks, and bring me two fine young goats. I'll use them to prepare your father's favorite dish. ₁₀Then take the food to your father so he can eat it and bless you before he dies." ₁₁"But look," Jacob replied to Rebekah, "my brother, Esau, is a hairy man, and my skin is smooth. ₁₂What if my father touches me? He'll see that I'm trying to trick him, and then he'll curse me instead of blessing me." ₁₃But his mother replied, "Then let the curse fall on me, my son! Just do what I tell you. Go out and get the goats for me!" ₁₄So Jacob went out and got the young goats for his mother. Rebekah took them and prepared a delicious meal, just the way Isaac liked it. ₁₅Then she took Esau's favorite clothes, which were there in the house, and gave them to her younger son, Jacob. ₁₆She covered his arms and the smooth part of his neck with the skin of the young goats. ₁₇Then she gave Jacob the delicious meal, including freshly baked bread. ₁₈So Jacob took the food to his father. "My father?" he said. "Yes, my son," Isaac answered. "Who are you—Esau or Jacob?" ₁₉Jacob replied, "It's Esau, your firstborn son. I've done as you told me. Here is the wild game. Now sit up and eat it so you can give me your blessing." ₂₀Isaac asked, "How did you find it so quickly, my son?" "The LORD your God put it in my path!" Jacob replied. ₂₁Then Isaac said to Jacob, "Come closer so I can touch you and make sure that you really are Esau." ₂₂So Jacob went closer to his father, and Isaac touched him. "The voice is Jacob's, but the hands are Esau's," Isaac said. ₂₃But he did not recognize Jacob, because Jacob's hands felt hairy just like Esau's. So Isaac prepared to bless Jacob. 24 "But are you really my son Esau?" he asked. "Yes, I am," Jacob replied. 25 Then Isaac said, "Now, my son, bring me the wild game. Let me eat it, and then I will give you my blessing." So Jacob took the food to his father, and Isaac ate it. He also drank the wine that Jacob served him. 26 Then Isaac said to Jacob, "Please come a little closer and kiss me, my son." 27 So Jacob went over and kissed him. And when Isaac caught the smell of his clothes, he was finally convinced, and he blessed his son.

30 As soon as Isaac had finished blessing Jacob, and almost before Jacob had left his father, Esau returned from his hunt. 31 Esau prepared a delicious meal and brought it to his father. Then he said, "Sit up, my father, and eat my wild game so you can give me your blessing." 32 But Isaac asked him, "Who are you?" Esau replied, "It's your son, your firstborn son, Esau." 33 Isaac began to tremble uncontrollably and said, "Then who just served me wild game? I have already eaten it, and I blessed him just before you came. And yes, that blessing must stand!" 34 When Esau heard his father's words, he let out a loud and bitter cry. "Oh my father, what about me? Bless me, too!" he begged. 35 But Isaac said, "Your brother was here, and he tricked me. He has taken away your blessing." 36 Esau exclaimed, "No wonder his name is Jacob, for now he has cheated me twice. First he took my rights as the firstborn, and now he has stolen my blessing. Oh, haven't you saved even one blessing for me?" 37 Isaac said to Esau, "I have made Jacob your master and have declared that all his brothers will be his servants. I have guaranteed him an abundance of grain and wine—what is left for me to give you, my son?" 38 Esau

pleaded, "But do you have only one blessing? Oh my father, bless me, too!" Then Esau broke down and wept.

⁴¹From that time on, Esau hated Jacob because their father had given Jacob the blessing. And Esau began to scheme: "I will soon be mourning my father's death. Then I will kill my brother, Jacob.

Chapter 27 Notes

Questions — Cross References — Observations — Discovery

Vs. 1   For the relationships between Isaac, Rebecca, Esau and Jacob, see Genesis 27:28.

Vs. 2   See the parallel between Isaac's request for an offering from his two sons and God's request from Cain and Abel. (Genesis 4:3-16)

Vs. 4   The theme of the firstborn: God often chooses the second son instead of the firstborn. What other siblings in the Bible does this pattern affect?

Vs. 8   For Rebecca, this was more than just playing favorites. See how God intervened in Genesis 25:21-26.

Vs. 24   I wonder if he yearned to be like his older brother. There are so many parallels to the way Jacob treats his own sons and how they interact with one another.

Vs. 26   Kiss of betrayal (Luke 22:47-48)

Vs. 27   Oh, what Jacob did for his Father's blessing! I love that because of Jesus, anybody that believes in Him get access to his blessings! We don't have to strive for it, for we are all like the firstborn son! See Hebrews 12: 23. What other blessings do God's children get in the New Testament?

Vs. 30   Look at how Jacob blesses Joseph's sons at the end of his life. (Genesis 48)

Vs. 32   He had already sold his rights as a firstborn for a pot of stew! See Genesis 25: 29-34

Vs. 33   'tremble uncontrollably'. This looks like a milder version of the way Jacob later reacts to bad news. What patterns do you see between Isaac and later Jacob in how they react to bad situations?

Vs. 41   Both Jacob and Judah flee from their father's home and start new families. What other parallels do you see between young Jacob in this chapter and Judah?

My Notes on Genesis 27

Shechem: The Revenge that Sparked Hostility

Much happens in Genesis 28-33. Jacob flees to his uncle Laban's house out of fear that his brother Esau will kill him. There Jacob meets Rachel, and falls in love with her. Laban capitalizes on this romance, and long story short, tricks Jacob into not only marrying Leah as well as Rachel, but working for him for fourteen years. There is much rivalry between the two sisters, and they give their servant wives to Jacob in order for them to give him children. The four women have eleven sons and one daughter. Eventually, after Jacob earns himself much wealth, he takes his family and leaves his uncles house. After a tense reunion with his brother Esau, we find Jacob and his family settled outside of Shechem.

Whenever I heard how Jacob favored Joseph, I always assumed it was because he was the son of his beloved Rachel and the child of his old age. That is a large part of it, but I wonder if part of his favor for Joseph had to do with his hostility towards the rest of the brothers. What happened in this chapter could have served as the event that sparked just that.

Genesis 34

One day Dinah, the daughter of Jacob and Leah, went to visit some of the young women who lived in the area. ₂But when the local prince, Shechem son of Hamor the Hivite, saw Dinah, he seized her and raped her. ₃But then he fell in love with her, and he tried to win her affection with tender words. ₄He said to his father, Hamor, "Get me this young girl. I want to marry her." ₅Soon Jacob heard that Shechem had defiled his daughter, Dinah. But since his sons were out in the fields herding his livestock, he said nothing until they returned. ₆Hamor, Shechem's father, came to discuss the matter with Jacob. 7 Meanwhile, Jacob's sons had come in from the field as soon as they heard what had happened. They were shocked and furious that their sister had been raped. Shechem had done a disgraceful thing against Jacob's family, something that should never be done. 8 Hamor tried to speak with Jacob and his sons. "My son Shechem is truly in love with your daughter," he said. "Please let him marry her. 9 In fact, let's arrange other marriages, too. You give us your daughters for our sons, and we will give you our daughters for your sons. 10 And you may live among us; the land is open to you! Settle here and trade with us. And feel free to buy property in the area." 11 Then Shechem himself spoke to Dinah's father and brothers. "Please be kind to me, and let me marry her," he begged. "I will give you whatever you ask. 12 No matter what dowry or gift you demand, I will gladly pay it—just give me the girl as my wife." 13 But since Shechem had defiled their sister, Dinah, Jacob's sons responded deceitfully to Shechem and his father, Hamor. 14 They said to them, "We couldn't possibly allow this, because you're not circumcised. It would be a disgrace for our sister to marry a man like you! 15 But here is a solution. If every man among you will be circumcised like we are, 16 then we will give you our daughters, and we'll take your daughters for ourselves. We will live among you and become one people. 17 But if you don't agree to be circumcised, we will take her and be on our way." 18 Hamor and his son Shechem agreed to their proposal. 19 Shechem wasted no time in acting on this request, for he wanted Jacob's daughter desperately. Shechem was a highly respected member of his family, 20 and he went with his father, Hamor, to present this proposal to the leaders at the town gate. 21 "These men are our friends," they said. "Let's invite them to live here among us and trade freely. Look, the land is large enough to hold them. We can take their daughters as wives and let them marry ours. ²²But they will consider staying here and becoming one people with us only if all of our men are circumcised, just as they are. ²³But if we do this, all their livestock and possessions will eventually be ours. Come, let's agree to their terms and let them settle here among us." ²⁴So all the men in the town council agreed with Hamor and Shechem, and every male in the town was circumcised. ²⁵But three days later, when their wounds were still sore, two of Jacob's sons, Simeon and Levi, who were Dinah's full brothers, took their swords and entered the town without opposition. Then they slaughtered every male there, ²⁶including Hamor and his son Shechem. They killed them with their swords, then took Dinah from Shechem's house and returned to their camp. ²⁷Meanwhile, the rest of Jacob's sons arrived. Finding the men slaughtered, they plundered the town because their sister had been defiled there. ²⁸They seized all the flocks and herds and donkeys—everything they could lay their hands on, both inside the town and outside in the fields. ²⁹They looted all their wealth and plundered their houses. They also took all their little children and wives and led them away as captives. ³⁰Afterward Jacob said to Simeon and Levi, "You have ruined me! You've made me stink among all the people of this land—among all the Canaanites and Perizzites. We are so few that they will join forces and crush us. I will be ruined, and my entire household will be wiped out!" ³¹"But why should we let him treat our sister like a prostitute?" they retorted angrily.

Genesis 34 Notes

Questions   Cross References   Observations   Discovery

Vs. 1   See 1 Kings 12 for the separation of the tribes of Israel that happens at this very location.

Vs. 2   See Genesis 33:19 for the connection between Hamor and Jacob.

Vs. 2   Where else in the Bible do we see rape happening?

Vs. 5   Why do you think he waited?

Vs. 7   I love how clearly the Bible puts this!

Vs. 13   It doesn't say whose plan this was specifically, but it appears all the brothers were in on it together and then Levi and Simeon carried out the majority of it.

Vs. 15   Isn't it fascinating to what extend the brothers went to protect their little sister, compared to what lengths they went to get rid of Joseph?

Vs. 21   The women of Jacob's family must have been so beautiful for the entire village to agree to get circumcised for them! See Genesis 20 for the trouble Dinah's grandmother's beauty caused.

Vs. 25   Do you think this *was* revenge or justice? Why?

Vs. 26   Do you think Dinah was surprised by this, or was she in on the plan? Did it make her embarrassed or feel loved and protected? Why?

Vs. 30   In my opinion, this is probably what defined their relationship from here on out.

My Notes on Genesis 34

The Dreams of Joseph

After the massacre at Shechem, Jacob moved his family to Bethel. There they purified themselves and worshipped God, and God gave Jacob his new name- Israel. After that, the family left Bethel and moved to Ephraim. On the way there, Rachel went into labor. After a very hard delivery, Benjamin, Jacob's twelfth son, was born but at the cost of Rachel's life. The family mourned and buried her in Bethlehem. Then they went to live with Abraham and Isaac in Hebron, which is where we meet them in this chapter.

When I heard this next story as a child, Joseph was always portrayed as the perfect son and his brothers were seen as cruel and jealous. In many ways that was true, but I couldn't help but feel sorry for the brothers. They clearly knew where their father's affections lay. Clearly, Jacob was not shy in expressing his love for Joseph. Whether you've heard this story or not, as you read it this time, try to see it from the brother's perspectives.

Genesis 37

So Jacob settled again in the land of Canaan, where his father had lived as a foreigner. ₂ This is the account of Jacob and his family. When Joseph was seventeen years old, he often tended his father's flocks. He worked for his half brothers, the sons of his father's wives Bilhah and Zilpah. But Joseph reported to his father some of the bad things his brothers were doing. ₃ Jacob loved Joseph more than any of his other children because Joseph had been born to him in his old age. So one day Jacob had a special gift made for Joseph—a beautiful robe. ₄ But his brothers hated Joseph because their father loved him more than the rest of them. They couldn't say a kind word to him. ₅ One night Joseph had a dream, and when he told his brothers about it, they hated him more than ever. ⁶ "Listen to this dream," he said. ⁷ "We were out in the field, tying up bundles of grain. Suddenly my bundle stood up, and your bundles all gathered around and bowed low before mine!" ⁸ His brothers responded, "So you think you will be our king, do you? Do you actually think you will reign over us?" And they hated him all the more because of his dreams and the way he talked about them. ⁹ Soon Joseph had another dream, and again he told his brothers about it. "Listen, I have had another dream," he said. "The sun, moon, and eleven stars bowed low before me!" ¹⁰ This time he told the dream to his father as well as to his brothers, but his father scolded him. "What kind of dream is that?" he asked. "Will your mother and I and your brothers actually come and bow to the ground before you?" ¹¹ But while his brothers were jealous of Joseph, his father wondered what the dreams meant. ¹² Soon after this, Joseph's brothers went to pasture their father's flocks at Shechem. ¹³ When they had been gone for some time, Jacob said to Joseph, "Your brothers are pasturing the sheep at Shechem. Get ready, and I will send you to them." "I'm ready to go," Joseph replied. ¹⁴ "Go and see how your brothers and the flocks are getting along," Jacob said. "Then come back and bring me a report." So Jacob sent him on his way, and Joseph traveled to Shechem from their home in the valley of Hebron. ¹⁵ When he arrived there, a man from the area noticed him wandering around the countryside. "What are you looking for?" he asked. ¹⁶ "I'm looking for my brothers," Joseph replied. "Do you know where they are pasturing their sheep?" ¹⁷ "Yes," the man told him. "They have moved on from here, but I heard them say, 'Let's go on to Dothan.'" So Joseph followed his brothers to Dothan and found them there. ¹⁸ When Joseph's brothers saw him coming, they recognized him in the distance. As he approached, they made plans to kill him. ¹⁹ "Here comes the dreamer!" they said. ²⁰ "Come on, let's kill him and throw him into one of these cisterns. We can tell our father, 'A wild animal has eaten him.' Then we'll see what becomes of his dreams!" ²¹ But when Reuben heard of their scheme, he came to Joseph's rescue. "Let's not kill him," he said. ²² "Why should we shed any blood? Let's just throw him into this empty cistern here in the wilderness. Then he'll die without our laying a hand on him." Reuben was secretly planning to rescue Joseph and return him to his father. ²³ So when Joseph arrived, his brothers ripped off the beautiful robe he was wearing. ²⁴ Then they grabbed him and threw him into the cistern. Now the cistern was empty; there was no water in it. ²⁵ Then, just as they were sitting down to eat, they looked up and saw a caravan of camels in the distance coming toward them. It was a group of Ishmaelite traders taking a load of gum, balm, and aromatic resin from Gilead down to Egypt. ²⁶ Judah said to his brothers, "What will we gain by killing our brother? We'd have to cover up the crime. ²⁷ Instead of hurting him, let's sell him to those Ishmaelite traders. After all, he is our brother—our own flesh and blood!" And his brothers agreed. ²⁸ So when the Ishmaelites, who were Midianite traders, came by, Joseph's brothers pulled him out of the cistern and sold him to them for twenty pieces of silver. And the traders took him to Egypt. ²⁹ Some time later, Reuben returned to get Joseph out of the cistern. When he discovered that Joseph was missing, he tore his clothes in grief. ³⁰ Then he went back to his brothers and lamented, "The boy is gone! What will I do now?" ³¹ Then the brothers killed a young goat and dipped Joseph's robe in its blood. ³² They sent the beautiful robe to their father with this message: "Look at what we found. Doesn't this robe belong to your son?" ³³ Their father recognized it immediately. "Yes," he said, "it is my son's robe. A wild animal must have eaten him. Joseph has clearly been torn to pieces!" 34 Then Jacob tore his clothes and dressed himself in burlap. He mourned deeply for his son for a long time. 35 His family all tried to comfort him, but he refused to be comforted. "I will go to my grave mourning for my son," he would say, and then he would weep.

Genesis 37 Notes

🗝 *Questions* 🔑 *Cross References* 💡 *Observations* 🔒 *Discovery*

Vs. 1 🔑 This is the land his forefathers were promised by God, but at this point in time they still lived there as foreigners. (Genesis 17:8)

Vs. 2 💡 Little tattletale! That must have been so annoying for Judah and his brothers. When they desperately wanted to please their father, having his favorite tell on them.

Vs. 3 🔒 What was the significance of this robe?

Vs. 3 🔑 For robes in the Bible, see Isaiah 61:10, Zechariah 3:4, Matthew 27:28 and Revelation 19:8.

Vs. 4 🔒 What parallels do you see between Joseph, his brothers and Jesus and the Pharisees in the New Testament?

Vs. 5 🔒 Who else had God spoken to through dreams at this point in history?

Vs. 8 🗝 What type of things do you think Joseph was saying about them?

Vs. 9 💡 I find it hard to see why Joseph kept sharing his dreams! Was he really naive or did he enjoy angering his brothers?

Vs. 12 💡 This was same place they killed the entire village just a few chapters earlier.

Vs. 17 🔑 What else happens in Dothan later on in the Bible? (2 Kings 6:8-23)

Vs. 18 🔒 In what ways does Joseph symbolize Jesus?

Vs. 22 🗝 Why do you think Reuben did this? Was this out of genuine care for his brother or was he trying to win back his fathers approval after he slept with Bilhah?

Vs. 25 💡 It's very hard to believe they sat down to eat after doing this to their brother, especially if the food they were eating was what Joseph brought for them

Vs. 26 🗝 Do you think Judah's idea here was motivated by greed, or hatred, wanting to make the worst possible scenario for Joseph? Or do you think he suspected that Reuben wanted to rescue him? Or do you think he was trying to help him, thinking he would do better as a slave then dying in an empty cistern? Why?

Vs. 28 🔒 What is the significance of this payment?

Vs. 28   For origins of the Ishmaelites, see Genesis 16: 1-15 and Genesis 21:8-21. What is the family relationship between Judah and these Ishmaelites?

Vs. 31   Since this happened before Moses and the law of sacrifices, isn't it interesting that a sacrifice of a lamb was still made?

Vs. 31   What did the law of Moses say killing a goat would atone for? (Leviticus 4:22-24)

Vs. 31   How was Jesus symbolized here? See Hebrews 9:12-14 and Hebrews 10.

Vs. 31   What does the Bible say about the blood of the lamb in the Old Testament? What does it symbolize in the New Testament?

Vs. 32   They say your son, not our brother.

Vs. 33   Do you think that Jacob really did not suspect anything?

Vs. 34   What must have it been like for Judah and his brothers to see their father losing hope like this?

Vs. 34   Burlap and tearing of the clothes: what did this symbolize?

Vs. 35   What is the original word that Jacob uses that is translated as 'grave' and what does it mean?

Viktoriya Lorimer

My Notes on Genesis 37

Judah and Tamar

To be completely honest, after around a year of studying this chapter, most things in it I still do not understand. We are told very little about Tamar, Er, Onan, Shelah, Judah's wife, or Tamar's parents. As what I wrote into this book is fictional, I want us to pay attention closely to what really happened in this chapter.

Genesis 38

About this time, Judah left home and moved to Adullam, where he stayed with a man named Hirah. 2There he saw a Canaanite woman, the daughter of Shua, and he married her. When he slept with her, 3she became pregnant and gave birth to a son, and he named the boy Er. 4Then she became pregnant again and gave birth to another son, and she named him Onan. 5And when she gave birth to a third son, she named him Shelah. At the time of Shelah's birth, they were living at Kezib. 6In the course of time, Judah arranged for his firstborn son, Er, to marry a young woman named Tamar. 7But Er was a wicked man in the LORD's sight, so the LORD took his life. 8Then Judah said to Er's brother Onan, "Go and marry Tamar, as our law requires of the brother of a man who has died. You must produce an heir for your brother." 9But Onan was not willing to have a child who would not be his own heir. So whenever he had intercourse with his brother's wife, he spilled the semen on the ground. This prevented her from having a child who would belong to his brother. 10But the LORD considered it evil for Onan to deny a child to his dead brother. So the LORD took Onan's life, too. 11Then Judah said to Tamar, his daughter-in-law, "Go back to your parents' home and remain a widow until my son Shelah is old enough to marry you." (But Judah didn't really intend to do this because he was afraid Shelah would also die, like his two brothers.) So Tamar went back to live in her father's home. 12 Some years later Judah's wife died. After the time of mourning was over, Judah and his friend Hirah the Adullamite went up to Timnah to supervise the shearing of his sheep. 13 Someone told Tamar, "Look, your father-in-law is going up to Timnah to shear his sheep." 14 Tamar was aware that Shelah had grown up, but no arrangements had been made for her to come and marry him. So she changed out of her widow's clothing and covered herself with a veil to disguise herself. Then she sat beside the road at the entrance to the village of Enaim, which is on the road to Timnah. 15 Judah noticed her and thought she was a prostitute, since she had covered her face. 16 So he stopped and propositioned her. "Let me have sex with you," he said, not realizing that she was his own daughter-in-law. "How much will you pay to have sex with me?" Tamar asked. 17 "I'll send you a young goat from my flock," Judah promised. "But what will you give me to guarantee that you will send the goat?" she asked. 18 "What kind of guarantee do you want?" he replied. She answered, "Leave me your identification seal and its cord and the walking stick you are carrying." So Judah gave them to her. Then he had intercourse with her, and she became pregnant. 19 Afterward she went back home, took off her veil, and put on her widow's clothing as usual. 20 Later Judah asked his friend Hirah the Adullamite to take the young goat to the woman and to pick up the things he had given her as his guarantee. But Hirah couldn't find her. 21 So he asked the men who lived there, "Where can I find the shrine prostitute who was sitting beside the road at the entrance to Enaim?" "We've never had a shrine prostitute here," they replied. 22 So

Hirah returned to Judah and told him, "I couldn't find her anywhere, and the men of the village claim they've never had a shrine prostitute there." ₂₃ "Then let her keep the things I gave her," Judah said. "I sent the young goat as we agreed, but you couldn't find her. We'd be the laughingstock of the village if we went back again to look for her." ₂₄ About three months later, Judah was told, "Tamar, your daughter-in-law, has acted like a prostitute. And now, because of this, she's pregnant." "Bring her out, and let her be burned!" Judah demanded. ₂₅ But as they were taking her out to kill her, she sent this message to her father-in-law: "The man who owns these things made me pregnant. Look closely. Whose seal and cord and walking stick are these?" ₂₆ Judah recognized them immediately and said, "She is more righteous than I am, because I didn't arrange for her to marry my son Shelah." And Judah never slept with Tamar again. ₂₇ When the time came for Tamar to give birth, it was discovered that she was carrying twins. ₂₈ While she was in labor, one of the babies reached out his hand. The midwife grabbed it and tied a scarlet string around the child's wrist, announcing, "This one came out first." ₂₉ But then he pulled back his hand, and out came his brother! "What!" the midwife exclaimed. "How did you break out first?" So he was named Perez. ₃₀ Then the baby with the scarlet string on his wrist was born, and he was named Zerah.

Genesis 38 Notes

Questions   Cross References   Observations   Discovery

Vs. 1   What else happens in Adullam later in the Bible? See 1 Samuel 22:1-2. What is the significance of this?

Vs. 2   This was something that was disapproved of in his family. (Genesis 24: 2-4)

Vs. 6   We are told nothing about Tamar or her background. What do you think would cause Judah to choose this girl for his firstborn son?

Vs. 7   I still do not understand this but I know God is always just, always loving, and always good.

Vs. 7   Was there anyone else in the Bible that this happened to?

Vs. 8   Where did this law come from?

Vs. 9   Where else in the Bible do we see this custom for a brother to marry his widowed step-sister? If Onan gave Er an heir, what would this mean for him?

Vs. 10   Why do you think the Lord considered it evil to deny Er a child if he was so wicked?

Vs. 10   The deaths of Er and Onan are still a mystery to me. I wonder why did the Lord intervene in this way specifically this time? Were there certain natural causes involved?

Vs. 12   The Bible is unclear about why she died. I wonder if it was from grief?

Vs. 12   What happened to the tribe of Judah in Timnah later on in the Bible? (2 Chronicles 28:16-25)

Vs. 14   I love how symbolic her widow's clothing is, representing our past, our mistakes.

Vs. 14   What do you think her motive was? Why?

Vs. 15.   Where else in the lineage of Jesus can you find prostitution? What do you think this says about Jesus for choosing these women to carry His line?

Vs. 18   What would our cultural equivalent be of Tamar asking for Judah's seal, staff and cord?

Vs. 20   It appears Judah was too ashamed to go himself and face her again. He seems to really care about his reputation.

Vs. 24   Most pregnancies are not able to be seen at 3 months, especially not with the clothing they probably wore. I wonder how this was discovered?

Vs. 25   She sent a private message instead of publicly humiliating him, which she could have easily done.

Vs. 26   Could this be Judah's turning point? The reputation he cared about so much in the previous few verses, he is putting on the line.

Vs. 27   This verse says that it was discovered she was carrying twins when it came time to give birth.

Vs. 28   This is not the proper way for a baby to come out! How painful must this have been?

Vs. 30   See Genesis 25:22 for how Jacob and Esau rivaled within the womb.

My Notes on Genesis 38

The Famine

While Genesis 39-41 focus on the life of Joseph in Egypt, the next place we meet Judah is in Genesis 42. At some point between these three chapters, Judah must have taken his three sons and most likely Tamar, and gone back to his father's home. The Bible doesn't say anything about this, but I can only imagine what it was like to face his family that he has departed from so many years ago. In some ways, Judah was a prodigal son. A life transformation happened for him somewhere between this time. He went from a man who was willing to sell Joseph into slavery, one who abandoned his family, to the man we see in the next few chapters.

Genesis 42

When Jacob heard that grain was available in Egypt, he said to his sons, "Why are you standing around looking at one another? ₂I have heard there is grain in Egypt. Go down there, and buy enough grain to keep us alive. Otherwise we'll die." ₃So Joseph's ten older brothers went down to Egypt to buy grain. ₄But Jacob wouldn't let Joseph's younger brother, Benjamin, go with them, for fear some harm might come to him. ₅So Jacob's sons arrived in Egypt along with others to buy food, for the famine was in Canaan as well. ₆Since Joseph was governor of all Egypt and in charge of selling grain to all the people, it was to him that his brothers came.

When they arrived, they bowed before him with their faces to the ground. ₇Joseph recognized his brothers instantly, but he pretended to be a stranger and spoke harshly to them. "Where are you from?" he demanded. "From the land of Canaan," they replied. "We have come to buy food." ₈Although Joseph recognized his brothers, they didn't recognize him. ₉And he remembered the dreams he'd had about them many years before. He said to them, "You are spies!

You have come to see how vulnerable our land has become." ₁₀ "No, my lord!" they exclaimed. "Your servants have simply come to buy food. ₁₁ We are all brothers—members of the same family. We are honest men, sir! We are not spies!" ₁₂ "Yes, you are!" Joseph insisted. "You have come to see how vulnerable our land has become." ₁₃ "Sir," they said, "there are actually twelve of us. We, your servants, are all brothers, sons of a man living in the land of Canaan. Our youngest brother is back there with our father right now, and one of our brothers is no longer with us." ₁₄ But Joseph insisted, "As I said, you are spies! ₁₅ This is how I will test your story. I swear by the life of Pharaoh that you will never leave Egypt unless your youngest brother comes here! ₁₆ One of you must go and get your brother. I'll keep the rest of you here in prison. Then we'll find out whether or not your story is true. By the life of Pharaoh, if it turns out that you don't have a younger brother, then I'll know you are spies." ₁₇ So Joseph put them all in prison for three days. ₁₈ On the third day Joseph said to them, "I am a God-fearing man. If you do as I say, you will live. ₁₉ If you really are honest men, choose one of your brothers to remain in prison. The rest of you may go home with grain for your starving families. ₂₀ But you must bring your youngest brother back to me. This will prove that you are telling the truth, and you will not die." To this they agreed. ₂₁ Speaking among themselves, they said, "Clearly we are being punished because of what we did to Joseph long ago. We saw his anguish when he pleaded for his life, but we wouldn't listen. That's why we're in this trouble." ₂₂ "Didn't I tell you not to sin against the boy?" Reuben asked. "But you wouldn't listen. And now we have to answer for his blood!" ₂₃ Of course, they didn't know that Joseph understood them, for he had been speaking to them through an interpreter. ₂₄ Now he turned away from them and began to weep. When he regained his composure, he spoke to them again. Then he chose Simeon from among them and had him tied up right before their eyes. ²⁵Joseph then ordered his servants to fill the men's sacks with grain, but he also gave secret instructions to return each brother's payment at the top of his sack. He also gave them supplies for their journey home. ²⁶So the brothers loaded their donkeys with the grain and headed for home. ²⁷But when they stopped for the night and one of them opened his sack to get grain for his donkey, he found his money in the top of his sack. ²⁸"Look!" he exclaimed to his brothers. "My money has been returned; it's here in my sack!" Then their hearts sank. Trembling, they said to each other, "What has God done to us?" ²⁹When the brothers came to their father, Jacob, in the land of Canaan, they told him everything that had happened to them. ³⁰"The man who is governor of the land spoke very harshly to us," they told him. "He accused us of being spies scouting the land. ³¹But we said, 'We are honest men, not spies.

³²We are twelve brothers, sons of one father. One brother is no longer with us, and the youngest is at home with our father in the land of Canaan.' ³³"Then the man who is governor of the land told us, 'This is how I will find out if you are honest men. Leave one of your brothers here with me, and take grain for your starving families and go on home. ³⁴But you must bring your youngest brother back to me. Then I will know you are honest men and not spies. Then I will give you back your brother, and you may trade freely in the land.'" ³⁵As they emptied out their sacks, there in each man's sack was the bag of money he had paid for the grain! The brothers and their father were terrified when they saw the bags of money. ³⁶Jacob exclaimed, "You are robbing me of my children! Joseph is gone! Simeon is gone! And now you want to take Benjamin, too. Everything is going against me!" ³⁷Then Reuben said to his father, "You may kill my two sons if I don't bring Benjamin back to you. I'll be

responsible for him, and I promise to bring him back." But Jacob replied, "My son will not go down with you. His brother Joseph is dead, and he is all I have left. If anything should happen to him on your journey, you would send this grieving, white-haired man to his grave."

Chapter 42 Notes

Questions   Cross References   Observations   Discovery

Vs. 4   How do you think Benjamin reacted to his father's affections? Why?

Vs. 6   The dream Joseph had over two decades ago has come true!

Vs. 7   Why do you think Joseph pretended that he didn't know his brothers?

Vs. 8   What would have happened to them if Joseph's accusation was met with the appropriate punishment?

Vs. 13   Joseph was still at the forefront of their minds!

Vs. 17   What does them being in the prison for three days symbolize?

Vs. 19   I wonder if he wanted to know which one they would choose?

Vs. 22   'answer for his blood' Their guilt, after decades have passed, is still so dominant.

Vs. 24   Earlier, he had given them a choice in who would stay in prison, now he told them it was to be Simeon. I wonder what changed?

Vs. 24   It appears Simeon had two wives, one of whom was a Canaanite. See Genesis 46:10 for Simeon's wives and sons. Who else in the family of Abraham takes a Canaanite wife?

Vs. 28   What they saw was God punishing them, but what was God actually doing?

Vs. 29   see Genesis 46: 8-25 for the numbers and names of Jacob's sons.

Vs. 32   'we are twelve brothers' Wow!

Vs. 36   Over two decades have passed, and we see Jacob still wallowing in the depths of despair for the loss of Joseph.

Vs. 37   Why do you think Reuben said this? See Genesis 46:9. Reuben has four sons. Why does he say that Jacob can kill two of them?

Vs. 38   Jacob still doesn't trust Reuben.

Vs. 38 I wonder what it was like for the entire family to see their father, grandfather, even great grandfather, so marked with grief? How can Jacob, the one who saw God, wrestled with him, asking for a blessing, and was told he would be blessed and protected by God himself, be so marked with grief? Why do you think it was so hard for Jacob to let Benjamin go?

My Notes on Genesis 42

The Feast

In this chapter, we see the first part of Judah's transformation. Where Reuben puts his son's lives at stake for Benjamin's, Judah places his own. When a choice he made many years ago put Joseph into slavery, his courage here releases something in Jacob, where the grieving old man finally releases his youngest son to Egypt for a chance to save his entire family.

Genesis 43

But the famine continued to ravage the land of Canaan. ₂When the grain they had brought from Egypt was almost gone, Jacob said to his sons, "Go back and buy us a little more food." ₃But Judah said, "The man was serious when he warned us, 'You won't see my face again unless your brother is with you.' ₄If you send Benjamin with us, we will go down and buy more food. ₅But if you don't let Benjamin go, we won't go either. Remember, the man said, 'You won't see my face again unless your brother is with you.'" ₆"Why were you so cruel to me?" Jacob moaned. "Why did you tell him you had another brother?" ₇"The man kept asking us questions about our family," they replied. "He asked, 'Is your father still alive? Do you have another brother?' So we answered his questions. How could we know he would say, 'Bring your brother down here'?" ₈Judah said to his father, "Send the boy with me, and we will be on our way. Otherwise we will all die of starvation—and not only we, but you and our little ones. ₉I personally guarantee his safety. You may hold me responsible if I don't bring him back to you. Then let me bear the blame forever. ₁₀If we hadn't wasted all this time, we could have gone and returned twice by now." ₁₁So their father, Jacob, finally said to them, "If it can't be avoided, then at least do this. Pack your bags with the best products of this land. Take them down to the man as gifts—balm, honey, gum, aromatic resin, pistachio nuts, and almonds. 12 Also take double the money that was put back in your sacks, as it was probably someone's mistake. 13 Then take your brother, and go back to the man. 14 May God Almighty give you mercy as you go before the man, so that he will release Simeon and let Benjamin return. But if I must lose my children, so be it." 15 So the men packed Jacob's gifts and double the money and headed off with Benjamin.

They finally arrived in Egypt and presented themselves to Joseph. 16 When Joseph saw Benjamin with them, he said to the manager of his household, "These men will eat with me this noon. Take them inside the palace. Then go slaughter an animal, and prepare a big feast." 17 So the man did as Joseph told him and took them into Joseph's palace. 18 The brothers were terrified when they saw that they were being taken into Joseph's house. "It's because of the money someone put in our sacks last time we were here," they said. "He plans to pretend that we stole it.

Then he will seize us, make us slaves, and take our donkeys." 19 The brothers approached the manager of Joseph's household and spoke to him at the entrance to the palace. 20 "Sir," they said, "we came to Egypt once before to buy food. 21 But as we were returning home, we stopped for the night and opened our sacks. Then we discovered that each man's money—the exact amount paid—was in the top of his sack! Here it is; we have brought it back with us. 22 We also have additional money to buy more food. We have no idea who put our money in our sacks." 23 "Relax. Don't be afraid," the household manager told them. "Your God, the God of your father, must have put this treasure into your sacks. I know I received your payment." Then he released Simeon and brought him out to them. 24 The manager then led the men into Joseph's palace. He gave them water to wash their feet and provided food for their donkeys. 25 They were told they would be eating there, so they prepared their gifts for Joseph's arrival at noon. 26 When Joseph came home, they gave him the gifts they had brought him, then bowed low to the ground before him. 27 After greeting them, he asked, "How is your father, the old man you spoke about? Is he still alive?" 28 "Yes," they replied. "Our father, your servant, is alive and well." And they bowed low again. 29 Then Joseph looked at his brother Benjamin, the son of his own mother. "Is this your youngest brother, the one you told me about?" Joseph asked. "May God be gracious to you, my son." 30 Then Joseph hurried from the room because he was overcome with emotion for his brother. He went into his private room, where he broke down and wept. 31 After washing his face, he came back out, keeping himself under control. Then he ordered, "Bring out the food!" 32 The waiters served Joseph at his own table, and his brothers were served at a separate table. The Egyptians who ate with Joseph sat at their own table, because Egyptians despise Hebrews and refuse to eat with them. 33 Joseph told each of his brothers where to sit, and to their amazement, he seated them according to age, from oldest to youngest. 34 And Joseph filled their plates with food from his own table, giving Benjamin five times as much as he gave the others. So they feasted and drank freely with him.

Genesis 43 Notes

Questions   *Cross References*   *Observations*   *Discovery*

Vs. 1   Jacob's household was not the first to experience such a famine. For the famine that affected Abraham in his lifetime, see Genesis 12:1-20, and for the famine that affected Isaac, see Genesis 26:1-11. What patterns do you see in God's actions during a famine?

Vs. 1   What other people later in the Bible were affected by famines? What other similarities do you see between the famine effects?

Vs. 2   How long did this journey take? How long was Simeon left in jail for?

Vs. 3   In what ways can you see that Benjamin symbolizes Jesus and Jacob symbolize God's fatherly heart?

Vs. 8   Maybe reminding Jacob that if Benjamin was not sent with the brothers to Egypt, the entire family would die, was exactly what Jacob needed to hear.

Vs. 14   Is Jacob finally trusting God? What do you think finally caused this change? Why do you think he agreed to let Benjamin go with Judah, not with Reuben?

Vs. 16   I love that Joseph declared a feast in the middle of a famine.

Vs. 17   The manager must have been very confused by his Master's behavior!

Vs. 19   Their integrity is very apparent. Whether out of fear or not, their honesty here shows they are changed men.

Vs. 24   What patterns do you see between these 12 brothers feasting together in this passage and the last supper Jesus had with his 12 disciples? (Matthew 26:17-30)

Vs. 30   Notice the contrast between Joseph's outwardly demeanor and inward emotions.

Vs. 32   What was the historical relationship between the Egyptians and Canaanites/Hebrews?

Vs. 34   5 times more: Why do you think Joseph favored Benjamin in this way?

My notes on Genesis 43

The Silver Cup

Judah's speech is the last thing Joseph hears before he reveals his identity. I can only imagine the tension that hung in the air at this time. Judah, knowing he can be killed instantly for his words, still speaks. He defends his youngest brother with his life. Foreshadowing Jesus, Judah's valiance releases not only Simeon from prison and reveals Joseph's identity, but redeems the entire family of Jacob, the origins of Israel.

Genesis 44

When his brothers were ready to leave, Joseph gave these instructions to his palace manager: "Fill each of their sacks with as much grain as they can carry, and put each man's money back into his sack. Then put my personal silver cup at the top of the youngest brother's sack, along with the money for his grain." So the manager did as Joseph instructed him. The brothers were up at dawn and were sent on their journey with their loaded donkeys. But when they had gone only a short distance and were barely out of the city, Joseph said to his palace manager, "Chase after them and stop them. When you catch up with them, ask them, 'Why have you repaid my kindness with such evil? Why have you stolen my master's silver cup, which he uses to predict the future? What a wicked thing you have done!'" When the palace manager caught up with the men, he spoke to them as he had been instructed. "What are you talking about?" the brothers responded. "We are your servants and would never do such a thing! Didn't we return the money we found in our sacks? We brought it back all the way from the land of Canaan. Why would we steal silver or gold from your master's house? If you find his cup with any one of us, let that man die. And all the rest of us, my lord, will be your slaves." ⒑"That's fair," the man replied. "But only the one who stole the cup will be my slave. The rest of you may go free." ⒒They all quickly took their sacks from the backs of their donkeys and opened them. ⒓The palace manager searched the brothers' sacks, from the oldest to the youngest. And the cup was found in Benjamin's sack! ⒔When the brothers saw this, they tore their clothing in despair. Then they loaded their donkeys again and returned to the city. ⒕Joseph was still in his palace when Judah and his brothers arrived, and they fell to the ground before him. ⒖"What have you done?" Joseph demanded. "Don't you know that a man like me can predict the future?" ⒗Judah answered, "Oh, my lord, what can we say to you? How can we explain this? How can we prove our innocence? God is punishing us for our sins. My lord, we have all returned to be your slaves—all of us, not just our brother who had your cup in his sack." ⒘"No," Joseph said. "I would never do such a thing! Only the man who stole the cup will be my slave. The rest of you may go back to your father in peace." ⒙Then Judah stepped forward and said, "Please, my lord, let your servant say just one word to you. Please, do not be angry with me, even though you are as powerful as Pharaoh himself. ⒚"My lord, previously you asked us, your servants, 'Do you have a father or a brother?' ⒛And we responded, 'Yes, my lord, we have a father who is an old man, and his youngest son is a child of his old age. His full brother is dead, and he alone is left of his mother's children, and his father loves him very much.' ㉑"And you said to us, 'Bring him here so I can see him with my own eyes.' ㉒But we said to you, 'My lord, the boy cannot leave his father, for his father would die.' ㉓But you told us, 'Unless your youngest brother comes with you, you will never see my face again.' ²⁴ "So we returned to your servant, our father, and told him what you had said. ²⁵Later, when he said, 'Go back again and buy us more food,' ²⁶we replied, 'We can't go unless you let our youngest brother go with us. We'll never get to see the man's face unless our youngest brother is with us.' ²⁷"Then my father said to us, 'As you know, my wife had two sons, ²⁸and one of them went away and never returned. Doubtless he was torn to pieces by some wild animal. I have never seen him since. ²⁹Now if you take his brother away from me, and any harm comes to him, you will send this grieving, white-haired man to his grave.' ³⁰"And now, my lord, I cannot go back to my father without the boy. Our father's life is bound up in the boy's life. ³¹If he sees that the boy is not with us, our father will die. We, your servants, will indeed

be responsible for sending that grieving, white-haired man to his grave. ³²My lord, I guaranteed to my father that I would take care of the boy. I told him, 'If I don't bring him back to you, I will bear the blame forever.' ³³"So please, my lord, let me stay here as a slave instead of the boy, and let the boy return with his brothers. ³⁴For how can I return to my father if the boy is not with me? I couldn't bear to see the anguish this would cause my father!"

Genesis 44 Notes

Questions   Cross References   Observations   Discovery

Vs. 1   It seems that joseph is trying to recreate the situation his brothers put him in.

Vs. 5   What did Joseph do with this silver cup?

Vs. 9   Although quite extreme, this statement shows that the brothers are going to stick together. If one is found guilty, they all offer themselves as slaves. They really have changed!

Vs. 13   They were so distraught that they tore their clothes in despair. They could have easily gone home. They were outside the city, they had grain for their families, they had Simeon. They were not bound by anything to go back for Benjamin, but they did.

Vs. 13   For where other people in the Bible tore their clothes in grief, see Genesis 37:34, Numbers 14:1-9, and 2 Samuel 1:11-12.

Vs. 14   Again, here is the same scene from Joseph's dream as a seventeen year old: his brothers bowing before him.

Vs. 15   What do you think Joseph means here?

Vs. 16   Judah says God is punishing them. It looks like they lived their whole lives under this fear. But although they messed up, how good is God that He redeemed the entire situation?

Vs. 18   Judah's courage: he knows this man can kill him instantly.

Vs. 20   He says 'his brother is dead' to that very brother standing in front of him

Vs. 21   What are the key words in Judah's speech?

Vs. 32   He tells Joseph about the pledge he made to protect Benjamin. How do you think this made Joseph feel?

My Notes on Genesis 44

I am Joseph

How beautiful is the forgiveness that Joseph extends to his brothers! Rather than being filled with hatred and bitterness, he chooses to see things from a different perspective: God's perspective. There are people all around the world who, throughout thousands of years, have relied on the words Joseph speaks in this chapter, the promise that what was meant for evil, God turned for good. It was not easy for Joseph, but he is very clear in his extension of forgiveness. Not only does he not hold their actions against them, he goes as far to say that God sent him to Egypt. He says this three times in a row! Can you imagine being in Judah's shoes? Seeing the one choice he made that has marked his life with such grief and guilt, being turned into the salvation of his entire family? My mind cannot comprehend the goodness that God shows to Judah and Joseph. Both men were far away from their family for many years, have suffered immensely, and here God shows His nature by weaving every wrong thing for good.

Genesis 45

Joseph could stand it no longer. There were many people in the room, and he said to his attendants, "Out, all of you!" So he was alone with his brothers when he told them who he was. 2 Then he broke down and wept. He wept so loudly the Egyptians could hear him, and word of it quickly carried to Pharaoh's palace. 3 "I am Joseph!" he said to his brothers. "Is my father still alive?" But his brothers were speechless! They were stunned to realize that Joseph was standing there in front of them. 4 "Please, come closer," he said to them. So they came closer. And he said again, "I am Joseph, your brother, whom you sold into slavery in Egypt. 5

But don't be upset, and don't be angry with yourselves for selling me to this place. It was God who sent me here ahead of you to preserve your lives. ₆This famine that has ravaged the land for two years will last five more years, and there will be neither plowing nor harvesting. ₇God has sent me ahead of you to keep you and your families alive and to preserve many survivors. ₈So it was God who sent me here, not you! And he is the one who made me an advisor to Pharaoh—the manager of his entire palace and the governor of all Egypt. ₉"Now hurry back to my father and tell him, 'This is what your son Joseph says: God has made me master over all the land of Egypt. So come down to me immediately! ₁₀You can live in the region of Goshen, where you can be near me with all your children and grandchildren, your flocks and herds, and everything you own. ₁₁I will take care of you there, for there are still five years of famine ahead of us. Otherwise you, your household, and all your animals will starve.'" ₁₂Then Joseph added, "Look! You can see for yourselves, and so can my brother Benjamin, that I really am Joseph! ₁₃Go tell my father of my honored position here in Egypt. Describe for him everything you have seen, and then bring my father here quickly." ₁₄Weeping with joy, he embraced Benjamin, and Benjamin did the same. ₁₅Then Joseph kissed each of his brothers and wept over them, and after that they began talking freely with him. ₁₆The news soon reached Pharaoh's palace: "Joseph's brothers have arrived!" Pharaoh and his officials were all delighted to hear this. ₁₇Pharaoh said to Joseph, "Tell your brothers, 'This is what you must do: Load your pack animals, and hurry back to the land of Canaan. ₁₈Then get your father and all of your families, and return here to me. I will give you the very best land in Egypt, and you will eat from the best that the land produces.'" ₁₉Then Pharaoh said to Joseph, "Tell your brothers, 'Take wagons from the land of Egypt to carry your little children and your wives, and bring your father here. ₂₀Don't worry about your personal belongings, for the best of all the land of Egypt is yours.'" ²¹ So the sons of Jacob did as they were told. Joseph provided them with wagons, as Pharaoh had commanded, and he gave them supplies for the journey. ²² And he gave each of them new clothes—but to Benjamin he gave five changes of clothes and 300 pieces of silver. ²³ He also sent his father ten male donkeys loaded with the finest products of Egypt, and ten female donkeys loaded with grain and bread and other supplies he would need on his journey. ²⁴ So Joseph sent his brothers off, and as they left, he called after them, "Don't quarrel about all this along the way!" ²⁵ And they left Egypt and returned to their father, Jacob, in the land of Canaan. ²⁶ "Joseph is still alive!" they told him. "And he is governor of all the land of Egypt!" Jacob was stunned at the news—he couldn't believe it. ²⁷ But when they repeated to Jacob everything Joseph had told them, and when he saw the wagons Joseph had sent to carry him, their father's spirits revived. ²⁸ Then Jacob exclaimed, "It must be true! My son Joseph is alive! I must go and see him before I die."

Genesis 45 Notes

Questions   Cross References   Observations   Discovery

Vs. 2 How many times has Joseph wept on the account of seeing his brothers before? What is the significance of this?

Vs. 3 What are the original words used for 'speechless' and 'stunned'?

Vs. 4 I love how he beckons them to himself. They were probably too shocked to even approach him.

Vs. 5 He tells them to not be angry with themselves, because he has heard them talking amongst themselves, saying how God is punishing them. And here he is, telling them that God has sent him to Egypt.

Vs. 8 Joseph repeats that it was God that sent him to Egypt three times. What is the significance of this?

Vs. 8 God's sovereignty: this outcome was one Judah and his brothers never saw coming. This story just sings praises to God!

Vs. 10 What does the name 'Goshen' mean?

Vs. 16 It is interesting that Pharaoh and his officials were delighted to hear this. If the Hebrews were despised by the Egyptians, maybe it was Joseph's status that made this revelation on his identity a positive one.

Vs. 22 They had ripped their clothes from grief earlier, and now they were given new clothes. What did giving someone a new pair of clothes signify in the East?

Vs. 22 See Genesis 41:42 for the time where Joseph himself received a new pair of clothes.

Vs. 24 Do you think this was Joseph being concerned about Benjamin's welfare after the extravagant present that he received or was it a joke, since he knew they would go to all costs to defend his brother?

Vs. 27 In the previous chapter, Jacob finally let go and trusted God with whatever happened to his sons. How faithful is God? Not only did Jacob's beloved Benjamin return, but he found out Joseph was alive- probably the greatest miracle in his life, something he never thought was possible. We can always trust God, no matter what our circumstances appear to be.

My Notes on Genesis 45

Tribe of Jacob, Line of Jesus

Judah is the one who is asked to go ahead of the entire family and prepare for their arrival, a task that was showing his status as the firstborn son. Maybe it was because of the courage that Judah showed, or maybe because the older three sons disqualified themselves, it is Judah who is given this right. In Genesis 49, when Jacob blesses all his sons before his death, it is Judah's blessing that the promise of Jesus gets spoken into. Here is a portion of that blessing:

> *Judah, my son, is a young lion that has finished eating its prey. Like a lion he crouches and lies down; like a lioness- who dares rouse him? The scepter will not depart from Judah, nor the ruler's staff from his descendants, until the coming of the one to whom it belongs, the one whom all nations will honor. (Genesis 49: 9-10)*

Genesis 46

So Jacob set out for Egypt with all his possessions. And when he came to Beersheba, he offered sacrifices to the God of his father, Isaac. ₂ During the night God spoke to him in a vision. "Jacob! Jacob!" he called. "Here I am," Jacob replied. ₃ "I am God, the God of your father," the voice said. "Do not be afraid to go down to Egypt, for there I will make your family into a great nation. ₄ I will go with you down to Egypt, and I will bring you back again. You will die in Egypt, but Joseph will be with you to close your eyes." ₅ So Jacob left Beersheba, and his sons took him to Egypt. They carried him and their little ones and their wives in the wagons Pharaoh had provided for them. ₆ They also took all their livestock and all the personal belongings they had acquired in the land of Canaan. So Jacob and his entire family went to Egypt— ₇ sons and grandsons, daughters and granddaughters—all his descendants.

28As they neared their destination, Jacob sent Judah ahead to meet Joseph and get directions to the region of Goshen. And when they finally arrived there, 29 Joseph prepared his chariot and traveled to Goshen to meet his father, Jacob. When Joseph arrived, he embraced his father and wept, holding him for a long time. 30Finally, Jacob said to Joseph, "Now I am ready to die, since I have seen your face again and know you are still alive."

Genesis 46 Notes

Questions   Cross References   Observations   Discovery

Vs.1   What is the significance of what happened to Abraham (See Genesis 21:31) and Isaac (See Genesis 26: 33) at Beersheba?

Vs. 1   What else happens later on in the Bible at Beersheba?

Vs. 2   What other times does God come to Jacob in his dreams? What does he say? Do you see a pattern? (See Genesis 28:10-20 and Genesis 32:22-32)

Vs. 2   'Here I am' What other people in the Bible respond to God in this way?

Vs. 3   When I see this verse, I am confused. Yes, it was in Egypt that God made Israel into a great nation, but it was at the cost of their freedom. Its often hard for me to put the two together- the goodness of God and His sovereignty. He knew the oppression that would happen here, but led them anyway. He even predicted this to Abraham while telling him of his descendants (Genesis 15:13-14) Many times, we do not understand God's ways, but what this story shows me is that God really does work all things together for good, and that his ways are above our ways (Isaiah 55:8)

Vs. 28   Judah is the one Jacob trusts to proceed the family. What does this signify?

Vs. 29   A father and son are finally reunited. Again, when I imagine this, it makes me think of the prodigal son being reunited with his father. (see Luke 15: 11-31) Although under different circumstances, both sons are finally back in the arms of their father.

Vs. 29   This reunion also makes me think of the way God embraces any of His children in his arms.

My Notes on Genesis 46

Restored

The reunion of Joseph and his brothers is one of the most beautiful stories of family restoration in the Bible. One of the reasons I wrote this book was in hope that the relationships in my life and the lives of my readers would feel God's touch of restoration. I believe that right now, God is outstretching his hand to you with that invitation. Whether you believe in God or not, why not take this moment to reflect on any severed relationships. Maybe a family member we haven't spoken to for a long time, or a long lost friend. No matter the size of the offense, let's take example from Joseph and do our best to search for the reunion of those relationships.

Here are a few specific areas God is showing me that he really longs to bring restoration. These people and situations were at the forefront of my mind as I was writing this book: yes, they are specific, but the Jesus I know often stops for the single person in the midst of a crowd.

I see a few women who have not spoken to their sisters in a really long time, and I think it is something to do with what your father did. God is offering his heart of forgiveness to you to extend to your family. Go call your sister right now. She has been wanting to reach out to you but feels afraid. Your entire families will become a safe harbor for the hurting, and I actually see children being adopted into the family, shown their identity and given hope.

I see a grandmother who has grandchildren that she can't see for some reason, and I think that reason isn't your fault and it breaks your heart. God wants you to know that He is right there in your room with you. I see him holding your hand, placing a ring on your finger, and holding your hand next to his cheek. You are so deeply loved.

I see a man who identifies himself as gay. I see you going to church, and being so afraid to share with people what you are really feeling. I want you to know that God loves you so very much, and he sees your struggle, your sorrow, and the hurt you have experienced. Ask God for a name of the person in church you need to talk to. God has been preparing this person's heart to support and mentor you. You need to be honest about how you are feeling, but let this person work through with you despite of your feelings. Ask this person to do some prayer ministry with you. You have a powerful voice. I see you as a spokesperson for those who don't have a voice, those who feel afraid. God will turn everything in your life into a story of hope to bring freedom to hundreds of people! I'm so excited for what God has prepared for you, freedom carrier!

I see a man who cheated on his wife and now you are loosing your hope in life. God sees you, He knows how remorseful you are. Ask Him what restoration looks like for you. I see you working with young men that have made some bad choices. I see you becoming a father figure to those whose father walked out on them and dedicating your life to these young men. You will be vulnerable yet your life will point them straight to Jesus. He will turn your weakness into His strength.

To any parent that has lost their child, no matter what the circumstance, I feel God wants to draw you close to Him in this moment. I see a picture of you as an infant, and God is wrapping you tightly in a swaddling cloth and holding you next to His chest. Slowly, your tears stop and your breathing steadies. I see God holding you as you sleep. He understands the pain, He grieved with you. Allow Him to see what is in your heart- even if some of the feelings are against Him. He wants to journey it all with you.

I see a man named Jack sitting in a prison, wearing a red shirt, that has a major back problem. You are deeply loved, your life has more value than you could ever imagine. Stand up and walk. Salvation will come to many in that prison and beyond because of the love and hope that Jesus has just given you.

I see a few people in wheelchairs. The names that come to mind are Carol and Brenda. Stand up and walk in Jesus name. Try doing something you couldn't do before. God has placed so much inside of you. It is time for you to be brave and share this with those around you.

If you've been living with an overwhelming sense of guilt, whether justified or not, I see Jesus giving you a large red present. The present is too large for you to carry, so you have to set it down on the ground. You say "I don't deserve this." He says "The price has already been paid." You hesitate, not sure whether to open to present or not. Eventually, maybe curiosity gets to you or because you feel ready, you open the gift. Inside is a freshly baked piece of bread in the shape of the cross and a jug of wine. Jesus smiles. You look away. He takes your hand and slowly you turn your face back to Him. When your eyes meet, you begin to cry. As Jesus gazes into your eyes, the guilt loses its power over you. When you look down, you see the guilt you were wearing transformed into a gleaming robe of white. Jesus serves you the bread and wine, his broken body and shed blood, and says "I have paid the price for your sins. Now live in freedom!" You smile, then begin to laugh. You understand that through Him, you now have not just the desire to live the life worthy of your King, but the power as well.

And any person who has been abused- mentally, physically, sexually- my heart breaks for you. You inspired this book. You are so brave and every breath you take is a testimony of hope. I can't even imagine the depth of your hurt, how so many things in your life may be colored by what has been done to you. But even though most people won't understand, I feel God saying that He does. He was there when it happened, He never left your side. He wept. He is furious on your behalf. Yes, He is a God of compassion, but just as much is He a God of justice. You can trust Him. I believe in you. With God's strength, you will overcome this. Your life has a million possibilities: each one filled with hope and restoration. You are not broken goods, you are loved. Your story is like a water jug that God will fill and use to bring to life those who are needing hope.

Whether any of those words were for you or not, why don't you take a moment now to ask God if there is a specific area in your life where He wants to bring restoration. Be brave, dear friend.

A Timeless Call

God didn't just see Judah at the time that he decided to sell Joseph into slavery: He saw the man who fathered the entire tribe of Judah, chosen to be the line that brought the promised Messiah into this world. God didn't just see the Jacob that was anxious and wallowing in despair at the loss of his son Joseph: he saw the man 'Israel' who became the father of the twelve tribes of Israel, God's chosen nation. God didn't just see Tamar as an outcast Canaanite: he saw a woman made righteous and adopted into God's great family, whose courage carried the line of Jesus.

God didn't just see my sin, failure, rebellion, and anger. Instead, He saw a woman who He has chosen to bring hope and victory to many and the story of hope that He twined into my life, long before I was even born. Our God is timeless: He sees this all at the same time: our past, present, and future.

God sees you. From before you were born, every single moment of your life, He was, *is*, there. And now at this moment in time, our timeless God holds out His hand in opportunity: Will you surrender your life into the one who was able to take all the mess in the lives of Judah and Tamar and turn it into a beautiful story twined with hope and restoration? The God that is everlasting can turn any path into one that leads straight into His arms.

What He wants you to know right now is that anytime you need, He will come running. He will embrace you and be as overjoyed as Jacob was when reunited with Joseph. He will love you selflessly; His love is not about our failures or mistakes, His love is about the blood that He shed that can turn any sin, failure, mistake or hurt into a righteous robe of white.

In this story we discovered the tribe of Judah, but this story is just a small part in the great story of the Bible; the entirety of which leads to Jesus. Jesus' heart that runs so deep for people, a heart that has never changed. He is pursuing you.

He loves me and you so incredibly much, that He accepts us just the way we are, but also loves us too much to let us stay the way we are. He is always good, no matter the circumstances. He wants to love you in this transformational, life altering way: and now the choice is in your hands. He asks for everything- your life, your family, your emotions, your finances, your time, your hopes and dreams. But the pleasure of knowing Him is far greater than any of those things.

Run to him. He is waiting.

Viktoriya Lorimer

A Story of Hope

I believe that God is shifting something in His sons and daughters in the area of writing. More and more people that I have talked to have felt a stirring in their heart to share their thoughts in a creative way with those around them. I believe that God, the ultimate Author of all, is rebirthing in His sons and daughters the passion, desire, and talent to write. A mighty shift is coming. From children writing books of hope to their peers, to people who think the best days of their life are long past, to single parents, to people much too busy, to couples writing together, and many more, this industry is looking at a powerful move of God, a move of God happens when individual sons and daughters chose to say yes to the calling God placed on their lives. Books, blogs, poems, magazines, children's books, journals, devotionals, songs, movie scripts, TV show scripts: God's breath of life is waiting to be breathed into you afresh.

I believe this to be true, but to get to the place where I can include myself 'in' on what God is about to do took quite some time. Even though I always knew that one day I wanted to write a book, I loved and hated writing in equal amounts. Time and time again, I felt like God was inviting me to write with Him, but there were many excuses in my head. Writing felt like throwing a tiny pebble into a gigantic ocean; no impact other than a tiny splash, insignificant like a pebble fluttering to the depths of the ocean floor of the internet. But God was persistent. It was almost impossible to talk to Him without Him bringing up this topic. I resisted, but ended up trying to write little blogs, but the set aside time consisted me being extremely frustrated at myself and my computer; jittery from all the coffee I drank as a distraction.

Now I know all the people who support me in my writing, but back then, I felt extremely isolated. Writing wasn't something I told people I was passionate about. There was nothing to show for my passion, so I kept quiet. This desire within me was too vulnerable to share and too large to contain inside. But by God's mercy, I wrote even though I felt misunderstood and even though I honestly could not see the point. It was a hard choice of obedience. Every word felt like a battle, even when I knew this was what God was asking of me.

On Easter of 2016, during the worship at my church, Causeway Coast Vineyard, I felt like God was asking me if I was ready to stop fighting Him about writing. At His words, this unshakable mountain in my heart slowly began to shift. It was nothing I did, but somehow He just shifted my heart. Here is what I wrote in my journal that day:

> *"Today is a line in the sand type of day. Today is a new beginning. After fighting God for so long about blogging, writing, being an author, today I surrender. I choose to say 'yes' to you, my Lord. Today I am starting to believe that I am an author, just like my Father. I am an author of life, joy and hope."*

This day began a massive shift in my life. Even though writing was extremely difficult and frustrating, I knew that I had already given it all to God. There was no going back: and I would do what He asked of me.

A few months later, on July 4th 2016, I was journaling with God and I began to think about this question: "What wonder what it would look like to write Bible stories as fictional stories? What if... I kept what I know the same, but filled in fictional feelings, and told the story that anyone, no matter their knowledge of the Bible or God, could read, as easily as any other book?"

At this point in my life, I was an apprentice at Pais Ireland, where one of the core values is studying the Bible. Through the book 'Haverim' by Paul Clayton Gibbs, founder of the movement, I had learned how to study the Bible thoroughly. In his book, Paul unpacked four ancient levels of studying the Bible. From day one of studying the Bible through this method, I was captivated. There was so much more to every single story in the Bible that I could have ever imagined in my wildest dreams. All throughout my three year internship, I studied the Bible through Haverim every day with my team. Where the first and second level focus on context and cross references, the third level has this saying: "Fill in the gaps, don't change the facts."

Having this basis of Bible study for the past three years, on July 4th, 2016, I began the first discoveries of Genesis 38, the foundation of this book. I used all four levels of Haverim and my imagination to put together all I could find out about this passage. That day, I began to type out the first words of what is now 'The Palm of Judah'. Writing a book seemed like a huge task, but somehow I was more excited than overwhelmed. I could finally see that maybe there was a point to this whole writing thing!

Another few months later, I found out that there was much more to the dream that God had for me than just this single book. I was meeting for a coffee with one of beloved friends, Katharina Dube. We sat drinking our coffee and dreaming together, and when I told her about the book I was writing, she told me she was doing the same! After chatting for awhile about what in the world we were to do with our near finished books, she said, laughing, "I wish God would speak to someone in our church about publishing books! That would help us both out so much." As soon as those words came out of her mouth, it was like the fog cleared and the task ahead of me lay clearly before me.

I ended up telling her that God actually was speaking to someone about this, and that someone was me! For on July fourth, next to asking God what it would look like to write Bible inspired fictional books, I had written down that maybe one day, I can help release other people's books, help them step into the dreams God has for them. That casual coffee with Kate turned into the beginning of me looking into what it would look like to help and inspire other people with this process of writing.

After much research, thinking and dreaming, I decided on following what God has spoken to my heart in this way: creating a community for writers where we can encourage them to go after the dreams of writing God has placed in their hearts. At this point in time, 'A Story of Hope' is nothing more than Kate and I coming together as authors to encourage and champion each other, share resources, ideas and techniques. But I want to place my dreams and the words God has spoken right back into His hands, and say yes even though I don't know what this community of creatives will look like.

Authors, creators, dreamers, if you have felt a stirring in your heart to be part of the hope God wants to bring to the world through writing, do not be afraid. Lean in to that little fascination, that spark of creativity, that fluttering of your imagination. You have your own unique story of hope to tell. Whether it's in family, adoption, business, education, science, fiction, art, medicine, travel, humor, history or any other area, take a deep breath, and if you are ready, surrender. Say 'yes'. Against every excuse running through your head, surrender. Against the isolation, the insignificance, the fear of not knowing what to do, surrender your 'yes'. Against the unyielding thought that you aren't qualified, surrender.

I believe that this is a line in the sand type of moment for many of you reading this. You've felt the stirring in your heart, but maybe you haven't known how, maybe you've not had the time, or maybe you hear God's call, but feel you don't have anything to say. Wherever you find yourself, just say yes and let God do what He does best. Allow Him to show you that He is the God of miracles.

Some of you need to put this book down and go start writing right now. God has been calling you to do this for a long time. He has given you the name for what you are to do and specific instructions. No more excuses. Go write the first words or continue what you started long ago. Some of you need to go deeper into your study of the Bible before you can take the next steps. His word is lamp to your feet, and you need to let it shine. Just ask God specifically where in the Bible to read and then go there. It is as simple as that, but if you are struggling, I would definitely recommend 'Haverim' by Paul Clayton Gibbs to give you a great foundation or a Bible study at a local church or even online devotionals. Some of you need to journal, writing first to God. He wants to first build that deeper relationship before anything else can happen. For others, it is not yet time. Just relax, know that God is working in your life through every ordinary hour of your day, and that you can rest assured knowing your time will come. Be patient and enjoy this season. He will not delay in telling you when it is time. And lastly, some of you, you just need to know that it really is God that is calling you to write. Go into a quiet room, close the door, lay down on the floor, with your hands outstretched, and wait.

In ten years, I can't wait to look back on this day and see what God can do with the open hearts of those who love him, love people, and are willing to do whatever God is asking them to do. But for now, let's make the small choice of saying 'yes' to God whenever He speaks, pushing deeper into His presence every day. But even more importantly, know that we are all loved more than we could even understand, whether we write or not, whether something comes out of our obedience or not, whether our words touch one life or millions. To Jesus, there is no life too insignificant. We are all loved in a way that isn't based on what we do, but based on the love and goodness that our beautiful Father has for us. Nothing, not our fears, doubts or dreams, our failures or successes, can ever separate us from the love that God has for us.

I believe in you, but more importantly, our God Himself, is championing you. The world is eagerly waiting for the words yet to be spoken by the chosen sons and daughters of the Author of hope, our Lord Jesus Christ.

Acknowledgements

First and foremost, I'd like to thank my mother Nina. Mamochka, thank you for believing in me from before I was born and speaking God's love into my heart my entire life. You are my greatest supporter, the one who gets most excited about all my ideas for writing. You always believe in me, and from you, I discovered my passion for the Bible, God's heart for the outcast, and the power that my words carry. You gave up everything for me, and I am forever grateful.

My dearest Ricky, the love of my life, this book would not be possible without you. You champion me to pursue my dreams, show me grace in my lowest moments and love me unconditionally at all times. You make me laugh when I want to cry and are always there to enjoy life by my side. You are my best friend, the eagle with whom I can soar.

I am forever grateful for your strong support of prayer, papochka, and my family in Minnesota, Ireland, Germany and Russia. You helped shape who I am today. I know that you all are always there for me. I'd also love to thank all at Revival Baptist Church, Causeway Coast Vineyard and the Pais Movement. You adopted me into your communities and helped me understand who God made me to be. You inspired me to believe the difference one person's surrendered life to God can make. Your DNA of hope runs through my veins.

And to my beloved friends: Irene Litvinovich, Tanya Glushko, Alina Zvereva, Natali Bulycheva, Katia Demchenko, Annika Mueller, Amanda Busswitz, Shannon Swanson, Kate and Anna-Lena Dube, Kiki Lorimer, Moni Knoch and Anna Dawson. You girls are my best friends, my sisters. You were always there, and I love you with my entire heart.

And lastly, special thanks to Dan Brown, my editor, who is able to really see what I am trying to write on a page and bring out the very best, to Jenny Harte, for the stunning cover design and creativity, to Irene Litvinovich for editing the Bible notes, Steffen Sharikov, for the incredible cover image, and Rhoda and Andy Fearon, pastors of Carlisle Vineyard, for their kindness and championing of all people, being faithful to God no matter the cost, pursuing God's dreams for Carlisle, and always seeing the very best in all people.

All of you have made this book possible. I am more grateful than I could ever express.

More from A Story of Hope

<u>Astoryofhopebooks.com:</u> The place for upcoming books, writing inspiration, and stories of God's restoration around the world.

Follow Viktoriya Lorimer

Instagram: Viktoriyous

Twitter: Viktoriyous

Follow Katharina Dube

Instagram: katharina.dube

Twitter: KatesCreativity

Coming soon from A Story of Hope

The Nameless Book Project by Katharina Dube

The nameless book project aims to give those who love Jesus and are hungry for more of Him an overview of the supernatural. Whether it is hearing God's voice or reacting to His presence, having a deep and intimate relationship with Him or partnering with Him in our everyday lives, God is extending an invitation to see and adventure in His world - the one we were made for. Written by Kate, it is framed by a collection of art and photography contributed by artists from Sweden, Germany and Northern Ireland. It is being designed to come in the form of a single edition magazine.

www.ingramcontent.com/pod-product-compliance
Lightning Source LLC
Chambersburg PA
CBHW051440050726
47593CB00005B/1866